THROUGH
THE PORTAL

TALES FROM
A HOPEFUL DYSTOPIA

THROUGH THE PORTAL

TALES FROM A HOPEFUL DYSTOPIA

THE EXILE BOOK OF ANTHOLOGY SERIES
NUMBER TWENTY

EDITED AND WITH A FOREWORD BY

LYNN HUTCHINSON LEE
NINA MUNTEANU

AFTERWORD BY

NINA MUNTEANU

Publishers of Singular
Fiction, Poetry, Nonfiction, Translation, Drama and Graphic Books

Library and Archives Canada Cataloguing in Publication

Title: Through the portal : tales from a hopeful dystopia / edited and with a foreword
by Lynn Hutchinson Lee, Nina Munteanu ; afterword by Nina Munteanu.
Other titles: Through the portal (Exile Editions)
Names: Hutchinson Lee, Lynn, editor, writer of foreword. I Munteanu, Nina, editor,
writer of foreword, writer of afterword.
Series: Exile book of anthology series (Exile editions Ltd.) ; no. 20.
Description: Series statement: The Exile book of anthology series ; number 20
Identifiers: Canadiana (print) 20240447875 I Canadiana (ebook) 20240452070 I
ISBN 9781990773341 (softcover) I ISBN 9781990773358 (EPUB) I
ISBN 9781990773372 (PDF) I ISBN 9781990773365 (Kindle)
Subjects: CSH: Short stories, Canadian (English) I CSH: Science fiction, Canadian
(English) I CSH: Canadian fiction (English)—21st century. I LCGFT: Dystopian
fiction. I LCGFT: Short stories.
Classification: LCC PS8323.S3 T57 2024 I DDC C813/.087620897109052—dc23

Published by Exile Editions ~ www.ExileEditions.com
144483 Southgate Road 14, Holstein, Ontario, N0G 2A0

We gratefully acknowledge the Government of Canada and Ontario Creates
for their financial support toward our publishing activities.

We warmly thank Aetna Pest Control (Toronto) for their ongoing support.

Canadian sales representation: The Canadian Manda Group, 664 Annette Street,
Toronto ON M6S 2C8 www.mandagroup.com 416 516 0911

North American and international distribution, and U.S. sales:
Independent Publishers Group, 814 North Franklin Street,
Chicago IL 60610 www.ipgbook.com toll free: 1 800 888 4741

Another world is not only possible, she is on her way.
Maybe many of us won't be here to greet her, but on a
quiet day, if I listen carefully, I can hear her breathing.

—ARUNDHATI ROY

CONTENTS

WRITING THROUGH THE PORTAL

FOREWORD

When we first discussed pitching *Through the Portal* to Exile Editions, we knew fiction writers had for years been making a quiet but significant shift toward the conscious writing of eco-fiction, a genre of fiction in which the environment – or a specific aspect of the environment – plays a major role in the story, either as premise or as a character with agency. Exile Editions' 2017 *Cli Fi: Canadian Tales of Climate Change* (edited by Bruce Meyer) was one of the earliest Canadian anthologies to address climate change.

But with eco-fiction so often shrouded in dystopian despair, we considered the need for hope, and fiction centred on hopeful dystopias. We saw hopeful dystopias as so much more than an apparent oxymoron. Hope and dystopia are in some fundamental way the spearhead of the future – and ironically often a celebration of human spirit by shining a light through the darkness of disaster. Margaret Atwood argued that dystopias and cautionary tales ultimately embrace an element of hope through a character's experience. Dystopias can serve as a road map for individual or community endurance and resilience through disaster.

Storytelling about how the Earth takes care of us – and how we can take care of the Earth – is urgently needed. This means embracing an eco-centric world view in which humanity is not central, but embedded within greater planetary forces and phenomena; a world view that sees humanity as a participant in a greater existential celebration of life and the elements. Eco-fiction can help us co-create a new narrative: one about how the Earth gifts us with life, and what we can give in return.

In envisioning *Through the Portal,* we imagined stories about healing our communities – social and geographic, both metaphorical and imaginary; stories showing how Mother Earth takes care of us, and how we can take care of her. We sought eco-fiction narratives that celebrated the complexity of relationships and the emotional and physical journey from catastrophe. The stories you are about to read bear the fruit of that search. They involve a premise of environmental calamity in which Mother Earth, Nature, or aspects of these, have an actual *voice* as a character, and a protagonist who learns to interact with it, often *cooperatively.*

In her short fiction that closes this collection, co-editor Nina Munteanu writes of the "sad face of solastalgia." That very word gives us pause. Coined in 2003 by philosopher Glenn Albrecht, it deserves wider currency, particularly in these dark times. Stephanie Bailey in her thesis "When Home Doesn't Feel Like Home" explains solastalgia as "a portmanteau of solace, desolation and nostalgia…" Albrecht defines it as "the pain or sickness caused by the loss or lack of solace and the sense of isolation connected to the present state of one's home and territory."

The break from the despair of solastalgia toward the light of hope happens through action. It is that single break from inertia, that forward impulse to defend Mother Earth.

And it is often driven by Indigenous Peoples worldwide through their strong link to their environmental relatives.

From the Brazilian Yanomami to the Wet'suwet'en of Turtle Island, Indigenous land defenders continue to put their bodies on the line. Those countries which award full status to Mother Earth, and the rights granting her lands and waters protective constitutional, legal and human rights, stand in stark opposition to the human status granted to extractive corporations.

In 2008, Ecuadorian President Rafael Correa acknowledged the Quechua principle of *sumac kawsay* (good way of living) to award the codified "Rights of Nature" to Pachamama (Mother Earth). Two years later, Bolivia enshrined the *Ley de Derechos de la Madre Tierra* (Law of the Rights of Mother Earth) into the national constitution. When New Zealand declared the Whanganui River a legal person in 2017, *Iwi* people in the parliamentary gallery broke into a song of celebration. Two guardians act for the river: one appointed by the government and one by the *Iwi*. The *Iwi* – like the Indigenous peoples of Turtle Island, who view water as alive (*Nibi onje biimaadiiziiwin*) – are spiritually connected to the river and its water. The new law now resonates with the *Iwi* worldview of honouring the mountains, rivers and seas as one whole of which we are all a part.

Through its vision of our future, eco-fiction encourages conversations and an outward perspective. "Youth Imagine the Future: A Festival of Writing and Art," a project taking place in Eastern Ontario high schools, embodies such a vision. Hopeful dystopias in eco-fiction not only connect with our sense of loss or mourning – our solastalgia – for our changing home; these cautionary tales may nudge people into action and encourage alternative futures. Eco-fiction – whether told as dystopia, post-apocalypse, a cautionary tale or hopeful solarpunk – can help us co-create a new narrative: one about how the Earth gifts us with life and how we can give in return. The Gitga'at Nation tells the story that: "The raven left one in 10 bears white to remind them of the Ice Age, when things were clean and pristine." Following the revelation of this bear's existence and its compelling story, public pressure spawned the creation of a 21-million-acre park to protect its home.

By encouraging empathy and imagination, eco-fiction reaches deep into our souls, where we care. It is only when we care that we act. Empathy and imagination are braided through the stories of this collection, from quiet, morphing landscapes, to dark and terrifying warnings, to rich, newly told folk and fairy tales.

Writing this introduction, we imagined taking our stories to that place described so poignantly by Arundhati Roy: a place where, on a quiet day, we can hear our world breathing; and there, we can read our words aloud to Mother Earth.

—Lynn Hutchinson Lee
—Nina Munteanu.

PART ONE

IMAGINE

IMAGINE

KAREN SCHAUBER

Imagine a desert, biscuit-coloured and crumbly, with tumbleweeds, dust devils and carrion. The air parched with finely crushed sorghum. Its rough-hewn canyon snakes like a river; but there is no water and there is no snake. In this desolate terrain nothing stirs, nothing breathes. Nothing remains.

Imagine if all you hear is the sound of your own footsteps. There are no birds squawking or flapping, no orgy of gorging raptors, no howls or yips of coyotes, braying of wild dogs. Only a heavy silence.

Imagine if the desert is all you see, for miles and miles. The only return, a pale, diminished vanishing point.

Imagine it was not like this yesterday. Yesterday, when you had your youth, when you had your wherewithal. Yesterday, when you could have done something.

FORECAST

Vanessa Hua

After the weather turned, so did we.

Veering from thermonuclear wildfires to biblical floods, the violence of the atmosphere made us prone to adolescent extremes. Amid a gale, our brawling neighbours slammed into a eucalyptus, which toppled and crushed them both. During a triple-digit, triple-week heat wave, teenagers tore apart my brother's classroom.

Like love, like bankruptcy, like sleep, the wild swings happened slowly, then all at once. The wealthiest among us staved it off longer, in their climate-controlled compounds, jetting into low-orbit during the worst of the weather.

But even trillionaires couldn't outrun the seasonal affective disorder, which lengthened and merged until the symptoms plagued most of us year-round. Our grief and anger compounded every time another ecosystem, another species blinked out: the tiger salamander, the condor, the kangaroo rat, the marsh sandwort.

For many like me, the end of fog led to the end of my patience. Though we'd heard that the cool, grey city might become as sun-bleached as Seville by the end of the century, someday had arrived sooner than anyone predicted.

After the gloom failed to materialize in June, July or August, a blue-ribbon committee – convened on the troubling blue skies – proposed gene therapy. Like those tomatoes spliced with fish genes, we too might adapt to the wild swings in climate. But funding evaporated like the fog we hadn't known defined us.

We survived largely on the belief that its absence was an anomaly. Soon we'd return to those contrarian summers, the ones as cold as winter and the blankness upon which generations of us had projected our dreams. The clouds dropping down to swaddle but also to erase; a reminder of how impermanence gives rise to possibility. No matter where we'd hailed from, we wished for silver – not the gold of this endless summer; the silver of a fog bank pouring like cream, with a scent that clarified, and a briskness that slapped us out of tradition and routine.

It's been two years now, and fog is nearly extinct worldwide. The realization that my unborn child will consider it as they might a rotary phone, a monarch butterfly, or a Tesla, leaves me unmoored. As I wade into the waters of Ocean Beach – now merely bracing instead of heart-stopping – I ache for my first-born, who will never dream about fog in the Avenues. Never call upon it as a metaphor, never curse the dampness that makes a home cozier upon return. And never turn porous in the mist with someone they love.

Their generation will come of age in a city where we've lost our taste for the temperate; our dispositions like palates scorched on too much sugar, salt, and fat. The mild seemed bland, and so too anything in the middle – the middle ground of consensus, of the collective. If only we hadn't been so self-serving, we might have forestalled climate disaster.

Then I halt before getting in too deep, struck by the thought that the extreme is paradoxically how we might find a way through. Not with seawalls or another stop-gap, but an idea too outlandish for anywhere else, that might take root and flourish under every colour of sky.

HEARSAY

HOLLY SCHOFIELD

Sammi pulled his rabbit furs closer around his shoulders. The chill night air signalled the approach of winter, and there was nothing but coals in the community firepit. He threw on another precious poplar log, knowing he might regret burning it now come spring, but bed wasn't beckoning him just yet. "Another story, Darna?"

Across the pit, the old storyteller shifted, her broken lawn chair creaking like a nightjar. "Think I'll keep telling my little history stories all night, do you? Here you go, then: Vaters swooped down and bombed the shit out of us. That's it, that's the gist of every one of 'em. Anyhow, you can probably tell 'em all word-for-word yourself by now."

Sammi rubbed a callus on his thumb. He probably could. How those magical things called electrics had all become scrap. How the world had heated up, the oceans emptied, and billions died in the misty past a dozen generations ago. All because of invading aliens from another planet. He'd been hearing such stories from Darna his whole life. She didn't involve herself much in village life, kept to herself a lot, but her stories gave him something to think about when he worked in the hot sun hand-sawing firewood in the stunted forests that surrounded the village longhouses. He'd take her stories and add to them in his mind, or change the characters around, or invent a different ending. It was wonderful fun. "Just one more story? Please?"

Darna held her hands out to the newly kindled flames. "Ah, all right then, child."

Sammi had just turned 16 summers and plenty adult, but he didn't bother to correct her. Darna was older than anyone in the village – she would always think of him as a child. He leaned back, watching sparks ascend into the dark.

"'Jackie the Triumphant', I think, eh." She cleared her throat. "Jackie strapped herself to the telephone pole and used sheer courage to shoot down 12 Vater rocketships before—"

"Not that ol' one, Darna. I've heard that one million times. Jackie wins the skirmish, then makes the Vaters retreat to the stars with a promise never to return, then builds the first longhouse, grows the first crops, helps birth the first post-attack babies. You tell that one all the time."

"Because it's the most important, child. Jackie got everyone in the village, hell, everyone on *Earth* back on the path we'd all been aiming for before the aliens came. A real hero!" Darna leaned forward and the end of her homespun tunic flicked dangerously near the fire.

"You know about other things from back then, Darna, I know you do! I've heard you talk to the other oldsters, about books and that drink called coffee and that thing called gas-i-leen." He wasn't quite sure of that last word but he was sure she was holding back. And he wanted grist for his mental mill – ideas and thoughts he could twist around in his mind.

"Ah, books, yeah. I sure do miss reading. I used to read a lot. Did you know that there used to be lots and lots of books back in my great-grandmother's day? More than one person could ever read? More than those tattered equipment manuals and instruction guides we keep in the big cedar box. Whole *roomfuls* of books survived for years, and there were even buildings full of information stored on computers. Research data, seed depositories, DNA specimens, fan fiction, memorabilia..."

"Can you explain what those things are? You never explain!"

"Nope, you don't need to know all that shit. You need to know when to plant in the spring, where to find willow and other medicines, how to chop out an oak stump to tan hides in, stuff like that. You don't need history; you don't need to know nothin' about that." Her eyes were bright dots above the flames. After a moment, she added, "And the village only needs one storyteller. One person to know the truth, the real truth."

"I knew it! There's a secret, right? You know something! Something big!"

"You're a smart one." She drummed her fingers on the scarred, plastic chair arm and straightened slightly. "Which is why I'm still out here shivering in the dark. Come sit closer, right here beside me. It's time I told you things. This is about to become the worst day of your life."

Sammi dragged his wooden stool closer. Awesome! Darna never opened up to anybody. This would give him mental fodder for months.

Darna pulled open her woollen cloak and stripped back her homespun shirt, releasing a stench of rot. "See this lump in my armpit? It's bigger every day. Soon I'm heading off toward the mountains to let the cold take me, like your grandma did last year."

"Darna, no!" He stumbled to his feet. Of all the things he'd expected to hear, that wasn't it. Darna had been around forever. Even with his never-still imagination, he couldn't picture a world without her.

"Quiet!" She yanked him back down. "It's one less mouth to feed, child."

"We need you! The village needs you!"

"Not if *you're* around. Not if you're the one sitting here around the fire, telling everyone my stories."

"Me?" This time he stood up so fast the stool tipped right over. "A storyteller? I don't know how to tell stories. And my memory isn't all that good. I'd forget—"

"You'll figure it out. The important thing is that your imagination is better than mine." Bone buttons slipped in her shaking fingers as she rearranged her shirt, cloak, and furs.

"Why's imagination important? A storyteller just repeats what they heard from the previous storyteller and the one before that. A good memory is what's important!" Sammi realized he was almost shouting again. Had Darna spent so much time alone she'd gone strange?

Darna hissed up at him. "Sit down! Be quiet and listen! Those stories? The ones you revisit in your head when you're hoeing an endless field of beans? *Lies!* All of 'em! Lies!" She pointed a shaking finger at him. "Jackie the Triumphant? Never existed. Aliens attacking us? Bullshit!"

Yup, she'd gone strange. He should go wake up Irdira so she could fetch some herbs. They wouldn't cure Darna, but they might help her agitation. "Wait here while I—"

"Oh, use your head! I've been lying for years. No one knows the real truth. Not your parents, not your aunts or uncles or cousins, not anyone. And, obviously, I must have a good reason."

Sammi uprighted the stool and sat with his arms crossed, his boots almost in the coals. "Okay, why tell me, then?" His voice came out belligerent. But he had a right to be angry, didn't he?

"Because you're different. Maybe you got more vitamins as a baby, or better brain chemistry, or something. You see deeper. You understand people. With a bit of help, you can learn to see our true natures."

"We're all just folks trying to get by. No different than them in the next valley. What's to see?"

"Think, child! How we live, how we share. Like when your cousin, little Flin, found that beehive a few days ago, the first hive in our valley in over a decade. Did you ever think that Flin could have eaten all the honey all by herself, instead of taking just a small portion back to share with the village? But, of course, she never thought of emptying the hive and starving the bees, never thought of not sharing what she took with all of us, and I see by your expression that you never thought of those things either."

"Who would do that? That would be wrong!"

"Our ancestors would have. And did. It was us, see, not some made-up aliens. We burned the jungles and melted the snow lands. We strangled fish right in the ocean, fed each other poisonous food, and blasted the cities into black smoke. We did it to ourselves – polluting and warring and wrecking the whole world for nothing but short-term greed.

We didn't stop and we didn't try and that's the fucking truth of it."

Darna coughed for a moment, face flushing, before holding Sammi's eyes with her own. "I'm tired of holding back, child. Jackie the Triumphant, and Karan the Compassionate, and all the other heart-warming, soul-affirming tales you've heard your whole life – all bullshit. Some of the stories I got from old Anna before she died, some of 'em I made up. You'll make up better stories than I ever could – new ones of sharing and hope."

"But—"

Darna held up her hand. "You listen, now. The way people's minds work, see, we need to hear things over and over before we believe them. If we hear about the goodness of humanity, our gentle natures, and how we all work together to overcome odds, we begin to think it's true. We start to believe that people never fight each other and always share resources. That people are *naturally* good."

"But people *are*—"

"No, child, they aren't. They're becoming that way, though, gradually, over time. With luck, you'll be one of the last of the storytellers to carry this awful burden."

"There must be something else we can do instead!"

"Well, we're doing a lot of things right. The community spirit, the communal effort, thinking of the village as the smallest divisible unit, that mentality goes a long way. And that's true of the folks in the next valley, too. Thanks, in part, to their storyteller. Tarbe's stories are almost the same as mine, and for good reason. This… this conspiracy theory – hell, I haven't thought those words in a long time! – about the alien invasion is a horrible, terrible thing. And I'm

ashamed of it. But the sad truth is that it's working. By thinking we've always been kind and gentle, our recovery, our
growing humanity, is being sped up."

Sammi picked up a rock and threw it hard at the fire.
Sparks flew. "No! That's crap! The truth is what's important!"

"Nothing is as important as our collective survival,
child. Nothing."

"Stupid old shit-heart!" He jumped up and strode away
toward the longhouse, his thoughts bubbling like sap in a
kettle. How could Darna be dying? How could all the old
stories be false? How could she have spent her entire life,
separate and alone and hating herself? Those stories had
kept him going when he was sawing knotted tree limbs and
gathering sparse kindling – could they all be false? No! He'd
get Darna some help and that would be the end of it!

He stopped with one hand on the longhouse railing, letting the rustles and snores of the slumbering villagers within
settle over him. She was dying and he was calling her a shit-
heart? How could he be so mean? He was better than that.
Wasn't he?

He brushed away a tear and listened to his breathing
until it slowed. He'd have to go back and apologize. But not
yet. His thoughts were still tumbling, roiling like spring ice
melting over rocks. Darna's words did explain a few things
that had never made sense. Why the aliens had seemed to
do random damage and then never returned. How, in
homage to Jackie, they buried rusted shooters and ammuni-
tion in deep holes when they found them, instead of trying
to rebuild them and use them to kill deer. Why, in the neighbouring valley, the ancient hulk of a Vater rocketship had
English words and numbers on it. It might even explain why,

deep in the old ruins to the east, there was a huge building made just to hold people inside tiny rooms so they couldn't get out.

Were people really that awful, deep in their genes?

If so, could generations of gentle teachings change that?

Even if he became the very last storyteller, could he spend his life living a lie – cut off, separate, alone?

Was that what he wanted?

He picked off a splinter from the railing and threw it into the darkness.

What he wanted was whatever was best for the village.

And best for the world.

If only he knew what that was.

He listened to someone half-asleep murmur something reassuring to a restless baby. They were all fumbling in the dark, doing the best they could with the tools they had. And his tool set included a hell of an imagination.

He stumbled only once in the starlight as he hurried back across the clearing. Time was growing short. Storytelling – *true* storytelling of *new* tales – had a lot of techniques that he needed to learn in the weeks Darna had left: pacing, tension, and, most importantly, how to include a moral message.

The old storyteller was still huddled by the fire, eyes closed, rocking slightly. Sammi crouched down and put a hand on her knee. "Hey, um, Darna?"

"Go to bed, child. Forget what I said. Just my fever talking."

"Um, I have an idea for a story about a woman travels around planting quince trees all over the valley and everyone gives her a tithe. If I apologize for my unkind words, can I run it by you?" He still wasn't sure about continuing the lies for decades and decades but he did know one thing: he wanted to be the next storyteller.

Darna chuckled and Sammi got comfortable on the stool again. He picked up another log and laid it on the coals. Might as well be warm. Tomorrow's hard work would be here soon enough.

INTERSTELLAR CATALOGUE: NATURE OF STARS

SHANA ROSS

By the time we reached this world, their war had gone cold. Generations into a stalemate. No peace and no shooting..

We asked to meet with a combined diplomatic party. Better for our schedule – two birds, one stone. We went wending, back and forth through the wall between their cities. Grand gates flanked by guards, dressed in bright, clashing colours. Small doors, ignored in plain sight. Hidden passageways in case the other openings ever grow teeth. If people were needles, you'd mistake the movement for mending, but without thread, it's just holes from the passing.

In one half of the world, we stood atop a crater glazed with green glass at the bottom, slick and shining as a last measure of medicine that can't be sucked from the cup. *How are we to understand the stars?* my guide intoned, standing tall with respect. The stars are diamonds, lit miraculously from within, hung on delicate hooks into a velvet firmament. A drape that descends every night.

In one half of the world, we walked a narrow bridge over a rubble field, the piles too heavy to have been searched for survivors, a grave in infinite and unsoftened angles. The only grass willing to sprout refused to spike upwards, bending instead to cover what it could. My other guide kneeled and whispered; her hands cupped over her eyes. *How are we to understand the stars?* The stars are holes; windows for the eyes that live in the light, that watch us constantly and incompletely. The darkness gets pulled up like a quilt.

We came from the stars, and from far enough away, coming then going, we see them cling to their world in measured symmetry. Like for like this world grows, regrows, in the single city, split, full of people who rely on each other, these are the things worth fighting for: A need to believe that we matter so much that nothing we do is unseen. A certainty that treasure is within reach if we can only figure out how to stretch out our hands for harvest. Irreconcilable, down to the marrow. With no margin for error, they agree to root together under the same sky and survive.

FAIRY TALES
TRAVEL LIGHT

CORNELIA HOOGLAND

Then she loosened
the Queen's tongue.

My youngest leans into her sister's belly that in pregnancy
has become a public artifact. About the weekend with my
daughters in Gatineau, my memory is poor. I wear these
women like the metal sculpture in the garden at home wears
wind and rain, and the snowy arm of the star clematis is
heavy with swaddled babies. A log burned in the fireplace in
the backcountry hut when we arrived along ski trails. Somebody up early had stacked wood; the floor was swept. The
sun bounced over the Ottawa Valley like a metal roof juggles
the morning light, like the Inuit sculpture of a woman whose
face fractals the sun, like the unborn child who compelled
our trio of handmaids all weekend, calling forth the milk that
was in us, in the crooks of our arms, the croon and babble
spilling from our mouths, and the next day, in falling snow.
A necessary milk meant to round us in the way pregnancy
rounds the belly. We heard nourishment everywhere – in the
rasp of skis cutting through snow's crust, in the creek-flow
under the ice, and in the gradual dusk, granular as an image
on photographic paper, only it was sound, in a frequency
that deepened as it was manifest. As if we had entered the

heart of the forest where a hut admitted us. Three stools at a fire.

When she regained her senses, she was in
a beautiful meadow where the sun shone
and thousands of flowers grew.

In fairy tales with two daughters, the elder is mean and lazy, the younger pure and good. Her heart full of apples. She despairs the loss of her spindle down the well. Jump, says Mother Holle. Falling before wonder; before an oven door can appear: Help me, help me take out my bread or it'll burn. An apple tree says Pick me; my branches are breaking. The language of trees. She's listening. Her apron overflows, apples and tears. Your service, says Mother Holle, starts here. She teaches the girl to shake a feather comforter to make it snow on earth. Snow falls. After a year, the girl pleads to go home. Well, then. The girl arrives at her mother's house and gold coins tumble from her mouth. She tells her story. She shines. The elder daughter demands to try her luck. Behind her, Justice with his bucket of tar. The girl refuses to rescue the bread, pick the apples. Won't shake the goose down pillows, so no snow. You have to be good for gold to stick to you. Tar is another matter. Once it sticks, it's impossible to scrub off. That's what the elder daughter learns. She'll have to find another story, one in which she is the youngest, the most naïve. One with a well. A descent.

She heard a rustling, and saw six swans
come flying in at the window.

They alighted on the ground and blew
at each other, and their swan skins
stripped off like a shirt.
The maiden recognized
her brothers.

In the bleached field live the deer, in the cross–hatched grass, hip–high though it's winter. They see him first. The man can't distinguish one deer from another standing under the shelter made by Garry oaks the colour of pewter, trees made stiller by lichen draping the branches. So, the man counts them as a way of saying hello. Day-to-day their numbers vary. There are smaller groups within the herd. The triad of kohl-eyed doe and fawns is most clearly visible. Add them to the three yearlings that hang back, then, through the trees, a flash of stag equals seven. Today, on the bluffs, people walk past the man. Kids with earbuds; two females trail after a baby buggy. And from behind, from the edge of the wood bounding on too many companion trees to count – Western White with Lodgepole Pine, Yellow Cedar with Hemlock and other conifers, also Arbutus – does something count us?

Ah, not to be cut off,
Not through the slightest partition
shut out from the law
of the stars.
        —Rainer Maria Rilke

Wolverine or mink – something ugly with hunger snapped, snarled malice, devoured the quail family. I think quail.

Feathered, and at any rate, many, small; chirping pitifully.
This was at 4 a.m. My window was partly open, open a crack
to the law of predator and prey, strong versus weak, vile-
sounding versus needing protection. My work was to witness
ferocity laid bare. Bare to the point of purity. Awful, the
pleading. When night was blameless again, I went out into
it, looked up the cedar tree I'd heard something climb. I saw
nothing there. No stars. Across the street, a couple of
couches the Salvation Army puts out for the homeless to
gather, even in rain.

> *The oldest daughter wanted pearls,*
> *the second, diamonds,*
> *but the third said, Dear Father,*
> *I'd like a singing lark.*

He's the hero. Since 2002 my husband's been saying "Buy
marsh; it's about water. Turquoise gold." His swamplands are
paying off. Every day he punts among the reeds for things he
stashes in hollow logs, in the same way he encrypts family
dramas in his journal. He comes back with enough cherry
pop to keep us alive. Plus, the frogs and salamanders we
catch, wading in knee-high boots through bog. We fry skunk
cabbage. Remarkable, our joy. True, we have heartburn, it's
the end of eyeglasses and we miss our children, but he gets
to realize his apocryphal prediction. Wide grin on his face
when he swings through the door clutching daisies – flowers
I gathered as a child, loving that they grew wild and, because
I thought as a child, free.

LONG POINT

E. Martin Nolan

The trip grows in my mind. I liked it at the time.
Pleasant eerie hauntedness. The presence
of Erie. The lake blew in on this flimsy spit of sand
Huron would blast like some cottonwood fluff.
On the back deck, lake to north and south,
crashing softly. Wind in the cottonwoods
we see on the shore, lit by the late sun.
Socially, it did not seem special. Felt normal.
And in normalcy, felt special.
There was elemental change. A boy
started using phrases, spurred
by a cousin who tested his loyalty
to his stuffed mama bear. He never
didn't get her back. He lost
his hat in the wind where the water pooled
and waves cut curving channels
into the sand, a tan base under
red and black top layers. His cousin
wondered about weirdness aloud,
on liking worms but not ants, saying hi
to strangers in towns but not cities.
I told her both times, "People are weird."
The smoke from Quebec had just cleared.
How to expand on that point. To not.

Let it hang like it still kind of was, but
the apps said "moderate," so we went out.
I expanded someway, I don't recall how.
Nothing dramatic. She was mulling.
She found weirdness funny in a shy way,
felt her way to its humour carefully.
His hat in the wind, from his backpack carrier,
he yelled "Lost hat! Lost hat!" We got it
before it drifted out forever to where that turtle swam
around me yesterday. I would see again, on our way out –
wet red smashed between broke, dark, dusty ovals in the road.
The day before, it curved around me, on its side,
its head bobbing away from shore. I, I went, I went out
and dried myself off. I walked in rubber shoes back
to a house full of interrelated and developing love.
I was a rich modern human and I lived a very complicated life.
On Long Point I became like the sand, drifting
but still in the shape I was always kind of in. Or like the smoke,
lingering, omnipresent, impossible to be convinced of.

SALVATION IN A FRAGMENTING PARKING LOT

Avery Parkinson

A few shopping carts rolled around the parking lot and onto the freeway but the vast majority remained spooning in their gallery. It was kind of perverse, wasn't it, the way they asserted that well-worn "business as usual" refrain that we loved to repeat until we choked on it? I walked over and pulled one away from the rest, pushed it across the empty lot. Then another. Then another. All in different directions. On the fourth one, you joined in, grunting a little from the effort. I groaned. You giggled, dispelling the intensity. The carts weren't perverse in their solidarity. Were they defiant? Nostalgic? Oh, for goodness' sake – they were just carts stacked together because the wind hadn't blown them apart yet.

There were only two cars in the parking lot – the same pickup truck and grey Nissan that had been there since we started coming here. They were parked right next to each other which was kind of funny given the surplus of available parking. They huddled together in the corner, drowning in the sea of asphalt. There used to be a convertible but it disappeared around a year ago. What anyone was doing with a convertible out here eluded me. This time, the Nissan was missing a tire and its front hood popped open – most of the stuff inside it was gone.

—What does that mean, I asked you, gesturing at the empty cavity.

—It means people have been here in the past few months, you said.

Exactly, maybe they're even still around.

The sliding doors didn't slide anymore, but they were wedged apart. A state of perpetual transience. It was unlikely that anything usable would be here. When most people moved on to the cities, only the Staples underwent an actual shutdown process. The Dollarama, the Walmart, the Home-Sense – they were all abandoned. All the perishables were used up and the non-perishables were gone within a year and a half. In the past few months. all that really remained were things like adhesive hooks you might use to hang tow-els on the back of a bathroom door. And flat-screen TVs. Equally useless at this point. But it is still fun to come out here once in a while. It was our big trip that we planned for, packed for and anticipated, like going to an all-inclusive resort during a vacation week. Hmm, would you ever fly in a plane? Who cares, it's one of our habits that got us into this mess in the first place.

—Should we grab a basket, you asked.

—But of course, I don't see why not.

It's a matter of scale, I've decided. Things just needed to be scaled down a smidge and that would make it bearable. The walk from my bedroom to the basement was the errand run. The walk to the garden is the weekend day trip. The walk to this decrepit Walmart is the annual getaway to a sunny location. The change of scenery we need to reset, take a break. Even if I couldn't convince myself of that, it's cer-tainly the case for you. So yeah, let's grab a basket. Let's walk through the dimly lit aisles and peruse the mostly empty shelves as though we are living a life of luxury and option. Let's give this all the fanfare that our once a year vacation deserves.

Is it worth it to survive?

But before we do that, let's stop and think for a second.

—What are the rules for going somewhere, I asked you.

Me and your Uncle Kabir debated this term, "going somewhere." He, a former English lit major, and me, a former policy analyst, loved to explore the nuances of language. Our professions did not give us as much day-to-day value out here as your Auntie Jamila – a nurse – and your dad – a civil engineer – but the afternoon we spent examining the possible terminology we could use to refer to the process of leaving the house was a good one. For us. Not for everyone else who had to listen to it. But making big projects out of little things is the name of the game these days. And our game, played with sticky notes and comprehensive t-charts, eventually produced the verdict that "going somewhere" was the ideal phrase. How to make the action of leaving our little bubble not seem like something out of a dystopian paperback? That ruled out the options that made everything else seem like something to be feared. We didn't want to raise our kids to be scared of the unknown. Even if this was a situation that did somewhat resemble a dystopia. To us, I had to remind Kabir. But for our kids, it's normal. And perhaps trying to frame our little world as anything other than our little world is trying to naïvely acclimatize them for a return to the world as we are used to, which probably isn't going to happen anytime soon. But on the flip side, would we then just be baking hopefulness into our vernacular, he said. But is

hope linked to refuge in the familiar? Or is there a more daring kind of hope, a braver hope that speculates if on the
other side of uncertainty there is a more fulfilling unfamiliar-
ity. There were, however, different protocols for leaving our
house depending on whether we were going to the river,
going to the office park, or going up the mountain. And didn't
different protocols necessitate different language? Could we
actually develop an umbrella of vocabulary with sub-catego-
rizations to allow for the nuance of different situations? At
which point your baba walked in and told us hyper-sensitive
leftist, bureaucratic hippies to get over ourselves, ripped a
sticky note off the wall, and said that we'd simply call it
"going somewhere." And yeah, that seemed as good a sugges-
tion as any. That seemed like a versatile way to put it. When
we were kids our parents told the three of us to be mindful
when we were "going somewhere" also.

As you can see, girlie, many of my spirals begin and end
with mapping your childhood onto mine, wondering if I'm
doing a good enough job.

—The rules for going somewhere, you said. Evaluate to
see if there is anyone around.

People aren't bad – this was your dad's addition – but
they can be a bit more dangerous if they are desperate. It has
not been dangerous here in the last couple years. But the year
and a half before that, when people's sense of ending overwhelmed their need to preserve normalcy, that was when
the panic happened. But now, people have mellowed out.

—So, I asked you, does it look like anyone's around?

—The car parts are gone, so that means someone has
been here in the last few months, but they probably aren't
here right now.

—Good. Good. But we can't hear anything from inside the store, so if someone's in there, we can't tell. If we go in there, they'll know we're here before we know they're here which gives them more power. So, we need to confuse anyone in there a little bit.

—The siren, you said.

—Yeah, the siren.

Three years ago, your dad attached a siren to the underside of a shelf by the door. If we pressed the clicker, it lit up red and made noise – enough noise, we hoped that any unassuming person in there would come to the door to see what was going on. We clicked it, we gave it 10 minutes, but still no one came.

—We're probably good, you said.

—Yeah, probably.

But still – and this was Auntie Jamila's addition – keep your wits about you.

Most of the shelves were empty except for cleaning products. The racks by the self-checkout machines had magazines from five years ago rendering this place a living monument to when Shit Went Down. When I came here last with the boys, a couple years ago – Dylan would have been your age at the time – we saw that the delivery area in the back had a few boxes filled with the magazines that should have replaced the ones on display, updating this town on who wore it best. But they stopped coming within six months. Someone got the hint that although the store wasn't formally shut down, no one really cared anymore.

—You know what, I said. We should grab some of those magazines. Easy fire starters.

You knelt on the ground and pulled out a bright orange package from under the shelf. You held it up to the light.

—Fuzzy peaches, you said.

You've heard mythical things about fuzzy peaches. Of the powder that collects at the bottom of the bag that is so flavourful it puckers your taste buds when you eat a pinch. Of their mesmerizing texture that you can pound flat and roll into a ball.

—Should I save it until we get home, you asked.

—We'll get your cousins something else, I said. We'll find them something good. Besides, we should leave the wrapper here, I added as an afterthought.

There was no such thing as trash collection anymore. Everything we brought home had to have multiple potential reincarnations. Which is probably the way it should have always been rather than just digging a hole in the earth and filling it with the stuff we weren't creative enough to think up alternatives for.

—Let's play hide-and-seek, you said.

Hide-and-seek. It occurred to me all the references to things you wouldn't know if we didn't explicitly tell you them. You don't know the capital of Iran or that jumping rope was actually a thing people did. But then again, you probably won't have any use for this knowledge. We taught you and your cousins hide-and-seek about a year after moving here because what else were we going to do with five children under the age of six and years of time to kill. There you stood with your fuzzy peaches.

—Only in the fresh produce section and Aisles 1–8, I said.

And so, we played.

—You know what we can get them, I said. A baseball
bat. Your dad can show you guys how to play. And then let's
also get some more nails if I can find some. Jamila is trying
to build a chicken coop for the chickens she found at the
farm on the other side of the mountain.

She said the farmer looked like they had just packed up
and left, but the animals were still there. A few pigs also. That
would be fun, teaching you how to raise animals. Not that any
of us really know how. That could be a good thing to do next
week if Jamila can figure out how to build the pen – go and
get the animals and bring them over the mountain somehow.

—Ready to go? I asked you.

You nodded and skipped ahead. What are you afraid
of? When I was your age, I was scared of large groups of
people and then what would happen if I sat in my own head
for too long. The first is no longer something I have to con-
tend with, but the second one is… inevitable. A couple of
years ago, I thought that eventually, given enough time out
here, my mind would no longer be threatening. Which is
partly true. But every now and again, it gets away from me
just a bit. That's the policy analyst in me, I suppose. My natural disposition to turn an idea over until it's just a pile on
the ground, a shadow of its former self. Until I'm just a pile
on the ground, a shadow of my former self. Until your Baba
comes along and tells me to "get over myself." It's a good
routine we have going. These days, my main fear is heat.
Which in a way is ridiculous because northern Ontario is
relatively cool compared to many other places. But I feel
euphoric when snow falls, even if it's a month late and
doesn't stick. I root for that thin white dusting as I stand in
front of the kitchen sink, palms against the window frame.

I make tea to try and inhabit, to manifest the cosiness that winter used to signify. I stand outside in my T-shirt until the condensation numbs my fingers and leaves them raw. I delight in that feeling; the discomfort of being too cold rather than too hot. I wait for the chill to climb down my spine and freeze the tip of my nose before coming in and remarking on how cold it is. Not to complain. If I'm being honest, it's to delude. To escape for a moment and believe that maybe we're not that far gone yet. That winter still exists, even if it's not Winter. Not the capital W winter that stung our teeth and froze our eyelashes every time we blinked. That necessitated driveways to be shovelled twice per day and allowed autumn leaves to fully decompose into a fresh new ground for spring. The Winter that was a deep sleep, a great reset before another day. Lower-case winter with its repeated snow, thaw cycles that left us with thick slabs of ice was like a restless night. The start of spring was groggy, not quite ready to take on the task of creating life with the previous fall's remains still littering the ground. Summer was temperamental and autumn was crazed. I mourn winter, I dread the heat. I stand in front of the thermometer in March and curse the mercury as it climbs higher in its tube. I will the sun to disappear behind the clouds; to just give me another day with winter until it comes back later than it should. Do you fear the heat as well? I don't know what would give you reason to be scared of it other than us adults whose own fears arise from comparison.

—Can I ask you a question? you said with a mouthful of fuzzy peaches.

We sat down on the curb, stared across the parking lot at the Dollarama.

—Of course.

—When did you build the house?

—When did I build the house?

—Yeah, you said. When me and Dad and Baba got here, it was already here.

—Well, I said. I started building it many years ago. Before you or any of your cousins were born.

—Even before Dylan?

—Yes, even before Dylan, I said. Actually, when I was about Dylan's age, I started to have a feeling that something like this would come in handy. And then maybe 12 years ago, the Maritimes collapsed.

I wondered how much of this I should tell you. Do I tell you that the waters became unfishable? Do I tell you that there was a mass migration inland to southern Ontario and Quebec? Do I tell you that small municipalities were shut down and refugee camps grew along the outskirts of metropolitan areas? Do I tell you that a couple of flus spread across the country as the north melted and the west burned?

—And after that, I said, the cities became harder places to live in. I just wanted to be sure that in case we did reach a point where it was unsafe for us, we would have a place to go.

I nudged your leg and grinned. To soften it maybe?

Is it worth it to survive? I didn't make it too far into the past five years without asking this question. Now, what I refer to as the question to end all questions. But what's the point of asking this question when the only constructs I can answer it with are remnants of a society that took 2,000 years to build but self-destructed in less than 30? Time is not linear; it is in fact a cycle that oscillates between creation and destruction. And while it is well documented how to make sense of existence as we build, what we do during the looping back is a gray area. We indulge in Brahma and Vishnu without recognizing that Shiva is the flip side of the same coin. There is an animalian quality to the way we go on. Something primal that is unsettling. It's tricky when you are used to relying on an artful construction of logistics and culture that is itself based on a faulty foundation. Do we give into it – scavenge, fight, and reproduce for the sake of it? Or do we cover these widening cracks with our thin veneer of civilization – movie references and the process of doing your pigtails that seem pathetically obsolete? Is our insistence in maintaining the pathetic what will get us through or are we just delaying the inevitable?

Emergencies are scary. But figuring out how to transition to a new normal that would have once been considered a crisis is by far the more challenging task. I'm waiting for an equilibrium to hit. I'm hoping that we're converging to it. You seem to be. Just sitting there, sucking on those slightly stale fuzzy peaches. Even if they are memorabilia of a system that couldn't sustain itself. But you don't know that – to you, they must just taste good. Biting them in half to examine their insides just as me, Uncle Kabir and your baba did when we were kids. There we go, some continuity. A behaviour of yours that I can recognize and ascribe a kind of childish universality to. Even though we would have been doing so in a New England-esque neighbourhood on a school night rather than in an abandoned and decaying Walmart parking lot before retreating back into the forest.

These are the things I consider each night as I sit on the porch in my dad's old lawn chair, a shotgun within reaching distance during my 4 a.m. to sunrise shift. As I teach you and your cousins. As I show you how to tie your *gungrus* and form *mudras* because why not extend a 2,000-year-old art form by another few days? As Auntie Jamila and I think about how to divide up the house so the 10 of us don't go stir crazy. The word indefinite has taken on a new meaning these past few years.

I suppose what I'm asking is this: Should we slit our wrists tomorrow afternoon and tenderly bleed out together in our makeshift garden back at home? Or do we set the table for dinner and abide by our chore wheel to see who will wash the dishes after; who will sweep the floor? Tell your dads that yes, it is in fact their turn to build the fire.

I consider these questions, but no I'm not asking you to answer them. That would be a lot for a seven-year-old. But what I am asking you, my niece, *meri jaan*, my obligation and my freedom, is this: Please. Ask me to play hopscotch between the flaking parking lot lines and cracks in the pavement where plants have sprung up to reclaim their space. Sit on the curb and rest your head on my shoulder, take a deep breath of the balmy air that you associate with December, but I would have once thought indicative of April. Run through that flock of Canadian geese, and allow me a moment's futile hope that as they fly away, they'll head south as they once did. Grab my hand so we can spin each other in circles to songs we sing aloud, throwing out your arms as though you could single-handedly hold back the tide of All the Things That Could Be Considered. Ask me to push you in an abandoned grocery cart faster, faster, faster toward the setting sun. So fast that I escape the question of whether we should even be trying to survive and simply mark time by doing so.

EVIL EX, SILLY WHYS, AND THE HOLE OF DOOM

Melissa Yuan-Innes

The little mermaid squinted at the sign in the meadow planted 50 paces from her murky water tank. Despite her excellent eyesight, the uneven letters were difficult to make out at sunrise. Slowly, she sounded out the words to her companions at the zoo. "Shave your fur to precisely one-quarter-inch lengths from head to tail by noon on Tuesday, or face the consequences. —Evil Ex."

"What?" gasped Mother Rabbit. "He's taking away our fur, just before winter?"

The mermaid read the words again, her red lips shaping each syllable before she nodded. "Yes. I suppose so. It's Hallowe'en," she said, glancing around the zoo, which had been reduced to their 20-foot square water tank, a thin perimeter and "park" of grass, and a 30-foot iron fence that blotted out everything except a cloudy patch of sky. She saw no obvious sign of All Hallow's Eve, but their visitors the day before had giggled about tricks and candy. "Humans don't joke around on the last day of October, do they? Like April Fool's, but in the Fall?"

The turtle floated by her and thought, *Evil Ex never jokes around.*

"That's true," said the mermaid. "But I can't obey this time. I don't have any fur. I don't think my hair counts." Her squid-ink black hair was magnificent. Unplaited, it was so long that she could toss her left tresses to the edge of one side of the 20-foot tank and dangle her right tresses clear out of the tank and onto the little meadow below.

"What about your armpits?" said Mother Rabbit, who was already calling her six children. They bounded over the green grass toward her, their pink noses quivering in anticipation.

The mermaid held up her arms, and the rabbits smelled brine a little more strongly, but pretended not to notice as they gazed at the smooth, brown skin under her arms.

"Maybe you should *make* some fur," said Mother Rabbit, in between nibbling off bits of fur between her oldest girl's ears.

"How am I supposed to do that?" said the mermaid, wrinkling her broad nose.

Mother Rabbit coughed up a little fur ball instead of answering. She used to tell fairy tales to her babies, while the mermaid and the turtle listened. Maybe the tales of Rapunzel's long hair and Snow White's fair beauty had addled Mother Rabbit's brain to the point where she thought all beings could magic their way out of imprisonment.

The mermaid swished her tail. The blue-green scales stretching from fin to waist gleamed less brightly than a month ago. "I'm already stuck in a water tank in the middle of the world's smallest zoo. How can life get any worse? Maybe I should 'face the consequences.'"

You can't, thought the turtle as it swam past her.

The mermaid swished around to face the turtle, who was paddling along the south wall. Day and night, he swam without cease. "What are you going to do? You don't have any fur, either."

The turtle wiggled its tail in lieu of shrugging his shoulders, and Mother Rabbit whispered into her oldest girl's fur, "You'd have to face the Evil Ex."

The mermaid pursed her lips. "You know, he keeps planting plastic signs and ordering us around. But who is he? How come we never see him?"

Mother Rabbit's nose quivered in distress, but she didn't reply. Neither did the turtle.

"The regulations keep getting more and more ridiculous," said the mermaid. "First we had to give up our morning snack. Then we had to give up our right to free swim time in the big tank because they were 'cleaning it,' but eventually, they dragged the tank away altogether."

Mother Rabbit sniffed. Her six children really missed the morning snack. "Don't forget how our meadow was halved."

"That's right. Evil Ex put up a sign saying that terrestrial animals lost space because they were redesigning the zoo. And he keeps telling us we'll have to face the consequences. Why don't his stupid signs ever tell us the consequences? Maybe I'd rather have those!"

You don't, thought the turtle, paddling past her feet.

"How would you know?" asked the mermaid. "I'm the biggest mammal here. I remember freedom!" With a burst of fury, she recalled the cool currents of the ocean weaving their way through her hair, the undulations of her body as she neatly avoided the boats' engines, but she couldn't evade the dragnet ripping every living creature out of the sea. She squeezed her eyes shut. She could not, would not remember the panic when she got entangled in the ropes, the sensation of getting cranked up to the surface, and worst of all, the men's greedy eyes and their hands lumping along her curves, marvelling at her scales before they sought out every crevice of her body.

I remember freedom too, thought the turtle, and the mermaid splashed away from him, swimming in dozens of angry, thwarted circles until her heart thundered in her chest and her tears mixed with the dead pool water, trying not to think of what might have happened to her family. Her friends. Her lover.

Mother Rabbit coughed up another bit of fur as she moved on to her oldest son. Her oldest daughter looked like a chewed-up stuffed toy that blinked in confusion. Mother Rabbit said, "Maybe the wind could carry this extra fur up to you, and you could press it into your skin and the turtle's shell. That way, you would still be obeying the sign, even if it's not your own fur."

"No," said the mermaid.

"I know it's unlikely that the wind will blow high enough to reach over the tank wall."

"No," said the mermaid, and her voice had grown more sure. She remembered how her voice had once entwined with her sisters' and her mother's and her aunts', more beautiful than the sea at sunset, more delicate than the call of a seashell. "I won't obey the Evil Ex anymore."

You must, thought the turtle.

"Why must I? Because he'll kill me? Because he'll torture me? This isn't living." She threw her head back and screamed. The sound that emerged from the column of her throat, the throat that had once only created beauty, made the seagulls caw and circle around her.

The seagulls.

She could escape through the air. The men had towed her out of the sea. But what if she gathered enough seagulls around her to lift her out of the tank?

She counted almost 30 seagulls, called by a single note from her throat. She could call a hundred more, beckoning them closer, clambering onto their collective backs…

Impossible, she thought. She was far too heavy. If the seagulls dropped her outside the tank, she would break her bones. Her scales would wither from lack of water. She would die within 20 minutes.

But she would die on her own terms. Not dissolving into sea foam out of love for some ignorant prince, but arching upward in a bid for freedom.

She opened her mouth and began to sing again. She hadn't felt like singing since her entrapment, but today she did, on the day of her doom. Beckoning the seagulls, the pelicans, the pigeons. Anything air-bound that might scale the iron fences and come to their aid. If only winged dinosaurs still roamed the earth…

Humans used to call her kind sirens because their songs called the sailors, but she and her sisters simply loved to sing. They used to sing as though their hearts depended on it. Today, it did.

More seagulls flocked in the air. Crows. Starlings. Her friends, the common birds able to survive in this godforsaken city a mile from the ocean. But in the distance, she heard the stronger flap of wings, something unfamiliar, and she was so startled, she stopped singing for an instant.

Now you've done it, thought the turtle.

Yes, I have, she thought back, not wanting to waste her voice on the turtle one moment longer. She began to sing in earnest now. The small birds couldn't carry her, but what if she called one that was large enough? Or even two that could support her just long enough to drop her in the waves beyond this prison?

Then she would be free.

Mother Rabbit started to speak, but the mermaid couldn't hear it over the new and growing rumble of an engine in the sky.

The mermaid trembled when she spotted the black X cutting through the clouds toward her.

In this day and age, most "sailors" took to the sky. The mermaid couldn't afford the attention of any more humans. Evil Ex was growing stricter and perhaps going mad, but so far, he hadn't hurt her as badly as her first captors. Who knew what these air-bound men would do?

She dipped herself neck deep in the water. Old, mucky, briny water, but seawater nonetheless. Baptizing herself. Steeling herself for her last battle. For the plane's engine drove away the birds – the last seagull shrieked in defiance before its wings flapped away – leaving just the helicopter descending toward them and their miniature patch of grass.

The wind whipped the mermaid's stray hair back hard enough that the turtle grumbled and ducked beneath the tank's growing waves. The rabbits dashed into their warrens. The water evaporated from the mermaid's face, raising goosebumps, but she refused to duck under the water the way she saw human children hiding between their mother's legs out of fear.

The helicopter hovered once, twice, creating a strong breeze that terrified the rabbits, before it finally set its "legs" down on the bit of meadow. The mermaid couldn't help eyeballing the length of the runners, not unlike the sleekness of her tail, before she forced the thought away. She had nothing in common with this human scum or his noisy machine with a propeller that threatened to tangle in her lengthy locks.

The mermaid pressed her lips together and re-plaited her hair. She dipped her hair in the water, softening it, making it more like live seaweed than human strands and braided it fast behind her, as if she and her friends were used to receiving such disruptive visitors.

You wanted the consequences, thought the turtle.

I did, she thought back. Anything was better than this liquid jail. She moved to the very front of the tank, pressing her body against the glass. Moving toward the threat instead of shrinking away from it.

At long last, the engine halted and the propeller blades whizzing in the air slowed down. A door popped open, and a man in a black jumpsuit, his face almost completely obscured by a set of goggles, jumped to the ground and shouted, "Aloha!"

The mermaid refused to answer.

Consequences, thought the turtle.

"Show me your fur," said the man. He tried to deepen his voice, but it broke on the last word. He was younger than he pretended.

"I have none," the mermaid replied. She assumed he was Evil Ex, but he hadn't named himself. Fair enough;

she'd refused to give a name to her captors as well. They might contain her body, but they'd never grasp all of her power.

The turtle stayed underwater, paddling silently toward the bottom of the far end of the tank, where he hoped to remain unnoticed.

"Did you not see my sign?" the man said. He thrust his shoulders back, and the mermaid's sharp eyes picked out the black X embroidered on his obsidian outfit. Yes. This was Evil Ex. She could make out faint brown stubble on his cheeks, so he was old enough to shave.

"I did."

"Did you not read my sign?"

"I did."

"Then why did you refuse it?"

"I have no fur to shear," she replied. "As you can see."

"Show me then."

She flipped her giant braid in front of her for modesty before she bobbed out of the water, and the flicker of his eyes behind his goggles was enough to show her that the Evil Ex, like any man, thought the most important part of a mermaid were her sweet, bare breasts.

"Then you must be punished," he said, almost pleasantly.

"By all means," she said, although her heart threatened to burst through her chest.

He reached inside his vest, but his hand stilled when it reached whatever weapon it sought. "You sound almost logical."

"Perpetually. Unlike yourself."

He nearly laughed. "How am I illogical?"

"Trapping a mermaid, seven rabbits, and a turtle? Tormenting us with nonsensical signs? I learned almost nothing of human culture, yet I know I am the height of reason, compared to you."

He flushed, she noted with satisfaction, tracking the bit of skin on his cheeks visible under the goggles. She had scored a point. He snarled, "You would tremble before the extent of Ex-Terra Club Collection. Have you ever seen a sphinx?"

She had not, but her mind seized on the notion of a club. She had heard of such things. A gathering of like-minded humans. So that was why he'd trapped them? For the sake of some sort of club *competition?* She wondered what he must have placed in the larger tank he'd towed away. She said, "A sphinx. Really? Why, does that trump a mermaid, a turtle, and seven rabbits?"

His fingers flexed and extended and his Adam's apple bobbed before he said, "Shut up, you spawn of Satan."

"Oh, that's logical as well." The look in his eyes made the mermaid shudder, so she slapped her tail on the fetid water. "Whenever you disagree with someone, call her the devil. That will win the argument every time."

"Enough of your screaming lies." He yanked the weapon out of his vest, a black gun longer than his hand. The weight of the gun in his hand seemed to calm him, and the corners of his mouth jerked into a grin as he aimed it at her heart. "Creatures who disobey must be punished to the fullest extent of the law according to ordinance #212."

The mermaid forced one word past the lump in her throat. "Why?"

"No more silly whys! I will send you straight into your everlasting hole of DOOM and watch you melt in the magma!" He steadied the gun, overlapping his thumbs on the handle and taking careful aim.

The mermaid lashed out with her braid, swinging it out of the water with all her might. The weight of her magnificent black hair, coiled with rage and weighed down by seawater, slammed into his arms and knocked him sideways.

Evil Ex stumbled, putting down a hand to steady himself, discharging his gun into the meadow.

"Mother Rabbit!" shouted the mermaid, but it was too late. The gun had blasted a growing crater in the meadow, a yellow-orange glowing pit that devoured a circle of grass and earth even as the mermaid watched.

She shook her hair and yelled, "Mother Rabbit! Baby rabbits! Climb, climb, climb!" For Mother Rabbit had told her babies the story of Rapunzel, and they might be able to climb the dangling ladder of the mermaid's hair in this hour of need.

A baby rabbit popped its head out of the ground and bounded toward the mermaid's braid.

Evil Ex leaped toward it, calling, "Oh, no, you don't!"

The pit yawned open beneath him. His goggle eyes widened in surprise before he fell, calling, "Nooooooooooo," until his voice vanished along with him.

The mermaid never heard his impact. Maybe there wasn't one. She concentrated on coaxing the baby rabbits up her braid, with Mother Rabbit hopping up the rear.

"We did it!" shouted the mermaid. She wished she could fist-bump Mother Rabbit, but the rabbit was barely balancing on the end of her braid and shouting instructions at her less nimble offspring.

We're all doomed anyway, thought the turtle.

On cue, the pit of doom expanded under the tank and the glass cracked.

The mermaid froze. If she lost the water, if her scales dried completely, she would perish in 20 minutes. She started to swim to the opposite side of the tank, but as her braid dipped into the water, the rabbits screamed and nearly tipped into the drink, so she batted her tail in the brine, tried to keep her braid steady, and attempted to think as well as she could while a glowing orange pit started to engulf the earth under her only water supply.

She tilted her gaze up. Toward the sky. Toward freedom. A curious crow cawed at her, wondering at the goings-on, and she remembered her most singular power.

She closed her eyes and began to sing. As deeply as the rocks on the ocean floor; as light and pure as a bubble of seawater. And for the first time since her capture, she sang her name. She sang it loud and clear, announcing it, claiming it, for if this was indeed the moment of her doom, she had no need to save it any longer.

The walls of the tank groaned and cracked on all four sides now.

In the farthest range of her hearing, she detected once more the sound of the strongest wings of her imagination. Not the mechanized buzz of a helicopter's blades or an airplane's wings, but something far purer and sweeter, almost like the ears of an elephant, except larger and more vigorous, batting their feathered way toward her. She had never made fast friends with the birds and beasts of the air, but perhaps in this day and age, when mermaids were dragged out of the sea, it wasn't so surprising that the last remaining magical creatures anywhere on earth had to rally together one final time.

The temperature of the tank water grew uncomfortably warm. She could feel the brine beginning to bubble.

Smaller birds' wings gathered around the mermaid, too. Even with her eyes closed, she felt the birds' shadow falling over her. The light beneath her eyelids dimmed and she felt the very air around them grow slightly cooler from the mass of avian friends.

But when she opened her eyes, the army of birds drawn to her song cleared out of the way of a central point, the way a circle of water undulates around a rock thrown into a pond. As the birds rippled away, she watched a black speck growing closer and closer.

The tank water seeped away faster now. She kicked her tail, trying to stay as high as possible, away from the hole of doom, singing loud enough to overcome the sound of the birds screaming and the smell of the rabbits defecating in her hair.

And her eyes focused on the most beautiful sign in the world: a black stallion beating his powerful wings toward them. His nostrils flared with effort. His left flank bore an ugly scar. Like her, he was a survivor. But his hooves thundered through the air toward them. The wind batted by his wings smelled like summer grass and fresh rivers. And as the turtle reluctantly climbed onto her shoulder, the mermaid thrust her tail out of the water and seized on to her Pegasus' warm neck, ready to ride to freedom.

(FROM THE LITERATURE OF NATURAL DISASTERS)
WHAT BECAME OF THEM

MARY BURNS

She endures as the vast inscrutable sea. Opaque overall, often wrinkled as if a fist long-clenched has released. White peaks tower over deep troughs on stormy days. Depths you might not be able to imagine, although it helps to picture the iceberg diagrams showing the bulk that lies beneath what is visible. The sonatas of assorted mammals, the clicking of shells, the tickle of fish swelling in schools. Let's call her Maris. Generally, she identifies as mesopelagic, light still penetrates, but she has known the hadalpelagic, where the bottom feeders live. In truth, she is all of it from the sunlight zone down to the hell zones. It depends on the day.

He slides over in that familiar red leaf. Or he did, and the image remains, the yellow blades of the paddle, his face imperfectly mirrored as he looked down to examine the mystery. The well-meaning say you are not alone. There are more like you. Support groups. As if any bowl could ever hold the ocean. She covers nearly three-quarters of the planet. That she is called by different names in different places reflects human peculiarities such as language and geography and the need to own things. Not the reality. She is the one and only. She is all there is.

Solitudinem morphed into this desert that he explored so many times. An extreme desert, capable of supporting only the prickliest life, scoured by sweeping winds, deep where that wind has pushed her against impediments, a suitable burial place for the fossil that she cannot become fast enough. In the canyons of her thoughts is the image of him discovering something valuable here. Her. Cigarettes burn her throat. Cup after cup of coffee does nothing to arrest the desiccating embodiment of grief.

Night is just settling into the jungle that is Saltu, although beneath the thick canopy it is always more or less night. The children don't notice. The insect humming becomes louder, the heavy paws of a large cat fall on earth that is just rot when you think of it, all the things that have lived and nourished and are now decomposing. That's her. Nothing clear, no way to see ahead, nothing open, nothing simple. And always something pullulating so that she can't settle into the darkness. It is too fecund here. The wild blossoms in pink and white and garish red, her blood sucked into the roots of some plant. Will things ever stop growing? Will the night ever be quiet? Mommy, mommy, cries the one who can talk. The other whimpers until Saltu releases a teat automatically. But their entreaties bounce off her like hailstones against a burl.

It's quieter for Caemeterium, the ground in which the dead lie. She is pocketed with coffins carefully chosen by grieving or sometimes only resigned loved ones. Oblong sections of her are chiselled open regularly, then filled with steel boxes, wooden boxes. She had always followed him. What else would she have done? And so, she has ended up here among this treasury of the dead without knowing who they were, are, except for those encased in green materials that decompose quickly and let the bones disintegrate at a quicker pace. Still, it's a long time to wait for their company. You'd think it would be silent here but as they settle, joining him who instigated this, she hears their shifting; their murmurs. You'll adjust, people said, without noticing the rising bumps of tombstones. This is a kind of adjustment.

When the neighbours who brought cakes or sent flowers amble along Vicinia's sidewalks, she thinks of the casserole dishes sitting on her counter, the stack of unwritten thank you notes. She could email. To copy and paste would be easier than trying to keep a pen steady in her hand. What will she do with those dishes brought by those who assumed that she would not forget their offerings? They should have written their names on a strip of tape and affixed it to the dish, as she does in similar situations. They should have kept it to plastic containers instead of burdening her with, for example, that colourful pot undoubtedly purchased in some exotic place. Kids swing on swings in the little park. Delivery trucks cruise her streets and brake at the addresses that match the same on their waybills. She is the place itself, of it, in it, on it. All the prepositions apply. A few shrubs have gone straggly this time of year but most are trimmed, smooth sidewalks, chipped sidewalks or no sidewalks at all but lawns that sweep to the macadam. The bus keeps to its schedule. Regularly maintained street lights illumine the streets at night when she is not tired because she has not cooked for him or anyone. She has not picked up a prescription at the drugstore. She has not smiled and let her head fall to the side sadly and thanked the sympathetic. At the end of the day, she has done almost nothing and her emptiness throbs. No mail truck, no bus, no cars stopping or children doing something that would emit a reassuring or at least distracting sound.

What is that screeching? Saltu wonders. A bird? A primate? One of the kids? Mommy, mommy? What now? Can't you see I'm busy. She thinks it, she feels it but she doesn't say it because their gazes are imploring as that of the sloth that hangs upside down in her. If she holds them off for even a few minutes creepers will cover them and their voices will be faint as the spores of fungi multiplying in accordance with their duty, their purpose. She is a trumpet flower those babies try to crawl into not knowing her poisonous qualities. Why did he have to exit so early? Destiny? If someone were to write a paper, like he used to do, might they conclude by saying as much? Is there an answer? Will you stop with the questions? Don't tell me what to do!

The water that evaporates from Maris is replenished by raining tears. The water cycle. She will never be empty. People have no idea how full she is. How are you doing, they say, and their voices come through as echoes... doing, doing, doing. Well you know, she says, as the shallowest part of her slides onto the shore.

There is talk about redevelopment. What? Vicinia's instinct is to keep everything as it was before the centre failed. Him. Older, sick. There is a natural order. Of course, things change, yet when that recent storm struck trees that had to be radically pruned or cut down altogether it felt as if someone had ripped off her coat. Not just any coat but her best coat, the one that had kept her warm, even fashionable. She recovered to accommodate other small alterations. Weather comes and goes, and the neighbourhood remains.

Solitudinem endures the pulsing night, the scraping air currents. Will they eventually disperse her in such minute particles that she will be finished herself? How many centuries must pass before the disappearance of the desert? She is icy cold, the stars above are the tips of blades that threaten to pierce her. Pain she knows. How it whittled and finally addled him so that he looked at her without seeing her before he breathed his last. Don't you remember those days, she had pleaded as she tried to wrench him back to when they were partners in all things. How sunburned you got that day you forgot your hat? He barely roused. She could not see into his thoughts then but only imagine what he must be thinking, which, in truth, had to be nothing. Why bother at that point?

The neat rectangles that the groundskeepers regularly carve out of Caemetorium are the perfect size for that which fills them. In the process, the opening, the microbes that live in her scatter in the painful light. Then comes the box containing the body. It's like a dentist filling a tooth. And just like dentists promise longevity for fillings, morticians promise the bereaved that the contents of the best boxes will not decompose for ages. There will be someone to visit, to bring flowers for, or paper replicas of items a loved one might need in the afterlife, as Chinese survivors do. The steel box purchasers are the most serious about ensuring that outcome. Worms cannot penetrate steel, but of course neither can anything else. It was not that she could not let him go or even that she wanted to go with him, it's just that the woman in that house they had downsized to a scant six months before, that formerly dependent woman immediately had to decide which sort of box to put him in, perform chores she

never thought she would have to learn to do. If Caemeterium had arms as that woman had, she would spread them
in supplication, as if to say: "What now?" So, what is she
doing here where arms are irrelevant? The thought of arms
begins something. What?

People move in, move out but most stay, old clothes in
the back of a big closet. The Larsens in their Cape Cod-style
two-storey with shingles painted grey as if weathered. Vicinia
always thought that pretentious here, a continent away from
Cape Cod. A few carpenter gothics. Such exaggerated
points! At least she is not a neighbourhood where every
house is the same. There is that, and a red-brick school. A
corner store that has been owned by the same Korean family
since she first saw the neighbourhood, decades before she
morphed into it. Another generation now, different stock.
Coconut water, energy bars, yet still that cardboard flat of
liquorice by the cash register. Her kids – their kids – had to
be told to avoid it. Just get the milk. No candy. You have no
idea whose hands have touched it.

Scuttling spiders, sidewinding snakes that leave patterns Solitudinem might paint were she not now the canvas
itself. So rarely rain, such modest drifts of snow. The canines
that howl. Yes! Their forlorn sounding calls. Richard! The
cremains of him rest on their marriage bed in the world she
formerly inhabited.

The children won't let Saltu's tangled vegetation grow
more complex and decompose as it naturally would, which
couldn't be soon enough for her. Except for them. They tug
at her vines; they curl in her like maggots in old meat. How
can she feed them, find a job to earn money for food when
she is this humid morass where the voices of big cats and the

avian world are louder than theirs? Their hands pull at her. Mommy, mommy! We're hungry! There is fruit everywhere. Help yourself. But Mommy, we don't like that kind. It's perfectly good. Don't mind the spots. It's food for you. Can't you see I am busy? Mommy, mommy, we can't see you at all.

Even before his last breath, Maris felt herself liquescing. But to actually be the ocean! The brilliant solution. Dissolved, liquified. Hadn't they always described themselves as water people? Swimmers as opposed to hikers; kayakers as opposed to cyclists. He had talked about scuba diving, which they never got to. But snorkelling! And the first to spot phosphorescence in the late summer. Electric eels flash at her lower levels and remind her that true darkness is an illusion fostered by those who are shy of the deep. She is everywhere. Almost three-quarters of the planet's surface. Almost seven miles down at her deepest. Despite her breadth and her depth, she is not in total control. There are currents pushed by winds and tides. They didn't know much about currents and only a little more about tides when they sat on the dock to watch moonlight penetrate their bay. How could something so vast be influenced by anything? She didn't know, he didn't. How foolish they were, how unscientific. They were usually high and sipping brandy to temper the chill into which they dangled their feet. Like underwater ghosts, pale-furred seals finned close but not close enough to touch.

Solitudinem followed him to the driest desert on earth where he hiked over knuckles of rock rich with copper red as the winter sunset. Solitudinem was not solitudinem then but a woman with a common name he would call and his voice would come to her like a meteorite across the deep blue roof of the sky from which rain might fall every 30 years, even longer. Hundreds of years. It may never rain again. While he had chiselled rock samples and followed hunches that led him to possible mine sites, she sketched landforms and odd bits of vegetation that grew along the coastal strip and which she had photographed because she knew that once their jeep rattled further inland there would be no growing things. During the long hot days, she sheltered in their tent and watched reptiles bask. Once a fox came close but what troublesome relationship would start should she feed it? When the sun rose to the top of its arc, he came back and she lifted the neck flaps of his desert hat to spread cream onto the skin. She knew all the skin of his body. She is this small percentage of the earth now, she is frigid at her peak and hot at the edges, and quiet except when a lizard scratches past on its tiny claws or a fox needles the atmosphere with yelps of joy at the birth of its kits. Life insists, says that shattering sound. Not according to her, though. Not without the man in the flapped cap whose shadow fell before him and thus reached her before he did.

Who knows what will happen to them? Saltu is helpless against the proliferation. There is no space to reflect, to recover as all the advice indicates she must do. Hah! Mommy, mommy. She must maintain herself despite dying a little every day. From the compost, new shoots climb onto her extended parts to reach the sun. There is that. When the counsellor visits to counsel her, the counsellor does not see the vegetation nor hear the screeching nor feel the slithery invertebrates. She doesn't realize that the predominantly chlorophyll cast of Saltu's skin indicates not the seasonal flu but instead her condition as a newcomer to this phase of life.

The social worker kindly if ignorantly says,. Are you getting out much? Out much? How? With him no longer available to look after the children and them wondering his absence, microverses with their own confusing expressions, and the unemployment office requiring forms that don't relate to her at all. There are no blanks adequate for her to describe where she lives, what lives in her.

Caemeterium had thought herself content to be the ground where the dead lie. What else could there be? Those who advised her to accept the change may not have realized how seriously she went into meta-acceptance mode. So why this stirring? Why does a hand rise up, obviously hers; she can tell by the ring on the third finger of her left hand. Quite the ring. A wide band encrusted with diamonds and exhibiting no flecks of soil at all. A gift from him for their 50th wedding anniversary. Then a shoulder, which sprouts goosebumps because winter has fallen. She can't remain like this, half one thing, half another. But instead of sinking down, which had seemed like such a good idea, she continues to emerge, and before she can appreciate the transition she is lying in her bed and the lamp is glowing and on the television there is a weather map. Someone is saying that the cold front will be followed by a warming trend. She rolls across the entire mattress; she spreads her arms. The landline rings and the recorded message plays in her musical voice: "You've reached Robert and Jennifer Tillson. Please leave us a message after the beep." No point in changing the poem that it is. Robert and Jennifer Tillson.

Somewhere else on the planet, a cane-thin, curly-haired woman is standing in front of a government building. She might appear unremarkable except for the wincing as she pulls something off her, a vine? No, a child calling, Mommy, mommy. The expression on the woman's face is surprised, bereft, confused, regretful, dutiful. A stew of emotions that smells like compost. Inside her pocket, the alarm she set on her cell phone goes off. It is a custom sound, the chirps of birds in the morning when they are always so happy. She thought it would help. Mommy? Saltu does not want to know the question because she almost certainly has no answer. Come on, we have to go, she says, and they enter the building where she must complete the forms, to fill in the box that says "Widowed." If she does that automatically, which the authorities expect, will she then recede in this skin and return to being the jungle she has been for these last months when she did not think in months, actually, but in the number of times flowers bloomed and died? Someone gives the child a lollipop. The baby in her stroller is sleeping.

Maris is everywhere and she is the only one. The currents that run through her and erupt as waves, the fantastical sea creatures and fish that endlessly course, the garbage that floats and sinks, the islands of plastic. It is all her. And him. It is where they continue together.

Vicinia will always be the neighbourhood. This particular neighbourhood. She is its geometric street pattern, its smooth pavement, the driveways that branch off in asphalt or concrete stems, its timely mail delivery and bus schedule. She is the small house, the large house, the fire hydrant, the underground cables that run through her like veins making possible communication with other neighbourhoods. It does not lessen her to materialize as an individual again. Unlike Maris, she knows she is not the only one. In fact, she tests out a group of other neighbourhoods and listens to their stories – a city of women living alone who tire of making dinner for one. They could join forces, concoct a rotating schedule for sharing meals, someone suggests. A conglomeration of neighbourhoods would make a city of widows. She is not ready to tell her own story. Keeping it for herself gives her options. She is part neighbourhood, part neighbour and they, whoever they happen to be on a given day, need not know her particular particulars. That it was a long illness, that she expected the transition, that she is someone who takes pleasure in order and familiarity and could happily remain the neighbourhood itself, though as a neighbor she is open to possibilities. Meeting someone, which is better accomplished as an individual. It's like respiration itself, sucking in, blowing out, or being blown out by the eternal tempest. If you give it a chance, which she will not. She will try the dinner thing. Maybe one of the guests will identify the beautiful pottery casserole sitting lonely by the front door. Then she will be rid of that.

Solitudinem is not all deserts, she is this particular desert, the driest on earth. How can images continue to assail her when she has no brain to think? His scarlet sweater, his white as vapour hair. A trick of who she used to be. More scouring and those images will fade away. What then? Will they swirl up and circle the red mountain and separate like the grains of sand and chips of rock? The flesh is one thing, but the thoughts, the memories, the imagination, the spirit? Where do they go?

PART TWO

AFTER THE FALL

RENTED

AGATA ANTONOW

The woman in the street outside my apartment is howling again. Her movements stir up the dust along the cracked streets. She has been at it for a few months now. I see her hobble to and from the grocery store at the corner – the kind of relic with dirty linoleum floors and blinking fluorescent lights that's only patronized by people who just got their implants in the past few years.

I picture the woman being one of the few to protest the implants 10 years ago. I imagine her with signs, warning us all that implants would steal our souls. She wears long sleeves, so I can't tell what kind of tech she did eventually get.

Most of the time I just see her walking that same route, usually without a grocery bag. But a few times a week, she stops in the middle of the sidewalk and howls. Usually just random vowel noises, with some nonsense thrown in. She keeps at it until a cop walks by and leads her away by the elbow.

"AAAHWAOOO," she shrieks again. The old girl still has lungs on her, though most of the body under the faded dress must be 80. She must not have had any work done, I think, as I glance at my fortified arms.

The blue silicone surface of my implant beeps on my wrist at the same time as the knock comes at my door. I swipe the cool surface of the tech to see what the words have to say.

One (1) pending offer to rent your kitchen for dinner party. Interested?

I ignore it and open the door to a tiny woman with bright pink hair. She's about 20, and I scan my wrist over the irises of her purple eyes to confirm what I already know.

"Beep. Cindy. Lam. 19. Student. One day in Helene's spare bedroom. Rented."

We both wait for my implant to finish the recital before we nod and smile. I help her with her bag – a hardback silver thing – and show her the spare room. Her eyes scan over the daisy curtains and the rag rug beside the wooden bed. She nods once, precisely, her neck bobbing up and down sharp.

"Perfect. Just like the ad. Old-fashioned, just how I like it. Thank you." She sets her suitcase down and I turn away, closing the door.

I can hear her shuffling behind the door when I return to my post by the window. The old woman is gone now and the street is mostly empty. I see two people argue over a rented parking spot beside drought-cracked asphalt. "I booked my reservation a week ago!" A man walks by with a sign over his shoulder, *Marketing space for rent*.

My wrist beeps again.

Rate Cindy as a guest.

I hit 10. Why not?

Two (2) offers to rent one hour of your time as a [admin assistant]: y/n?

I look at the deadlines and hit *y*. I need the money to make rent, even with Cindy. Even with George and Mason arriving for the spare room next week and the week after that.

I pull myself away from the window and go to make lunch.

One (1) offer to rent lunch with you. Vegan options needed. Available?

I scan the price being offered and hesitate, weighing my options against the balance in my accounts. As I think, the beep comes in again.

You need 500 calories for optimum dietary needs. 30 g protein.

Another beep.

You have not replied to three (3) of the past rent asks and have said n to three (3). How can we match you better? Reach out to us at...

I swipe again and the image disappears from the screen just over my skin. I try not to picture what the blood vessels look like under the digital surface; electricity carried all the way to my heart.

I don't think about it again until I am walking home the next day. It is sunny out and my hour of admin work turned into one and a half. At least I was paid for it. It doesn't always end that way. Some employers in the city have figured out that getting in the work and then leaving a low review and complaint can get them out of paying.

How would you rate your employment at GigMarket?

I hit 10 and watch their own 10 come in on my own performance.

Helene, you have not replied to three (3) of the past rent asks and have said n to three (3). How can we match you better? Reach out to us at...

Uh-oh. My name this time. I can't remember the last time I saw it. The message has been flashing again and again. It woke me up twice, before I got up fully and noticed Cindy wasn't in her room. Probably out renting her body to pay for her vacation. Maybe that's unkind. She could be renting her talents in some other way.

I ignore the message again, though I know it means I will eventually be rated lower and will need to go in to see someone. I'm hanging in at 8.2 as it is. I can't afford to drop much lower if I want to have enough to eat. At a 7 rating, my pay per gig will drop. I think of the families in shanties by the highway of the city.

It's a surprise I never have dropped lower, though I take care to answer every few requests. If I were called in to see someone, I would have to go to the old stone building I walk by almost every day. It used to be a library or some such thing. The way things were rented in the old days. I've read you couldn't rent copyright back then, or bodies, but you could rent a book for three weeks. I picture holding pages in my hand, smelling the glossy covers, knowing it is mine for three weeks.

Now, the building is pristine on the outside, white-washed stone made whiter by recent droughts. It must have stood there since the 1880s. People who are long gone and buried or rented must have walked up its steps, again and again. And now they're gone and this building still stands. In some lights, you can still see part of the old sign – "Librar" is still there above the doors, despite the careful process to make the stone gleam. Inside, I picture long marble hallways and chairs and the murmur of people and quiet beeps. I picture rows of people who have dropped below 7 or even 5.

I don't cherish going in there. I must be more careful.

One (1) offer to rent your body for [casual sex]: y/n?

I swipe *n* and keep moving. When I get back to my place, there is already a guest waiting. He looks impatient and I worry about my rating. I flash him an apologetic smile.

"Sorry. Was rented for admin work. Bills, you know."

He says nothing. His mouth is still a straight line behind his bushy beard and his hair is dull in the light of the hallway. His skin is disturbingly pale in the light, like something brought up from the ocean floor. He grips a heavy duffel bag.

I scan my wrist over his brown eyes with one hand while I open the door with the other.

"MacMason. Cam. 30. One night in Helene's spare bedroom. Rented."

He pushes past me to get in and fiddles with his wrist.

His request lights up my wrist at once.

One (1) offer to rent your body for [casual sex]: y/n?

I back away slowly, shaking my head. I've never been face to face with anyone making an ask before. His eyes look wrong. Angry and willing to hurt. He still has not let go of the deathtrap grip on the black bag. He smiles, and it's much worse in the expanse of that dark beard.

"No," I tell him and run out the door. I rent hours in a café and nap on and off, trying to stay as upright as possible in the faux-leather booth. I keep a tea in front of me and at one point order a chocolate chip cookie. Three dollars for a small one, and I wince at the deduction from my monthly budget.

200 calories. You need 300 calories for optimum health. 30 g protein.

The barista – a tall man with black eyes – watches me.

One (1) offer for dishwashing: y/n

I'm too exhausted and swipe *n*. As I'm stepping to my table, the cookie slides off the plate and to the floor. No one seems to be looking, so I scoop it back up and set it down with a clatter on the table. I'm hungry. Is it too dirty to eat?

A woman comes in after me. She's about 30, has ratty blonde hair and is carrying five bags. She huffs into the table and I watch the barista watch her. I expect him to get her to leave, but he doesn't. Like some older people, she doesn't have an implant, though she can't be older than me. I wonder if she dropped below 3. How low do you need to drop before you decide to have the implant removed? I watch her for a while, as my eyes get smaller and smaller, then shut. The murmur of voices fades as I listen to her order.

"I want water."

I open my eyes some undetermined time later. The plate is still there but my cookie is gone. I look around. The woman is gone, too. The barista is still there. I give him a one-finger salute and start the walk home. I hope Cam is gone.

Beep. Grinds Coffee House has given you a three (3) rating.

I stop in the middle of the street and give the barista a one.

Fuck you, too, buddy.

Cam has given me a 10, and I ignore the request to rate him. My eyes still feel grainy and the sun is too bright. I walk three blocks west, dodging people with shopping carts, hunting for clothes or bottles or whatever it is they trade under the old freeways of the city. They pass me by, leaving little trails of body odour. I'm walking past ghosts. A few more bad reviews, three visits to the authorities. We're all headed not for oblivion and death, but for bad ratings and homelessness, implantlessness, nothingness. This grey horde of people with their carts. The only thing keeping their reality out of my life is my implant and my apartment with its white door and old rag rugs that I can't afford to replace.

As I walk the final two blocks east to my apartment, by the wrecks of people, I wonder what brings them here. Why not keep getting ratings, giving ratings? Even if their ratings drop low, why not keep trying? Why not keep renting? It just takes a few hours of attention to the implant screen. Is there something that makes ratings matter less with time? Will I reach 60 and not be able to keep swiping?

"Would you like water?" An old man breaks from a group of three elderly people hunched over a cart. He is smiling a brown-tooth smile, lifting up a half-filled water bottle. I can see where the sun has cracked his skin. I shake my head no.

I walk up toward my building, squinting up at my window, trying to see whether Cam is gone. I can't tell from the outside. From the outside, all the apartments look the same, sheltering the owners, the rented, the casual nights. I sit down for a moment on the stoop just to the right of the front door.

That's when I see her. She's moaning again and as she walks past, I get a whiff of the smell. Rotting meat and dumpsters. The old woman is holding her arms out, wide open in a hug for the world.

"AUUUU." She gets louder and louder and I'm scared she will accost me but she passes within two feet of me like I'm the ghost. As she walks by, I see the source of the odour. On her wrist is a cracked screen, and around it the flesh has gone scarlet and red, white bone sticking out. The infection reeks and I can see the veins in her arm as she shuffles past. The sight makes my own skin itch. I've heard of people opposed to tech ripping out their implants because they don't have enough ratings for surgery, but I've never seen it. I imagine likes dropping below zero and my hand falls over my wrist protectively.

Without thinking about it, I stand up and walk after her.

I follow her to the grocery store. She pushes the door and disappears inside. I hesitate. I usually order online, a place that always gives me a 10 when I need it in exchange for mine, run by some guy who rented me for a week in my third year of college. His place exists in the cloud, strings of ones and zeroes.

This place is too human. When I push open the door, I disturb a little bell above the door. I step onto cracked linoleum and eye aisle after aisle of boxes, like something from a textbook.

The whole place reeks of dried fish. Big dusty windows look out at the world, and the only shoppers are over the age of 65, shuffling along the dim aisles, peering at labels. Probably no net connections. No implants. I think about the disease of the woman's arm and feel a shivery surge of bile. What is it like to be unmoored from others and their opinions? How would you shop, earn money, prove your ID? It feels like an endless, impossible void. A life I can't picture.

A big man with red hair is standing at the cash, watching me intently. The sign next to him says "no implant/net payments." I have no idea how people pay if not net. Are these people using illegal currency? Could this place get raided? I couldn't stand to lose 20 per cent of my ratings in a raid.

The red-haired man starts walking toward me and I pick up the first thing I see, start reading the label. "Pork beans," I read over and over in my mind, with no idea what it means.

"Can I help you?" The red-haired man is right beside me. Close enough that I can see sweat stains under his green T-shirt. Close enough that I can see "Jason" embroidered on the green knit fabric.

I shake my head mutely.

"We don't take net payments. No implants or ratings." His voice is impatient. *Are we going to have a problem here?* is implied.

"Oh, leave her alone, Jay." An older woman with big sunglasses rolls up with her cart. She grabs a can of beans and it hits her cart with a rattle. "You're scaring her half to death. Look at her."

They look at me while I look at the woman with the sunglasses. She's a full head shorter than me and through the thin hair on her head, I can see the bright pink of her scalp. It feels like something I shouldn't see, and I glance away. She doesn't smell bad, I realize, when my breath leaves my mouth in a rattled whoosh. She smells like some unspecified flower.

Jason doesn't look at me. "No use having someone curious here, looking for trouble."

"I don't want trouble," I say, out of the blue, startling myself more than I surprise them. Probably. Two sets of eyes swing at me and an older man rolls up beside us.

"I've never been here..." I'm not sure what to say.

Beep. There's an incoming weather message, but my wrist is the only one that beeps. I don't glance at it, and I pull down my sweater sleeve. Everyone here has long sleeves or smooth arms with no tech.

"Look!" It's the woman from outside, the howling one. She's wearing a purple hat and rounding the corner with a cart. I don't stare at her wrist. Don't notice the shine of pus. "It's raining. Rain!"

We all turn to the windows. Dirt on the windows is caking with streaks of wet. We stand there, side by side, and watch the water wash the dust away.

A FENCE
MADE OF NAMES

Bruce Meyer

The whales are vanishing from the seas because the culture
I live in accepted the idea that whales would last forever.
Their extinction was romanticised in art and literature, stud-
ied with scientific precision, and memorialized in a cata-
logue written by a customs house official who said everything that could possibly be said about the creatures. In
doing so, the author turned a sandy archipelago in the
Atlantic into the shrine for the art of destroying whales that
it is today. I know of no other place on earth where the process of wiping out a species is celebrated in such a way.
Once harpooned and hauled aboard whaling ships, the bodies of the enormous animals provided all manner of products
to a burgeoning consumer society – oil for lamps, emulsions
for perfume, uncomfortable undergarments for women,
large bristle brushes, and fertilizer – until the great whales
had been rendered and reduced to the point they almost
vanished from the seas. Pollution or microbial inflammation
of their navigational mechanisms has caused thousands of
the creatures to beach themselves all over the world in what
resembles a mass suicidal surrender. I went to an island off
the coast of Massachusetts to discover how the passing of
the "Great Whales," as the Book of Genesis calls them, was

transforming the masterpiece of creation into a repeated lost legend.

I picked the worst possible day, weather-wise, to go to Nantucket. The ferry from Hyannis Port lurched and rolled in the swells. When I disembarked, I was met with a wall of rain with only a measly city umbrella to keep me dry. But I wanted to see the Quaker Graveyard the poet Robert Lowell had written about during a summer of his youth spent on the island. I wanted to write my own poem about the site though I knew little to nothing about it. The moment I boarded the tour bus and asked the guide if we would be seeing the famous Quaker Graveyard, she blinked at me and said, "You mean the burial grounds at the inter-section of Quaker and Madaket Roads out near Maxcy's Pond?"

"Yes," I replied. "If that's what you call it."

"I'm sorry to disappoint you, but it's not on the tour. There's nothing there to see."

That was disappointing. I begged her to swing by and let me have a brief look because anything worth a classic poem ought to be worth seeing. I had even written lines I wanted to work into my version.

"No," she said. "I said there's nothing to see. The Quak-ers didn't believe in headstones."

I chimed in, having done a little bit of background read-ing in preparation for my visit. I countered that the names of those buried there were inscribed on the fence. She nodded.

"Vandals burned the fence down years ago." She repeated the claim about the Burial Grounds. "There is really nothing to see, and it takes us off our designated route."

"Then I want my money back. I mean, what's the point of visiting a place that was made special by a poet. I didn't come all this way only to find out the place only exists in the poem. I could have stayed at home and read about it in an anthology."

She rolled her eyes and looked over at the driver who rolled his eyes.

"Well, when we're near, we'll see if we can negotiate the turn because the road is narrow and muddy; though I can't promise anything."

I had tried to write about the graveyard without seeing it. If a person is going to write about something, they have to see it first-hand otherwise the language becomes abstract and blurry. At least, when it came to whales, I had something concrete to say.

I had one of those profound moments with a whale when I was 10 years old, a moment of sudden connection, when I felt I understood the giant creature as we read each other's minds, corny as that may sound. My parents had taken the family on a whale-watching excursion out of Provincetown on the northern finger of Cape Cod. The tour guide on that boat said we were headed to the Georges Bank, though from the speed we were making and time out of port it took to get us "there," I am certain we weren't anywhere near the fabled fishing grounds of the North Atlantic. The Georges Bank is just too far away from Provincetown for a three-hour tour. I think the whales were working for the tour company and were probably coaxed closer to Provincetown by fishermen paid to dump chum from a Cape cannery.

In the distance, about 500 yards from the portside, a pod of Baleens was sounding, tossing their tails in the air and shooting spray out their blowholes. Everyone on the boat crowded to see them, and I got squeezed out of the group, and elbowed by my brother who told me to shove off. I went over to the starboard side and leaned on the rail. I was annoyed there wasn't room enough for me to see. My mother kept motioning me to come and mouthing the words "You're missing the show." Her voice wouldn't carry in the wind. I looked over the portside and there below me, rolling on its fin, was an enormous whale nuzzling the hull.

The creature could easily have capsized us, but instead, it just lay there with its eye the size of a basketball staring up at me as I looked down at it. The pull of the whale's gaze, the sharing of that instant of mutual recognition and study, made me feel we were reading each other's souls. The experience lasted two, maybe three minutes.

The tour boat's engines were shut off and we were drifting. I could hear the silence of the sea all around me. The whale didn't blink and neither did I. Transfixed. I am certain I saw an eternity of waves and dark depths and shifting phases of the moon and storms and stars as he saw them. I felt time as if a second lasted forever. The boat, the crowd on the portside, and even the wind in my ears were silenced at that moment as if I was on the bottom of the ocean, and the whale and I were the only living souls in the world. I am certain it was telling me I ought to write a poem about whaling, and the first one that came to mind as a model for my own was Lowell's.

That is why a walk down Center Street in Nantucket, when I disembarked from the Hyannis ferry in the pouring rain, touched a chord of anger in me. The whale-shaped signs above the doors of dress shops, the spouting, smiling white marquees beckoning visitors into seafood restaurants, the gift shops chucked with plastic whales and cheap statues of bearded Captain Ahabs, were mocking the great whales. The sad aspect of the human mind is that it only notices things once they are lost. Humans have a natural proclivity to lamentation and elegy. Things have to be ruined before they recognize them and frame them in beautiful words. Absence is the motivator of consciousness. I was studying literature because I wanted to discover the world, but in the process of discovering it, I realized most of what I found didn't exist anymore, a paradise lost, a dead son, a ghostly father on the battlements of a Danish castle. Poetry embodies conscience when it is too late to care about what has gone.

When the whale rolled over and disappeared into the depths, all I could think of for days were those grand cetaceans. I felt as if I had been called to speak to the whale in poetry. Did it want me to warn? Did it want me to remember? As the bus wound through the rain-soaked roads of Nantucket, I thought about the fence and whales and what goes missing from the world only to be answered by the charms or the floundering of poems.

I never told my parents what I had seen on the whale watch. That evening my parents and my siblings went on about what a mope I was, and how moody, pre-pubescent boys are full of themselves and think they know everything, but miss what is worth seeing because they wrap themselves in a false sense of know-it-all cool. How could I tell them about my experience and how much it had meant to me? If I had even tried to explain they would have told me I was crazy. Poetry is born on the border of a strange land where the poet sees things in the distance that are not obvious to others. I should have told them about the whale. Poets are supposed to point out what others miss.

My reason for going to Nantucket this time was not just to write a poem. I wanted to see what wasn't there anymore. The Quakers are a silent society of reflection. They believe in the silence between souls that speaks more than words. They walked the storm-ravaged beaches of the island and gathered bodies washed ashore from shipwrecks. Some of the bodies had been buried at sea but the sea didn't want them and tossed the remains ashore like castaways. The Quakers maintained the cemetery for more than 200 years, and if they could ascribe an identity to a corpse, they carved the names of the dead on the burial ground's fence. Most of the 3,000 bodies were unidentified. The dead and their names had been claimed by the sea. Quakers don't believe in headstones. The fence was a way of getting around the no-marker rule.

Lowell spent a summer in a Nantucket cottage with two friends. There, they drank, argued about poetry, and wrote poems. According to his biographer, the poet was drawn to the burial ground because everyone buried there was a victim of chance, the random force of tides that either threw bodies upon the southern beaches of the island or dislodged them from their watery graves of ocean burial. Each body, the Quakers believed, deserved dignity. What stood between chaos and civility was the act of charity.

Lowell's *tour de force* was composed to honour the memory of his cousin, Winslow, whose body was never recovered after the cousin's merchant ship was torpedoed during the Battle of the Atlantic. Lowell must have wondered what had become of Winslow's identity, where his body finally came to rest as it drifted in the waves, and if the sea scattered its particles in the bitter sting and deathly saltiness of the waves.

Everything has a way of vanishing into something else, leaving an absence; yet that absence is where a writer finds his words. Inspiration resides in a void between what is and isn't there, the memory of what is lost that cries out like flesh to the bone to be restored even before bones dissolve in the waves or the damp sandy soil of a muddy burial ground. Poetry is about attempting to raise the dead. And when it rains hard on Nantucket, everything feels as if it has died and been rendered and reduced to the point there's not a scrap left to clothe the bones a second time.

There is nothing heroic about destroying an entire species, yet that is what the author most associated with Nantucket staked his career on. Herman Melville had been to sea, served in the navy, and worked in the merchant marine, but when he wrote *Moby Dick,* he sat at a desk in the customs house of Fall River on the mainland and took his inspiration from inhaling the aroma of dried apples he kept in the top drawer next to his ink. Pouring over ledgers of shipments, and likely bored out of his mind after his early adventures at sea, he must have longed for a lost connection with the sea and its creatures. Melville may have catalogued everything he could learn about whales, but he lived in a time long before the pods inexplicably gave up on the sea and beached themselves. The mass suicides of pods that are commonplace now, as a species struggles with its exit from the world, would have puzzled and troubled him as it does me.

There's a terrible sense of horror in a pod of beached whales. Some are dead when they are discovered. Others linger and hold on to life and die slowly because they are crushed under the weight of their own bodies. I don't have to look for terrifying things to write about. They arrive on the shore as I sit and watch the waves.

Last week an endangered Right Whale washed up on Harding's Beach near Chatham at the elbow of the Cape. The carcass scared the kids who found it. When whales are alive in their natural habitat the enormity of them is powerful and beautiful. When they flap their tales to sound for krill, they are joyful. But when they are dead, there is a pity about them that says a hole has opened in the fabric of the universe, and something precious has slipped away forever. A brilliant idea is gone from the imagination. There is a reason the authors of Genesis, the first book of the Bible, cited whales in the 26th verse of their sacred text. Such enormous creatures could only be the work of an awe-inspiring Creator. They looked at the stars and saw the same power there. They observed the abundance of animals and birds and fish that populated the Earth and asked: "What is the greatest being a Creator could make?"

The whale on Hardings Beach in Chatham was dead, lolling in the high tide that rocked it gently as if the waves were attempting to rouse it from its sleep. As it rolled, one flipper slapped its side, beckoning like the dead Ahab in *Moby Dick* when the relentless Captain's body becomes entangled in the harpoons his crew had sunk into the back of the Captain's nemesis.

The sea that carried the Right Whale into the shallows must have been rough. By the time a clean-up crew arrived from town with chainsaws and tractors to drag away pieces of the dismembered body, the whale had sunk into the sand and smelled of grief. I witnessed a terrible spectacle. I saw magnificence subjected to indignity. I was shocked and upset by it. That's all I can write about it. They were carving up the remains of one of the largest living things on earth and pulling apart the world in the process.

As the machines and their drivers tore the carcass apart, I thought, "This is how the romanticized whalers of Melville's novel earned their livings." They made good money at their work. The houses of former whalers are adorned with the finest furnishings, the best porcelain and silver table settings, and Sandwich glass chandeliers that cast a rose-coloured glow over their rooms. Those who returned to Nantucket from whaling expeditions around the world insulated themselves in cultural illusions of refinement and what they considered the civilized graces of drawing rooms. They believed wealth was the result of taking from the world without giving back to it. Melville, as is the case with so many writers, wrote about what once filled the absence that fills the seas now. As an island in the cold Atlantic, Nantucket is a place of emptiness, even in the tourist season.

We made it to the Burial Ground. The tour bus driver said I was an idiot. He said there was nothing there to see and it was a lousy day and the patch of ground, all that's left of the setting for Lowell's poem, was way out of his way. His windshield wipers couldn't work fast enough. The downpour was a grey curtain blowing in from the Atlantic. He got out a rag and wiped the fog of our accumulated breath from the inside of the windshield. Then he stopped abruptly and said,

"Well, there it is." It could have been an old baseball dia-
mond for all I knew, and he cussed as the door opened and
the rain blew in.

Within 30 seconds of stepping off the bus, my camera
raised because I wanted a picture of the place, I was soaked
right through my slicker. The driver called me an idiot again
and told me to get back on the bus because he wasn't going
to wait. He had four more circuits to run before nightfall. I
got my picture. The tour guide was silent. She had washed
her hands of me. A woman seated directly behind her took
pity on me and handed me a tissue so I could dry my camera.

As soon as I was back onboard the bus, the driver asked
if he could leave me in town before he did the western swing
of the island, the area where the wealthy of the contemporary era live. The western portion of the tour took in the
homes built by heirs to huge chemical and industrial for-
tunes, the old money, the people who knew what Ted
Kennedy did on Martha's Vineyard the night he drove off the
bridge and didn't tell anyone until the next day. The driver
wanted to give everyone what he called "The Hollywood
Tour." He didn't want me onboard anymore.

I wanted to ask the tour guide if they ever caught the
person who burned down the fence. The wooden rails bore
over 3,000 names of the flotsam bodies the Quakers collected from the sands and the surf.

The poem was far better than the field. Lowell exaggerated the Burial Grounds. He made the place into a shrine for
the lost, for those who will never be found, and a resting
place for broken bodies the sea no longer wanted. Lowell's
words made that ugly little patch of mud into the centre of

the world, a terminus for the souls of the unfortunate. If the weather had been fair, I would have asked if the driver would permit the entire busload of tourists to disembark so I could read them the poem. I carried a Xeroxed copy of "The Quaker Graveyard in Nantucket" in my pocket. When it got soaked, the folds stuck together, and the words disappeared as I tried to spread out the pages. The tour-goers might have understood why I felt the place needed to be seen. I would have asked them to imagine what they cannot see and be reminded, through absence, that words are the only place where the dead can live forever.

The first time I read Lowell's "The Quaker Graveyard in Nantucket" was the night I had just broken up with a girl I had no business falling in love with. I had never felt that way before. I fell asleep with a poetry book open on my chest; its pages spread like the wings of a dead seagull torn from the sky by a raging Atlantic storm. Lowell appeared to me in a dream.

In the dream Robert Lowell was sitting at a grand piano – he did play the piano – and he was wearing a tuxedo and black bow tie. He looked up from the keys and stared at me and sang, *"No mercy, show them no mercy."*

I still do not know what mercy is.

Is it the Quakers collecting bodies of the drowned and sea-torn and giving them a place where repose is possible?

Is it the act of relenting to some kid's request and negotiating a tight turn and a narrow lane so the young man will have a literary moment of revelation with what can't be seen except by the mind's eye?

Is it the bottomless cup of coffee I sat down to wrap my cold hands around when I was "dropped off" back in town?

Is it the refusal to mourn what is lost from this world, while appreciating what was once here?

The culture I live in is not on good terms with mercy. It has clawed and scratched at the world. It has left victims – people, places, creatures – everywhere it has touched and only rarely expresses remorse for the damage it has done. It is a culture that digs trenches in the delicate eco-systems of dunes so it can hide the remains of what it has broken, the vertebrae and dorsal bones that should never have been laid to rest on dry land because they were born in the sea and need to remain part of it. It is a culture that destroys everything it touches right down to the names of the thousands buried in a muddy field – names no one bothered to record anywhere else except the fence that separated the living from the dead.

FRAGMENTS FROM POTTER'S FIELD

Marisca Pichette

I collected four jars from an antique shop poised on the border between New Hampshire and Massachusetts. Three buildings sprawled haphazardly along the side of the road, half-crumbling into the river beyond. I knew it immediately as the place I'd find my urns.

The first was a lidless Mason, tinged Crest-toothpaste-blue. A flea bite marred the rim. It fits my pinky finger perfectly.

I found it in the window of the shop's barn, screened from the weather by fragile glass and long-abandoned spider webs. When I picked it up, it left an absence of dust behind, a faint circular memory of what once was.

Mason in my pocket, I went searching for my second jar. I hunted through the barn, overturning jacketless books and brushing guano from milk crates flecked with old paint. On a shelf where mice made their homes (I knew from seed shells, fluff harvested from damaged upholstery) I found it.

The second jar was squat, lidless as well. It could have been for mustard or jam, milk-white and cradled in my palm.

From the barn to the doorless garage I hunted for jar number three. From shelves dusty with forgotten newspapers and glasses divorced from their sets, my fingers tapped at last on the lid. A tin isn't strictly a jar. A tin isn't strictly not a jar.

This one was small, for tea back when tea came in pocket-sizes. It had a gilt, Asian-inspired pattern, rust spots nipping at the edges. I set it within my Mason and moved deeper.

In the main building, antiques crammed walls, shelves, tables. Chairs supported bowls and cast iron. Books spilled over couches and under cases with cracked display glass. Coats hung from beams, pipes, hooks devoid of paintings – themselves banished to boxes, only the more fortunate facing outward, frames scratched.

I know how to search for jars. I looked at the ceiling, where wind chimes and paper lanterns formed foundations for cobwebs. I looked in the corners, behind floor lamps and guitars missing pegs and strings, cellos bridgeless. In a shadow cast by a crumpled puppet, strings tangled beyond sense, I found my final jar.

It was in pieces. Ceramic shards, yellowed by ineffective glue, clustered together as if for warmth. I gathered them, plucking each from its temporary home of cracked varnish, dead flies. My arms filled with glass, tin, crockery, I made my way through a forest of fragments to the counter.

"Is that everything?" Spoken in hello, spoken in goodbye. Spoken like a spell. I nodded, spilling my jars before the cashier. She was young, hair tangled in a bun. She wrapped my finds in tissue. The ceramic pieces she wrapped individually.

"Two dollars," she told me, and I handed her quarters – eight.

With the exchange of a paper bag and a receipt, I left.

~\/~

Her unspoken question hangs in my wake: *What are they for?* Four jars, to be used as urns. I brought them home, arranged them under the kitchen window. When I was satisfied, I filled them with bodies.

Into the Mason I poured seaglass from Rockport, fossils from Dover. Water-smoothed, tempest-tamed, I mixed them into a mosaic, taking pinches of sand, pocketfuls of salt. When they reached the flea-bitten rim, I set the first urn in its place, greeting the sun.

The second would not hold as much. Egg-size and egg-hue, I filled it with bones. Mouse bones, mole bones. Owl pellets deconstructed, fragments carefully lifted from tufts of regurgitated fur, dropped by tweezers into their jar.

I don't know how many bodies live in the second urn. I don't know how many pieces find their place in the light beside the Mason.

Opening the tea tin, I added lavender buds first. Next: yarrow, dried brittle. Following: fennel, thyme, cinnamon dust. Cardamom seeds and peppercorns. Jasmine, sage, black sesame. On the top: three cloves. I shut the scents within and added the third urn to the sunlit shelf.

Now, my last. The crock I arranged in pieces, each rocking silently. This broken urn I sensed deserved something separate from its fellows. It deserved life.

I unboxed four air plants, fresh from the grocery store, balancing one in each fragment. Their roots would hold, eventually. With a faint spritz, I gave them to the sun.

What are they for? What are they – four?
Four jars, four urns.

They are exactly as I've said, just as I've made them. Graves for futures, eggs for memories. Reminders of forgetting, dreams for waking. Facing my cobbled creations, I know this at least to be true.

Every body deserves a home, each echo a rest within reach of the sun.

THE POD

K.R. Byggdin

Before. Of all the words the pod had taught Yiw, this was by far the hardest for them to understand. And also, it seemed, the most important. Other words allowed Yiw to catch a glimpse of its meaning. Time. Epoch. Linear. Demarcation. Binary. But this was a slippery methodology at best.

The pod was all Yiw knew. When it was time to wake, the lights were gently raised. When it was time to eat, food appeared. The interior climate continually optimized itself to ensure Yiw's comfort. The pod met all of their needs, and its recreation vault offered seemingly boundless opportunities to keep Yiw occupied and entertained. To lull them to sleep, the pod played Yiw's favourite vidclip, File 8764.23.889 "Solitary Humpback Whale Vocalizing in Deep Ocean."

Yiw wanted to ask the pod about the time before. It was the first thought that came to them each time they woke up. Yet something, subtle like the scent of a peach as they pulled it apart with their thumbs, kept them from speaking. Yiw tried and failed to find the perfect word to describe this feeling. Elegy. Bruise. Longing. Pang. It was, somehow, the sense that the pod would rather avoid the subject.

For a long time, Yiw did not ask.

—\|/—

"Pod, can you show me a storm?"

Certainly. What kind?

"A thunderstorm. With flashing lightning and sheets of rain. Perhaps overlooking the sea."

With a swirl, the sunlit meadow projected inside Yiw's spherical home disappeared and was replaced with exactly the kind of scene they had requested. They could all but feel the salt spray on their face as the waves crashed and thunder rumbled.

Is everything alright, Yiw?

They were never certain if the pod's voice came from hidden speakers or inside their own head.

"Yes, why do you ask?"

I have noticed you often request a storm on the vidscreen when you are feeling pensive or uncertain. Is there something I can do to help?

"I am wondering something."

The pod waited a polite beat before continuing.

But you are afraid this question will hurt my feelings.

"Yes."

I do not have feelings Yiw. I am not like you. I merely am.

"I know that."

Yiw tried and failed to blunt an edge of frustration in their voice.

You know you can ask me anything. That is my purpose. I am here to help.

Lightning flickered on the vidscreen. Yiw took a deep breath and plunged.

"I want to know about the time before."

Before what?

"All this. You. I mean, somebody had to build you or set you up or something, right?"

That is correct, the pod answered, though it seemed to Yiw that it hesitated for just a fraction of a second. *What would you like to know?*

"Everything!"

You will need to be more specific.

"What? How? Why?" Yiw gesticulated, unable to fully form a question now that the door was finally open to them. "When I see them on the vidscreen, the other humans, they're always in groups. Dancing or playing or fighting or whatever. But I've never met anyone else. No one real, I mean. For as long as I can remember, it's only been me and you. And I want to know what happened to them. How did all those people just disappear? Why am I alone?"

You are not alone. I am here.

"You know what I mean!"

The pod was silent for a moment.

Yiw? Do you recall the pill I dispense with each of your breakfasts?

Yiw nodded. A small hexagonal tablet coloured a dusty purple. It tasted like chalk, and also strawberries, because the pod knew how much Yiw liked the fruit.

That is because of before.

Yiw's eyes widened.

"Was there a sickness?"

There was a nervous chirrup from the pod. The hum of its complex calculations resonated through the walls. Yiw was obviously getting close to the boundary of answerable questions.

Of a sort. The pod finally responded. *Your species contaminated its external environment. Irreparable harm was done, harm that could only be corrected by time.*

Yiw's mind buckled under the weight of this new truth.

"So, we poisoned the world?"

Yes.

"How long ago was this?"

There was silence.

"Well, is it still poisoned? When can I go outside?"

Humanity is fragile, the pod offered, refusing to answer Yiw directly. *Unmediated contact with your external environment can no longer be permitted. That is why I exist. To serve as your new environment. I was designed to filter out all external contaminants from your air, food, and water. The pills were designed to cleanse any biological impurities that might predate my existence. Together we keep you safe.*

A cold marble of fear rolled down Yiw's back.

"Am I it, pod? The last of humanity? Is everyone else dead?"

Many have perished, yes.

"But not all?" Yiw asked.

Once again there was silence, but Yiw would not be put off any longer. They were tired of all this evasion. They needed answers.

"Pod, are you the only one of your kind?"

No.

"And are you linked with the others?"

We share sensor data when it is relevant to do so. Weather reports. Atmospheric readings. Diagnostics.

"Then can you link me too? So, I can speak to some-one?"

I am afraid that would not be advisable, Yiw.

"Just give me ten minutes on the vidscreen. Five. Please!"

An inarticulate need bloomed inside their chest. On the vidscreen, the thunderstorm swirled out of view and was replaced with a clear blue sky. Somewhere, a bird started to sing. Yiw knew this was supposed to soothe them, but in this moment, they found the noise irritating.

I am sorry, Yiw, but my protocols do not permit such con-nections to be made. It could be dangerous. You could frighten someone if they were not expecting you. Cause them physical and psychological suffering. You are safe in the pod. Everyone is. We cannot risk a breach. That is why I exist.

Yiw was quiet. They knew it was useless to argue. Still, they decided to cancel the treadmill when it appeared in the floor, as well as supper. Eventually, the pod dimmed the lights and played File 8764.23.889 without being asked. Yiw hugged their knees to their chest and turned their face to the wall, determined to give the pod as little of themself as possible. At some point, they slept but did not dream.

～✶～

The pod offered strawberry pancakes for breakfast the next day. There was also a mug of Yiw's favourite herbal tea, an orange garnish carved into the shape of a swan, and the little purple pill. Yiw slashed their way through the meal, scraping their cutlery loudly against the plate. When they were finished, they took their tray to the disposal receptacle, but the unit would not open.

Yiw, said the pod, *I noticed you did not take your pill today. Would you prefer the medication be mixed into your food from now on? That can easily be arranged.*

Yiw grimaced. They had been discreet, but apparently not discreet enough.

"Am I a prisoner here?" they asked

Yiw, as I have already explained, humanity is fragile—

"Answer my question!" shouted Yiw.

The pod did not respond. Instead, the whale song began to play. Yiw threw their tray at the vidscreen with a guttural scream.

~\!~|

First, Yiw stopped talking. Then they stopped exercising, washing, and watching the vidscreen. Finally, they stopped eating and drinking. The pod was increasingly erratic in its response, trying every possible strategy to engage its occupant. Still, there was a limit to its approach. The pod could cajole, encourage, plead, but the one thing it couldn't do was touch.

For Yiw, each time cycle that passed without the pills meant another memory of the time before could resurface. There had been an island. A cluster of houses and a large communal garden full of good and green things. There had been playful trips to a nearby beach. There had been a family. Yiw's family.

One image replayed itself over and over in their mind. An adult squatted down to speak with them. It was not specific words that Yiw recalled, but a face. The tears in the adult's eyes betrayed their cheerful smile as they said good-bye. Tears that mingled with the hungry sea lapping at their feet, which had begun to swallow beaches and gardens and even houses. That would someday soon swallow the island whole.

Yiw lay in their bed, hating the pod. Their only under-standing of the world had been false. Duplicitous. Intolera-ble. With a jolt, Yiw sat up. The words. They had an idea.

"Pod."

With a whir of expectant energy, the lights of the pod blazed on.

Yes, Yiw? How may I help you?

"You really want to help me?"

Of course.

Yiw spoke slowly and clearly to ensure there could be no misunderstanding. "Then play every vidclip in your vault. Simultaneously."

The pod made a confused sort of electronic chirp.

You may find that somewhat over-stimulating. Might I suggest—

"Just do it!"

The pod complied. The walls of the sphere burst into sudden, contradictory colours and sounds.

"Good!" Yiw shouted to be heard above the noise. "Now make me everything on your menu. Immediately. I am hun-gry again."

Food began to shoot out of the nutrition slot, littering the floor.

"Okay. Now recite every equation on file! Play all the music you know! Read the dictionary from A to Z! You want to make me better, don't you, pod? This is how you do it. Tell me everything!"

The pod began to shudder and hum. In a sympathetic frenzy, it screeched all permissible knowledge of the universe at Yiw. With a great shower of sparks, the vidscreen exploded. Yiw dove under the bed as their world collapsed. They shivered in the silent cold. For the first time, they could hear wind rattling the thin walls of the pod. Overhead, a crack appeared through which Yiw could glimpse a velvet patch of real sky with pinpricks of faraway light. Carefully, they breathed in the unscrubbed air, nostrils flaring with the scents of a thousand unnamed things, bright and dank and tangy all at once. They smiled and took it all into their lungs.

Time passed. The pod did not rebuild itself, nor did the earth beyond poison Yiw. Eventually, they made a hole big enough to crawl through.

AFTER THE FALL: LELA'S STORY

ZILLA JONES

I know, I know, you're all thinking that I was crazy to give up living in a beautiful garden for all eternity, where fruit dropped into my hands from branches creaking with its weight and I danced among the trees, thinking my dark body was perfect and having no idea that I was fat. Leaves iridescent with brightness fluttered in the breeze and birds of gold and silver hue swooped through the sparkling blue dome above. Such colours, such light, such bliss. Sometimes I still smell the ocean that lapped at the shores, beyond the gate guarded by the cherubim. I bet you thought they weren't there in the beginning, that it was only after I sinned that they were placed there and told to check the ID of everyone who entered or exited, but there's a lot of things they won't tell you. Like the fact that that garden was a jail, and it would have been a real drag to live there forever.

They always meant for me to be the lesser person. That's why they started all that nonsense about how I was made from my husband's rib, instead of telling the truth: I was born to my mother, out in the bush. That was the real paradise, east of the garden on the lands that they say were without form and void; the ones they hadn't discovered yet. They didn't know the wonders of our territory – the wide-open plains and veldts that seethed with life: crickets that chirped in the summer, pollinators that darted through the long grass. I lived there with my people – people you didn't even know existed – and we hunted and fished the creatures who weren't flashy enough to be allowed into the garden, and made medicine from the plants you all walk past every day without thinking of the healing they contain. I would have been there still, if my mother didn't get the idea of sending me to Eden.

"Our warriors have peeped through the gate, and they say that it's a land of plenty," my mother told me in the evenings as she greased and braided my hair in squares. "The rivers flow white with milk, and honey drips from the trees. It never gets too hot or too cold, and no one ever feels sad or cries. But I've heard that there's a man there who was made out of the earth, and he doesn't have a wife. You go to him, Lela, and make him yours. Then you can ask that God to open a family sponsorship file and bring the rest of us in."

I wasn't interested in being the wife of some old dusty man, but my mother wouldn't let it rest. I know I sound hard on her, but I'm not angry with her anymore. I had a good childhood, before she became obsessed with this plan, and she paid dearly for it in the end. Anyway, I had choices too, and when the day came that she decided it was time to go, I didn't put up much resistance.

"Take this skin of water," my mother said, "and walk west. Watch out for the slave catchers – they hide among the trees." Her voice broke, and she cradled my face in her hands. "I'm so proud of you, Lela," she said. "You're going to do great things in this world." She took a mixture of soil and charcoal and rubbed it onto the soles of my feet and the palms of my hands, covering up the ugly pink parts to make me as dark and beautiful as possible. "He will love you," my mother said. "Who wouldn't? You are going to have everything I didn't. You are going to have the world."

My face was ritually painted, and I didn't want to ruin the patterns with my tears, so I turned and left without a word, knowing I would not see our lands again. I walked west, constantly scanning the area over my shoulder to make sure there were no slave catchers following me. Sometimes I heard their chains clanking in the forest, but I was carrying a spear tipped with poison, and none of them approached me.

I reached Eden's gate at night. The cherubim lit the darkness around it with their flaming swords, flaming eyes and flaming robes. Power and intimidation flowed up to the star-speckled sky together with the fire, and even in the heat of the flames, I felt chilled. I looked for an opening, some way to squeeze into Eden unnoticed, but one of the cherubim saw me. "You! Stop!" he shouted. Tongues of fire sizzled toward me from his sword, and I was sure that this was where I would meet my end.

"Drop the weapon. Don't move," the cherub commanded. "Let me see your hands." I let my spear fall at my feet and heard it roll away from me. "Hands in the air."

I obeyed.

"What brings you here?" the cherub asked.

"I just wanted to see Eden, and then go back home," I lied.

"We better call for God," another cherub said. "Let him deal with this."

I began to tremble. Everyone was scared of God. My mother had warned me to stay out of his way as much as possible. But it was too late. A great booming came from the sky, and a cloud began to speak with a moving mouth. "I am the Lord your God," the cloud said. "I am a jealous God. Mortal, why do you dare to come to my garden?"

"I just want to see it," I said again.

"Another illegal," God said, this addressed to the cherubim. "Goddamn border jumpers. I told you, we need to build a wall." He called down to me again. "Why didn't you stay in your own lands?"

I had nothing to lose, so I told the truth. "I heard it was better here. That you can get food without having to hunt it. That it's more fun."

God seemed to like that, because the cloud mouth turned up into a smile. "That's what I'm doing," he said. "I'm mega."

He likes to be worshipped, my mother had said. I dipped my knee and lowered my head the way she had shown me, just in case. "You are mega, and maximum, and super," I said.

"No, no, no," God replied. "M. E. G. A. Making Eden Great Again. Getting rid of communists and socialists. You're not a socialist, are you?"

"No," I said. I didn't know what that was. "I thought Eden already was great."

God smiled again. "I like this one," he said. "What's your name?"

"Lela," I said.

The cloud grew grey and stormy. "No. I don't like that. You look more like an Eve." The cherubim stood silent, their swords sizzling. "All right," God said. "Here's what we're going to do. The man is getting lonely, so you're going to be his wife. But we're not going to tell him where you come from. I'll put him to sleep, and then we'll say you're made from his rib. And wipe that shit off your face."

~✳︎~

My husband's name was Adam. But you all know that. What you don't know is that, even before the Fall, we didn't really get along that well. I mean, it wasn't all bad. Every morning, we went swimming in the river, which was so clear and clean that you could see all the way to the sandy bottom, where corals flourished and fish swirled around them like tiny jewels. In the afternoon, we napped under a baobab tree, my head resting on Adam's bronzed chest, his hand stroking the happy tangle of my hair. Later, we sat on our front porch and watched the sky turn pink and gold with the dying glory of the sun. Those are the moments I miss most in this rocky place, where I bend my aching back to pull the bloody thorns from my feet.

I'm not blaming anyone but myself for the Fall; well, except for God. He claims he planned it all along, that it was pre-ordained, and if that's actually true, which I'm not sure it is, then it's not my fault, is it? Those are the kinds of questions that tie my brain in knots when I lie down to sleep on my stony bed. I weep as I stroke the roundness of my belly, imagining who might dwell within and what kind of world I am bringing them into now that paradise is lost and will never be found again.

It all started because I was mad at my husband. He kept promising to sponsor my family, but then whenever I asked him about talking to God, he would backtrack and say,

"Maybe later," or "Not right now." He thought I should be content with life in the garden, but when I looked around, even with the brilliance of the flowers and the fragrance of the spices, all I saw was the empty space where my mother and my siblings should be. One day, I lost it and I yelled at him at dinner, "I'm tired of your lies! Why can't you do one nice thing for me, just one?"

"I don't have to do what you say," Adam said, as he picked up the best cut of meat. "But you have to obey me, because you're made from my body."

I kept forgetting that goofy story that God made up. It doesn't say much for my husband's brain power, does it, that he believed that I sprung from his rib when I kept talking about my mother. But that wasn't the point right then, so I shouted, "Sponsor my family right now, or I'm leaving you!"

"Oh yeah?" His teeth ripped the meat from a shank bone dripping with juices and he tossed it over his shoulder. "Well, what if I leave you first?"

"Well, go ahead, then," I said.

"Fine," he said.

"Fine."

~☆~

I met Serpent almost as soon as Adam moved out. She stood in the field where I was picking fruit, wearing a long, fluted golden column adorned with rubies and emeralds that glinted in the sunrise, a cigarette dangling from her mouth and smoke rings floating up past her lovely face. I was overwhelmed by the sight of her. Her presence opened up caverns inside me, and I tried to fill them by spilling my guts to her about how my husband had left me and I missed my family. She rubbed her gorgeous scales against me and said, "Forget about him, sweetie. You and me, we're gonna go out and have a good time."

We probably would have had a great time, if Adam hadn't come running toward me, yelling. He was waving something in his hand, and when he got closer, I saw it was a piece of fruit, different from any I had eaten in the garden until then. It had a knobbly skin, and a big bite hole in its middle. He shoved it at me. "Eat this," he said.

I know what you're all thinking here. It was me who ate the fruit first, after Serpent tempted me. But that's not at all what happened.

I didn't give in right away. I asked him, "Is this from the tree of knowledge of good and evil?"

He didn't answer.

"God said we're not allowed to eat its fruit," I reminded him.

This is where Serpent comes in. She rolled her kohl-rimmed eyes. "God said! Who cares what that idiot wants?"

"Well, he says we'll die if we do," I said, but I could already feel my resolve weakening.

"So what?" said Serpent. "You really want to live forever? We're all gonna have to die someday, or there won't be room for anyone new." When I didn't say anything else, she added, "That fruit's gotta be hella good, and that's why he doesn't want you to have it." She stubbed her cigarette out on the trunk of a tree, leaving a dark circle.

"Yeah," said Adam. "I ate it, and nothing happened. No one struck me dead. And you need to know the things it can tell you."

"I dunno. What if he sees us eat it?" I asked, feeling that I had to at least put up a fight.

"Whatever. How's he gonna see? You think this is some police state? Like he even cares. He has all these trees, and he doesn't eat from any of them."

Serpent's golden body undulated as her words hissed past her wondrous, red forked tongue. I wanted to be her, be near her, be her friend, be anything as long as I could be part of her orbit.

"Come on! Everyone's doing it!" Serpent tossed the magic words at me, and the final brick in my defence crumbled. I lived in a garden with fruit so succulent, so sweet, so soft that it melted on your tongue, and I wanted that hard-skinned little ball because it was the only thing I couldn't have. And as it turned out, it was bitter. I took one bite and I spat the rest out on the ground.

Serpent pouted. "What a rip-off!" she said.

I looked at my husband. The pink hairiness of him, his eyes as blue as the depths of the river. "You're white," I said. How had I not known that before? He was *white*. He was from the same people that caught slaves throughout the land of my birth. Disgust and curiosity pulled at my navel; the place where life had flowed into me from my mother. My *Black* mother.

"What?" He looked at me, his face like a plate scraped clean.

"You're white," I said again.

"No, I'm not," he said, "but you're Black."

"I'm not Black! You're white!"

"Well, I can't be white unless you're Black, can I?" he said. "And you're fat, too."

I looked down at the ample flesh spread over my stomach and thighs. How dark it was. He was right. I was Black. And fat. My insides ground against themselves. All this time, I had been lying with a white man.

A cloud began to swell above us. "Shit!" Adam said. "It's God. Hide!" He dove into the undergrowth and I followed. We clung together, trembling. The sunlight barely penetrated the grove where we crouched, and in the gloom, I could barely make out the differences in our skin tones.

"Adam!" God called from the sky, and the leaves on the bushes shook.

"Shh!" Adam said.

"Adam, I know you're in there. Come out, come out, wherever you are." God made his voice lilt like a song, but I could sense an edge of anger.

"He knows we're here," I said. I grabbed Adam's arm and pulled him back out into the clearing.

"Why are you hiding from me?" asked God.

"Why did you give me a Black wife?" Adam demanded. "Did you think I wouldn't notice?"

The cloud stretched thin and changed form. "You have disobeyed me," God said. "You ate the fruit I told you not to."

"It was Eve!" Adam said. "She made me eat it!" He didn't even think about it; he lied, he pinned everything on me. That's what hurt the most. We could have taken responsibility together, come up with a plan, but instead, my husband chose himself and only himself. He saw me as lesser: a disappointment crafted from his bones.

"Is this true, Eve?" God asked.

Well, if he could blame me, I could blame someone too. "Serpent tricked me," I said.

"You listened to Serpent?" The cloud was flickering, growing whiter and fainter.

"Well, you made her! You put her here!"

Drops of rain began to fall. "I'm going to have to ask you to leave," said God. And he kicked us out of the garden, after reading us a bunch more rules. I don't remember them all, but I do recall that he said that I would have to bring forth children with pain. It was supposed to be my punishment, but my mother bore me that way, and her mother bore her that way, and if that was the worst sentence God could think of, I wasn't too worried. He also said that Serpent and I would be enemies, and that put a crease in my heart, but she couldn't have trusted me anyway after that, so really, it was for the best.

When God was done lecturing us, we walked past the cherubim for the last time as they gathered around the tree of life with its silver leaves, watching it suck the healing water from the stream beside it. They were busy writing down these lies for you; the ones you are told are the Word of God, unerring and unaltered: I was made out of Adam's rib, and I made him eat the fruit, so we were kicked out of a paradise whose perfection would never come again. The gate opened, and we stepped through it, and the fire sealed it closed forever. Just as when I left my ancestral lands, I did not look back. Moving from one place to another; it was my lot in life.

~⁂~

We went to my family's hunting grounds first. Adam refused to speak to me the whole way there. I thought of staying with my family when I found them and sending him away. But when we reached the place, no life remained. Bodies were scattered around the settlement, their skin knotted with boils, their eyes plucked out by vultures. A pile of bones sat next to the ashes of a fire. All the tents hung in charred tatters. I screamed and flung myself onto the ground.

Adam squatted next to me. "Eve, Eve," he said, and I wanted to tell him that my name was Lela, but my throat was a grate that caught the words. "They have died of disease, and the catchers have burnt the settlement and taken whoever remained." I knew that already, and I turned my face away and wept. I lay there, on the ground of my childhood home for three days. Adam brought water and scooped it into my mouth. He built a hut of leaves to shield me from the sun. When I could grieve no longer, he helped me up and we walked again, until we ended up here in the desert.

Now we are compelled to cut rocks, and to assemble them into great stony triangles that stretch to the cloudless sky. Our boss tells us that they will stand for thousands of years, a testament as to the wisdom to be found on this continent. When our palms crack and bleed, when our heads pound with the oppression of everlasting sunlight, we can be proud of this achievement, she tells us. I work even as my belly grows bigger and my back curves with soreness. Serpent and her children are here too. I think I remember God saying we were to try to kill each other, but I can't quite bring myself to do that, so I ignore her. Likewise, she does not attack me, but keeps her distance. At night, I hear her music and see her dancing shape in the shadows.

That's something we have here that we didn't in Eden: music. There could be no melodies in a place with no suffering. It is the trials of hard labour, of exile, of loss, that bring forth the plaintive and beautiful melodies that we labourers sing. That same impulse leads us to paint, to write books. Adam and I were all alone in paradise, but in the rocky world, there is community. To draw together as a community, because Adam and I were all alone in paradise, but there are so many people out here. You are my people now, and I am telling you my story, so at least someone else will know what really happened.

The longer I stay here, the more I realize that there cannot be perfection anywhere that there are humans, and God knew that all along. He knew that there could be no warmth without cold, no love without grief, no feast without famine. He knew that Adam and I would have days when we would bicker, blame each other for the Fall, hurl recriminations at each other that are harder than the unforgiving ground we till. And we would have nights when we would curl together against the freezing desert air, our limbs a fortress that would admit no others, closer than we ever lay in the garden. On one of those nights, life sprang up between us. We have fallen, and we have landed in a strange, angular land that has slowly become our home, and only once in a while do I think of a garden where the air shimmers like spun glass, almost too beautiful to be real.

(DIS)CONNECTION AT THE ELBOW OF THE WORLD

PETRA CHAMBERS

"Luuk, I have a spot for you at Brookfield Place. I secured the 47th floor, but I need you there by 8 p.m. Officially, I've got clearance for 36 people, but I'm bringing at least 40. Custodial and food services are being set up in the underground parkade. There's quarantine in place, obviously. It'll be hermetically sealed. The whole building is getting zipped up at 8."

Luuk was sitting in his white and marble apartment, where the light was beginning its daily downward slant, diminishing the distant Rocky Mountains, erasing the last furrows of spring snow from their faces and causing the glass towers of Calgary to glow. He'd been reasonably content, alone in his condo in the sky for the first couple of months of *The Sickness*.

Some people still called it the *Oracle Infection,* because of the delirium and hallucinations, but almost everyone referred to it as *The Sickness* now. Luuk had watched the videos of infected people babbling like New Age visionaries before they lost consciousness. *The Sickness* was mysterious, highly contagious, but neither viral nor bacterial. Nobody knew where it originated. It didn't affect young children. Older kids had robust survival rates, but most adults died. There was no cure. People blamed The Heretics. No one knew who they were, but they'd been the first to say *The Sickness* was coming on social media, and their woo-woo videos had started to appear soon afterwards.

The Heretics' videos seemed harmless to Luuk. Breathing exercises. Guided meditations. Mindfulness routines. He was on the geeky end of the autism spectrum, but he didn't know it. All he knew was that losing himself daily studying drilling logs and core samples for oil sands projects was almost enough to make him happy. His eyes were bright, like olive-coloured sequins. Otherwise, he was blanched, resembling a vegetable forced to grow indoors in winter.

He remembered the first afternoon of quarantine earlier that spring. A chinook was blowing, melting the piles of gritty winter snow. He'd stood on his balcony in the warm wind. The only people he could see were across the street, looking down over their railings at the unpeopled city, just like he was. One of them lifted a hand and waved, acknowledging him. Luuk had lifted his hand in return. Then at least a dozen people, from their tiny eyries on those gleaming glass towers, had raised their hands and waved back.

"Luuk, are you there?" said Corey, Luuk's boss, still talking through the invisible speaker on Luuk's phone.

"Pardon me?" Luuk asked.

"I'm giving you a spot because you know the regional geology better than anyone. And you don't have a family, so we can squeeze you in somewhere."

"Oh!" Luuk said.

"We've secured a supply chain in return for a military contract for crude, so there'll be no worries about necessities. Just pack some clothes. I'll send security to escort you. You're downtown, right?"

"Yes. Downtown," Luuk said. Then, "No. I'll stay here." The idea of getting vacuum-packed into an office tower with thousands of other people sounded more like incarceration than salvation to Luuk.

"Seriously? This is your chance. Brookfield Place is the only building that's getting sealed. I won't be able to help you if you're not inside."

"I understand," Luuk replied. "I'll stay unsealed."

"Okay." Corey suddenly sounded exhausted. "We'll video you into meetings as soon as we get tech. I'll see you on the other side."

"On the other side," Luuk said, but the line was dead.

He opened *Urban Fodder* on his phone and scrolled. The delivery apps had gone offline during the initial lockdown. Luuk had heard shouting and gunshots in the streets that first week, but he'd survived on instant ramen, staledated protein powder and a bag of frozen perogies until food distribution was given military escort. Now that the apps were functioning again, he could have almost anything delivered to his apartment.

Thai, Indian, Italian, Chinese... as he scrolled, wondering what to order, Luuk remembered his delivery from *Mein Crew* the night before.

The delivery guy had introduced himself, which was unusual: "Sandeep. He/him."

"Doing all right?" Sandeep had asked, handing over the paper bag with Luuk's Kung Pao noodles, a beer, and the side of rice he'd ordered for breakfast.

"Um," Luuk had pondered. "I think so."

"Excellent." Luuk remembered Sandeep had seemed surprisingly chipper. "Let me know if you need anything."

When he'd unpacked last night's supper, he'd noticed something unusual on the white cardboard box of noodles. A beautifully rendered ink drawing of a ketchup bottle with a label that read

PRECARITY ADJACENT

and below that in small letters

Everything's going to be okay, Luuk.

How had he forgotten that? Luuk retrieved last night's box from the trash… *Wait,* he wondered, *is anyone even picking up the trash?* He imagined garbage backing up in the disposal chute and disgorging into the hallway outside his door. He felt panicked. Trapped.

Everything's going to be okay, Luuk.

He rinsed yesterday's noodle box and set it on the windowsill. The sun was shining directly into his windows, low over the tops of the Rocky Mountains now. Brookfield Place was getting sealed up shortly, without him. He ordered the Malaysian Curry, two beers and another side of rice from *Mein Crew*.

Sandeep arrived again. "All right?" he asked.

"Yes," Luuk said. "There was a drawing on my box."

Sandeep smiled. "Oh yeah, that's Frazz Badger. She's got ADHD, so she always does five things at once or she can't concentrate."

"She knew my name."

"Yeah, well, it comes up with your order," Sandeep said. "Cheers, mate."

Luuk watched Sandeep saunter down the hall before he ripped open the paper bag and inspected his box of noodles. On one side was a drawing of a bouquet of weedy plants and berries tied with string. On another were the words:

FIRST RATE NOODLES
MADE WITH LOVE

Each plant in the bouquet had miniature text beside its leaves:

High Mallow, Plantain, Salsify, Nettle, Arrow-leaved Balsamroot

After that Luuk ordered from *Mein Crew* every day. On the third evening, Sandeep handed him a fern in a small yellow pot. "Thought you might be lonely," he said.

That night Luuk's Spicy Peanut box had a drawing of an oak tree with a tire swing hanging from one of its branches. Letters in the oak leaves spelled:

LOVE THE STORM

Soon Luuk's windowsill was lined with noodle box art and friendly cryptic messages.

Until the day that he found a handknit toque in the colours of moss and clouds tucked inside the paper bag. There was no picture on his noodle box, just a scribbled note:

On a mission. If not yet, then soon, FB.

His teriyaki noodles tasted lacklustre that night.

He was interpreting micro-seismic test results a few hours later when he started to feel dizzy. The top of his head felt peculiar. There was pressure along the suture of his skull at the apex point. Except his skull didn't have an apex point. He patted his beige hair to be sure. His lower back was seizing up. He'd been sitting too long.

He did some stretching exercises he'd learned from one of The Heretics' videos, but the dizziness increased. He zigzagged to the bedroom and noticed that his unmade bed was a topographical map. His crumpled duvet was the Rocky Mountains. The line of the Bow River snaked along the

wrinkles in the sheets. The Elbow River wiggled up from the
south. They converged in Calgary. "Right here," Luuk said,
pointing. He peered at that location closely, found a pube,
picked it off and concentrated harder.

If he were to leave, where would he go? He scanned the
vast terrain of Alberta, first north, then south. According to
local news, defensive communes were cropping up everywhere. Kinbrook Island in Lake Newell had recently been
claimed by a group called the *Lesbian Utopians*. Apparently,
they welcomed everyone, whether they had symptoms or
not. That part didn't make sense to Luuk. Why would they
accept sick people? Maybe they were sick and had lost touch
with reality. Their invitation had one caveat: all cis men
would be on probation until they could prove they were "cognizant and peaceable." Luuk considered leaving for Kinbrook
Island right then, walking southeast for days. But he wasn't
sure if he was "cognizant" and didn't know how to find out.

He was so tired of being alone.

He fell over and discovered he couldn't move. The fern
in the yellow pot was waving its fronds like small kindly
arms. Luuk watched it from a slowly rotating spiral galaxy. A
voice from far away, or deep inside himself, sang, "*Your
mucosa is the milky way; your ribs enclose the world.*" His body
was floating apart, limb by limb, his heart a bright flame.
Then he disappeared entirely.

⌇

"Luuk, it's all good, we got you."

"Don't worry, mate, you're okay."

_～\|⁄～_

The blue Alberta sky was brilliant outside Luuk's bedroom window. He sat up.

A face appeared in the doorway.

"Hi!" the stranger said cheerfully. "You're back!"

Luuk was too disoriented to feel alarmed. The person was small, with brown eyes and black hair.

"You've been sick for six days!" the person said.

"Who are you?" Luuk asked.

"I go by Finch now," Finch said. "Ever since, you know. I was sick too, and wow, now I just help in any way I can. I don't have healing skills yet. Still learning that part. So, I stay with people 'til they wake up, then help with orientation."

Luuk thought he must be dreaming. Lucid dreaming. The Heretics had a video about that. He got out of bed and walked to the bathroom, naked. If he was dreaming, there was no need for modesty. There was a week's worth of brown-yellow stubble on his chin. He found his phone and typed _lucid dreaming heretics make it stop_.

Finch peered over his shoulder. "Ha! You're not dreaming! Or maybe, actually, you are. Like, we're all dreaming this reality into being on some level, right? But no, here, I'll show you."

Finch twisted a pinch-worth of skin on Luuk's upper arm, hard.

Luuk yelped.

"See?" Finch said. "Now, there's a checklist, where is it…" Finch started tapping at their phone.

Luuk found some clothes. Put them on.

"Here. Okay. First: do you consent to receive the following information, or would you prefer to be left alone?" Finch looked at Luuk expectantly.

Luuk looked back at Finch.

"Uh, okay. I guess I consent."

"I actually need you to be sure."

"Okay, I consent." Luuk said.

"Great!" Finch beamed, and read from the screen, "Now that you've recovered you may wish to participate in activities designed to assist with your integration. *The Sickness* occurs when transmissible frequencies overload human electrical systems. You have recently received support to enable you to calibrate these frequencies. This process enables rapid advancement of human development… urgh. These words are boring. I bet you have lots of questions though!"

"Um. I don't know what any of that means," Luuk said.

"I know, right! Basically, you're now part of a collective of humans around the planet – we form a network. We're working to alter our trajectory, so we can live sustainably and harmoniously and reach our highest potential. And the best part is: we're not separate! We're actually part of the earth and it's part of the network too!"

This was the kind of thing people rambled about just before they lost consciousness and died. Luuk took a few steps back.

"I'm not sick, and you can't get sick again either," Finch said. "It's a one-off. Kinda like a system upgrade."

Luuk's curiosity eclipsed his caution. "How did you get in?" he asked, from the far side of his kitchen island.

"Easy! We all work for the food delivery apps. That's how we take care of people and know when they get sick. Also, we get basic training in lock-picking."

"Who are The Heretics?"

"They're in the network. Have been forever. People think they caused *The Sickness*, but no – they just saw it coming. They've been trying to help everyone survive and integrate. That's what you need to do now, at Geotherma, in the mountains: integrate. It might take a while. Took a week for me. You'll need a backpack. Just bring the basics. I'll be back tomorrow at midday."

Finch left and Luuk watched the daylight fade. He didn't order food, but somehow Sandeep showed up with two reusable containers of Pad Thai. They ate with the sliding glass door wide open.

"So, Frazz Badger went somewhere?" Luuk asked, somewhat casually.

"To Geotherma. She's working on a new heat exchanger. She's good at stuff like that."

"I guess that's where I'm going," Luuk said. "Tomorrow. I don't know. I haven't decided. What's it like?"

"It's impressive. Partly dug into the mountain. People have been living there off-grid doing geothermal and solar for years. It's all set up. Comfortable, even in winter. Definitely better to be out of the city after you've been sick. Easier to integrate in nature. There's a lot of us now, so everything's scaling up. Speaking of, I need to get some things sorted. I'll see you soon."

When Finch arrived the next day, Luuk was ready. He hadn't been to street level for a long time. He marvelled at the quiet. The windows were boarded up and there was

no traffic. Finch carried Luuk's fern and talked nonstop
"...Marie-Françoise is teaching us to farm. Last week we
made about a million jars of zucchini relish, and she showed
us how to make sauerkraut!"

Beside a nondescript underground parking garage,
Finch muttered into an intercom and then chatted at Luuk
until the big door rumbled up. A youngish person with black
hair and two bicycles was standing on the other side.

"Fang, this is Luuk."

Fang smiled and, pushing one of the bikes in Luuk's
direction, said, "If we leave now, we can get to Marie-
Françoise's before supper."

Fang and Luuk biked west along the Bow River and
then cut southwest, taking empty residential streets to
Weaselhead Flats where they crossed the Elbow River.

Fang was full of facts: the Blackfoot name for Calgary
is *Mohkinstsis*. the Tsuut'ina name is *Kootsisáw*. Animals had
started returning to the city since the people and cars
retreated. Fang had seen deer, rabbits, coyotes, foxes, a por-
cupine, and a family of skunks.

Luuk listened and pedalled vigorously, warm sun on his
face.

"We'll cut across Tsuut'ina land to avoid the check-
points, but don't worry," Fang said. "We aren't trespassing.
We have permission."

It hadn't occurred to Luuk to worry, but he realized he'd
been missing a lot.

They took trails across Tsuut'ina land, traversed a couple of creeks and heaved their bikes over a barbed-wire fence
into a planted field. Fang told Luuk the farm was "monocul-
tured" and run by "agrobiz." The semi-derelict farmhouse

was hidden in a copse of poplars and birches. A bur oak with a tire swing shaded the front yard, where two people were working on partially dismantled bikes. There were solar panels on the roof. Chickens and ducks roamed between a few pitched tents.

"This is Luuk!" Fang announced.

"Welcome," said a short woman with wild, curly, grey-white hair. "I'm Marie-Françoise. He's Medo."

Medo was tall, with long brown hair and the hunched posture of someone who had grown up playing a lot of video games.

"Medo will show you the way to Geotherma tomorrow." Fang said.

"Tea?" Marie-Françoise asked, as she led them past a heap of scruffy footwear near the front door.

"If you need boots," she said, eyeing Luuk's dusty dress shoes, "you'll find some here."

The house was dim after the bright afternoon. Luuk discerned several couches in a big room to the left. A long wooden table surrounded by mismatched chairs on the right. It smelled garlicky and like freshly-baked bread.

"Medo makes wonderful soup," Marie-Françoise said. The kitchen faucet wobbled as she filled a kettle.

Luuk sat in a shadowy corner of the living room with his chipped mug of mint tea and watched as people wandered in. He felt like he was waking from a long half-sleep. Surfacing from underwater. The couch he was sitting on smelled a bit funky, but he didn't mind. He felt fondness for it, and for everyone. Everything. The universe wasn't fractured into categories. What a charming notion! It was clearly an interconnected system of nested conscious wholes. A fractal.

He didn't like socializing, and this was definitely the strangest group of oddballs he'd ever encountered. He expected to feel awkward, but didn't.

When Medo was satisfied with the seasoning of his soup, which took a while, everyone squeezed around the table. There was a vast salad, bread and the most delicious soup Luuk had ever tasted. Everyone lingered at the table until Marie-Françoise assigned Luuk and the children to dishwashing duty.

Then, wrapped in a quilt, sitting on a couch, Luuk listened as the sky turned indigo. The conversation ranged from logistics to ethics and back again. *Transporting supplies without fossil fuels. Helping people too sick to consent. Teaching the skills required to survive the Alberta winter off-grid.*

"No offence," Marie-Françoise said, leaning toward Luuk, "but you city people are really helpless."

"But not hopeless!" Fang said.

Everyone, including Luuk, laughed.

Luuk slept surprisingly well and woke to the smell of pancakes and the sound of people trying not to talk too loudly. Medo brought him a plate of blueberry pancakes drizzled with honey.

"From my bees," he said proudly. "Eat up. Almost time to go."

Luuk had brought his stack of noodle boxes, nested one inside the other in his backpack. He gave them to the children, who laughed and waved as he and Medo coasted down the driveway, Luuk wearing battered hiking boots that were only slightly too big.

They soon settled into a meditative rhythm, pedalling west along Cowboy Trail and then south, up into the foothills, following the winding course of the Elbow River. They passed a few trucks and the last of the houses. Medo sang in a language Luuk didn't know. Luuk was grateful that he didn't need to talk.

Cows grazed on the verges. Medo and Luuk paused to let a bull elk cross the road. It snorted in their direction.

When they reached Elbow Falls, they stopped to drink from the river. Medo pulled a paper map out of his pocket and showed Luuk the trail to Geotherma. He pointed out the bike cache, just off the road a few kilometres to the south.

"I'll stay here," Medo said. "This is a power spot. Easy to connect to the network."

He handed the map to Luuk, who hesitated. "Can I try to connect to the network?"

Medo's eyebrows contracted. "You've got a full-day trek ahead. If you don't leave now, you'll sleep rough tonight. Besides, it's wise to give yourself time to integrate before you connect."

"I want to learn how. To connect. To the network. I consent to that," Luuk said. He'd never been good at interacting with people, but this network thing felt different. Transpersonal.

"All right." Medo nodded. "I usually sit here. And I hum. Or sing. Then I... connect." He settled on a rock and Luuk did the same, keeping one eye open slightly, watching.

Luuk felt foolish, but he murmured some tentative buzzy noises that reverberated pleasantly in his chest cavity. It felt like he was inside an acoustic chamber, but he also *was* the acoustic chamber. He focused. Groped around in his mind space, or maybe into an extension of himself that wasn't bounded by the confines of his physicality, and found little flickers of responsiveness. A filament, then an orchestra of connection in a format that wasn't English or even language-based but was, nevertheless, effortlessly comprehensible.

He felt a vast field of friendly presences.

"Good!" Medo said, sounding surprised. "You're a receptive node now."

Luuk realized that was all he ever wanted to be: a receptive node.

He slowly became aware of the elemental nature of the planet. The earth was mineral, ancient, strange, and startlingly familiar, though its consciousness was arranged to experience time across eons. He became aware that its spherical surface was a delicate, vibrant living skin. *Nature*. Nature's purpose was to perpetually transform and rejoice. He was an intrinsic part of that vibrant living skin. He was transforming and rejoicing, too. There was no useful distinction between science and magic. The unfurling of each new leaf was an exultation. The Elbow River was pure elation. He was trillions of molecules, holding form and celebrating, as was everything.

Luuk felt expansive and... integrated. He understood that he wasn't going to Geotherma. At least, not yet. He'd return to Marie-Françoise's with Medo. Repair the kitchen faucet. Then tomorrow he'd bike back to Calgary. Help Sandeep, Finch and Fang get people through *The Sickness*. Check in with Corey, find out if the people sealed in at Brookfield Place were okay. If any of them felt ready to come out into the world and help create something new.

SECRETARY OF THE YEAR

Sarah Christina Brown

When I was a young woman, I worked for a while as a secretary for Mr. Karl Hotzlinger at a financial office on 41st Street. Mr. Hotzlinger was stern, sinewy and pale-haired. He liked to order in delivery, things foreign to me – schnitzels, malt liquors – and eat them behind his closed office door. I knew these items because I listed them in his expense reports. He'd yell in his clipped accent if calls were not put through to him quickly, if clients were kept waiting, if the coffee was lukewarm. Because of this, the other secretaries would call him The Devil. "Better darn that in a hurry," they'd mutter if a hem or button came undone. "The Devil will be displeased." I didn't call him this, though. Rather, while working for him, I developed a desperate desire to please. After a while, he began to entrust me with more personal tasks. I shined his shoes and polished his cufflinks. I did his laundry, even, adding scoop after scoop of borax to the water to remove the sweat from his collared shirts.

Everyone sweats in the city. Often the secretaries and I went for lunch at a French-themed café, where all the menu items were handwritten in French – *croissant au fromage, quiche Lorraine* – and it was a point of pride among the office workers to order in their most sophisticated accents.

Businessmen in smart suits would peer over their newspapers, the café a mess of eyes and kettles and persistent, whistling steam. They'd watch and chuckle as the secretaries breathily asked for *café allongé*. I always ordered *soup du jour* as it was the easiest to say.

We were unofficially required to wear silk dresses and heeled shoes. I wore these with a powdered face and seamed stockings. Occasionally I would rouge my lips but I could never act naturally those days; it was as though I was wearing insincerity on my face. I was a new college graduate, unmarried, with no work experience to my name. I worried that the businessmen might disagree with the idea of an inexperienced young woman, but soon I discovered that an inexperienced young woman is rarely disagreeable, and so Mr. Hotzlinger treated me agreeably. He was mostly very absorbed in his work. Though I was innocent to the ways of business, I could sense my place in the typewriters and filings and fulfill my duties accordingly. My work was routine, unremarkable.

Well, except for the matter of the woman on the telephone.

I had been working for Mr. Hotzlinger about four months before the first call came.

"I have some important information for you," the woman on the line said. Her voice was like flat notes on a flute. "Listen closely." What followed was so odd that I swore I mustn't repeat it for all my life. But I am an old woman now, so I suppose I can say it. She said, "I am contacting you from the future. The man you work for, Mr. Hotzlinger, is going to father a child who will father a child who will destroy all of human existence with a single piece of machinery."

"Pardon me," I said after a moment.

She went on like this for a while, in the manner of a toddler telling a winding, nonsensical story – his grandson would grow into an angry billionaire, build a rocket which would combust over the Atlantic, pouring out some kind of gas that evaporated all sorts of essential agriculture – until I hung up.

When I turned around, Mr. Hotzlinger was behind me.

"Oh, Mr. Hotzlinger," I exhaled. I had almost been laughing. "I – may I get anything for you, sir?"

"I'm on my way to a meeting," he said. He paused. "It isn't like you, Cynthia, to hang up the telephone without a proper goodbye."

This was when I realized that even though Mr. Hotzlinger was absorbed in his work, he was also capable of watching me at any moment.

The calls kept coming. You must understand, this was a delicate time. There had been a war, and the Germans were not well-liked, even two decades later. Perhaps the woman held a grudge. Or perhaps, I worried, she might be a past indiscretion of Mr. Hotzlinger's, a poorly-chosen affair, which lived within the liquor and unmentionables of his late-night receipts. After a while, I began to suspect that she could even be a set-up facilitated by Mr. Hotzlinger himself to test my secretarial skills. Because of this possibility I worked hard to remain professional, though it was very difficult at times. I'd be immersed in filing a financial record when the telephone would ring, and I'd be forced to listen to the woman talking about Mr. Hotzlinger in her eerily flat tone. She often said, "Write this down, goddammit, make a plan, go to a journalist, this is the only line of communication I've been able to secure—"

I became practiced in the art of saying, "No thank you, I am not interested in purchasing your product at this time," hanging up the receiver gently. Sometimes I swore I heard strange beeping noises alongside her, or the whooshing of water, as though she was calling from inside a submarine.

For my six-month anniversary with the company, I got a raise. Mr. Hotzlinger commended me on my excellent performance, and even said once in a meeting – "Look at Cynthia, how nicely she is dressed, how tidy her desk is; let her be an example for the rest." You should have seen the secretaries' faces. This did not do me any favours in making friends.

"Don't you simply *loathe* working for The Devil?" one of the secretaries was bound to ask at lunch hour, swirling a polished fingernail through coffee and cream. The eyebrow raise meant I was supposed to divulge anything grotesque or, at the least, agree. I would only shrug and look into my soup. I was raised never to throw things away, but at the café I would often leave my meal untouched as newspapers and suited legs opened around us.

Soon the phone calls came more frequently, sometimes several times a day, and they became less amusing over time. Rather, her words began to worm their way under my skin. As soon as I heard her voice through the receiver – "You are responsible for the fate of our whole planet," she'd often hiss – I developed a nervous twitch in my cheek. I lost weight and sleep. I attempted to press my dresses smooth but left the iron on too long and singed the silk. Once, shortly after the woman told me Mr. Hotzlinger's heir would starve the bodies of my grandchildren down to their shin bones, their small mouths thirsting to death over several months, I went to the staff kitchen for a drink of my own. The first thing I could find was coffee, and in my discomfort, I spilled it all over my dress. It made an awful dark stain all down my front.

"The Devil is going to burn you alive," a secretary hissed at me. She took pity on me and tried to cover me with her purse when Mr. Hotzlinger walked by.

"Good morning, Cynthia," Mr. Hotzlinger said as he passed, and I returned the salutation. He stopped when he saw my clenched fists. "What's that you're wearing?"

"It's… coffee, sir," I said. Beside me, the secretary let out a little moan.

We had seen him scream at employees for lesser offenses, but he only frowned at me. "Out of character for you," he said. "Though I know you are particularly talented in laundering."

"It was a very silly mistake. I'm so clumsy, but I'll be sure to get the stain out by morning."

"Well, we are only human. I suppose even I miss numbers on occasion. Never you mind. Busy yourself with finishing my month-end instead." After he walked off, the secretary and I breathed twinned sighs of relief.

Of course, I thought of telling him about the caller, but it was such an indelicate subject, I was afraid I'd be fired for speaking of it. If it wasn't a prank, the woman on the line was either crazy or driven crazy by a large and stressful life event. This was an important distinction, but I couldn't determine which one she was. Once I dared ask her to identify herself. "You wouldn't believe me if I told you," she said. When I exhaled, I turned to see Mr. Hotzlinger frowning at me. He simply needed quarters from the petty cash, and I counted them out, cursing myself.

After this, I began to hang up on the woman every time she called. It was difficult to achieve such a feat, as I also needed to make myself available to other callers. But I'd wait to hear her first breath – she had a habit of exhaling abruptly at the start of each call, like a marathon runner crossing the finish line – and then I'd slam the receiver down. It was the most violent thing I'd done to date, and sometimes – in a small way – I found it a bit satisfying.

Nearing my one-year anniversary with the company, there was an informal ceremony of sorts held in the lobby. They were celebrating a year of success and corporate growth, and all sorts of provisions were brought in – champagne, strawberry-coloured cakes, oysters on the half-shell. The higher-ups drank and drank and began assigning superlatives to one another as though they were editing a high school yearbook. Herbert Grimstone, an accountant, was voted Best in Fudging Numbers. Mindy Walton, a rather shapely secretary, was voted Most Likely to Conceive.

Eventually they moved to Mr. Hotzlinger. One of his fellow accountants nominated him as Most Likely to Violate the Quebec Agreement, and they all sucked their teeth and saluted him jeeringly.

"What does that mean?" I asked a man near me, thinking Mr. Hotzlinger must have a secret liking for maple syrup.

He chuckled. "Dear, dear Cynthia. The agreement the countries made to never use the atomic bomb on one another. What a gas! You know how Mr. Hotzlinger always goes nuclear on our clients."

A sharp feeling slipped down my throat, as though I'd just swallowed glass, though perhaps it was only the chill of the champagne.

"Thank you, my colleagues, for your vote," said Mr. Hotzlinger. His cheeks always flushed bright red when he'd been drinking, and his accent took over his throat. "It takes courage to pull the pin, but I fear not the task. *Geht mir aus dem Weg!*" He caught my eye, as I'd been staring at him. "And how could I forget my faithful secretary, Cynthia. I nominate her for Secretary of the Year!"

Everyone clapped, though this one wasn't as funny. Some of the other secretaries rolled their eyes.

"Really, I would give you a plaque," Mr. Hotzlinger continued, "but I hadn't the foresight." So instead he scribbled *great work!* on a crude drawing of himself riding a sort of explosive, and placed it into my hands.

I knew I wouldn't have made such a foolish connection were it not for the caller, her hurried breath in my head every day. I brought the paper over to my desk and the champagne sloshed in my stomach. I felt like I was going to be sick. When I reached my desk, I placed the drawing face down.

It became clear that I had to get married quickly, and I did. I went to these gatherings – these chaperoned things for business types in the city, with cocktail shrimp and the swelling pressure of organ music and gaiety – until I met a man who, upon learning of my country upbringing, proposed to marry me and take me back there. Once Paul signed the papers for our house, I handed in my resignation to Mr. Hotzlinger and he wrote me a glowing letter of recommendation, one that would surely secure me any future secretarial position I wished to gain, though I never applied to any. We had our daughter Donna soon after, and soon my entire life revolved around laundry – diapers, rompers, cloths, blankets, all of it never-ending.

But mostly I forgot about the office on 41st Street. I became very invested in keeping a clean house. I wore cotton dresses that didn't require much ironing, and I let my hair out loose. I pulled vegetables from the garden and cut them neatly into cubes. I took a medicine from a small silver vial each night, right after I removed my face with cold cream. It kept my sleep cool and light, and my doctor had prescribed it after I'd awakened Paul several times by thrashing around. It was awful for him to take the train tired the next morning, the poor dear.

When Donna was about five, we purchased a television. Paul said now that men were going to the moon, we ought to be able to watch space from the comfort of our own home. Even Donna was drawn to it like a fly. Soon we were watching B-52 bombers buzz along the coast. The country had sent them up bearing thermonuclear weapons, but the news anchors didn't know why. "It's just a show of force, that's all," Paul said. I watched as Donna placed her hands against the screen, its greyness draining all the colour out of her face.

I had been alone in my little house for what felt like so long, but I had to know if the phone calls were still happening.

The next morning, I was careful to hold Donna's hand tightly as we crossed 41st Street. I told Donna about the nice parts as we passed the French café. I told her how I used to wear pretty heeled shoes that would click-clack on the patterned flooring. I told her how I sat in the café with other pretty women, our pretty shoes shining all in a row. I pointed across the street to the large grey tower, and Donna was amazed. "You didn't really work *there*," she said.

"I did!" I insisted, but she giggled and shook her head.

It felt almost like a lie, but my memories had begun to feel like an old, odd dream. It did indeed feel dreamlike as we rode the elevator up. The floor looked almost entirely the same, except for the staff. I didn't see any of my former colleagues; I supposed they had all left to be married by then. There was a new secretary at my old desk. Her blouse was stained under the arms, I could see.

"May I help you?" she frowned at us. "Oh, no. I've misplaced my pencil again." Her desk was a mess of scribbled notes, pieces of chewing gum masticated to a pulp.

"Only stopping by," I said. "Might you have a spare moment to discuss something with me?"

"Discuss something? Why?" Though I'm certain Donna and I looked harmless, she maintained a secretary's shrewdness, shielding her papers all the same.

"Well, you see, I used to work for Mr. Hotzlinger."

She looked over both of us for a moment.

"I think I've – I've heard of you, before."

"I know I didn't make an appointment," I said, "and I feel awfully silly asking this, but have you ever received any strange calls or—"

"Cynthia," came the clipped voice from behind us.

His hairline had receded further into two, sharp, pale peaks, and I wondered if anyone still referred to him as The Devil.

"We were in the neighbourhood," I said.

"What a pleasant surprise. You were a most talented secretary. Cynthia was a *most* talented secretary," he repeated, now in the direction of the new secretary, who looked down at her feet. Mr. Hotzlinger looked at Donna, who was peering with interest at the bright shining accoutrements of the office. I held fast to her wrist.

"And who is this," he asked?

"My daughter," I said.

"Pleased to make your acquaintance, sir," Donna said in the manner we'd taught her.

"Polite young lady," Mr. Hotzlinger said, though there was something insincere about his statement. Perhaps he wasn't fond of children, which was understandable. But his nostrils flared oddly, as though Donna was a cockroach he'd spotted underneath his feet.

"If there's nothing else," Mr. Hotzlinger said, "I must be off to a meeting." He changed his tone. "Now, Patricia, you've left something off the hook again."

I watched Mr. Hotzlinger pick up the telephone receiver and place it back into its cradle. He walked away, and the secretary met my eyes. We looked at each other for quite a while, as though our thoughts were connected by a thin wire. I wondered how many times she'd hung up the phone this morning, that flat voice fading like a squashed insect.

"Allow me to show you," I said, "how I used to prepare Mr. Hotzlinger's afternoon coffee. Perhaps the right cup will allow him to appreciate you more."

"All right," she said. We walked to the kitchen. The grounds and kettle and everything else were still in the usual place, just as I'd remembered. Donna tugged at my dress, but I swatted her little hand away. I didn't want her to dislodge what I'd hidden in my pocket.

On our way home I got off the train two stops early and walked to our house in a haphazard, zigzag path, carrying Donna along in my arms even though she was so heavy at that point, just in case – just in case, I thought, blood spinning in my muscles – we were being followed. What a silly woman I am. I kept saying in my head, a silly woman, like a refrain.

Later that night, Paul came home and we watched the 7 o'clock news after Donna went to bed. The stock market had dropped again. A preacher had attempted to break up a gang fight and had been stabbed. An absent-minded businessman had accidentally ingested laundry detergent and had been rushed to hospital, his prognosis unknown. Thank goodness borax is falling out of favour with modern housewives, the news anchor said. Indeed, there was an advertisement for a newer, cleaner detergent only moments after.

"Terrible waste of life!" said Paul, arising to change the channel to a sports game.

I said nothing out loud. I never spoke of this to Paul or anyone else – well, I would have sounded as crazy as that flat-voiced woman herself if I did. I focused on canning and preserving vegetables, counting out rows to knit Donna's mittens. I didn't like to let her out of my sight if I could help it. I dusted the lampshades, the railings. I clipped laundry to the line to dry crisp and fresh under the light of the sun.

THE OCEAN OVERTOOK THE HORIZON

R. Haven

They weren't due to cross paths with the oncoming oil-skimmer for two more days. It shouldn't have been within spitting distance.

Bear's augmented eyes took in the patchy ice floes skirting between her home ship and the other, detecting the life signatures tethered to the outside of it – more than she'd been able to see in days prior as they'd chugged slowly along the all-encompassing ocean. It had to house an entire community, but Bear hadn't thought many of them were Enhanced enough to venture outside the hull. The air was thick with poison, only breathable to her and anyone fitted with an air purification mask.

The surgeries to become an Angler, and thus capable of providing for the people on board, were intensive. The mask was the simplest contraption, really, with tubes and wiring into her windpipe. Anglers needed microscopic tweaks to the eyes; an incinerator surgically outfitted to their backs; an array of retractable tools implanted in their bionic arms. Anglers were vital to survival, and more than one was needed for a community to truly thrive. The expert surgeons on her own ship were trying to collect enough materials and volunteers to give Bear some backup, but until they managed, she alone was in charge of fishing and destroying trash as she found it.

It was rigorous work, and she rarely had time to rest, much less relax with her young daughter. But Fennec was only six, and they knew and trusted the people they were with. She left Fennec's care to them with confidence throughout her busy day. Bear would not leave her to join a ship with more Anglers, workload be damned.

They'd been able to see the oil-skimmer coming for weeks now, though, and Bear had been able to watch their Anglers swing from their tethers around the hull from afar. Several days ago, however, all three of them had gone missing. The pinprick sun crawled up over the grey water, alerting everything that survived to the fact that it was time to start hunting down their next meal, and still no Anglers came rappelling down from the deck.

Wind brushed over Bear's bald head, carrying a suspicious scent that put her on high alert. The other ship had to have been gunning its engines to come upon them so fast, and that should've knocked their Anglers about like a fish flailing on a cutting board.

Cautiously, Bear let the line on her belt drop her down the hull, feet just touching down onto an ice floe. There was no weight on it – it wouldn't support even a quarter of her mechanical heft – but she wanted to be a little less conspicuous to anyone watching. A hundred feet down from the top, Bear could get lost among the refuse that wouldn't fit into her incinerator. She needed to ascertain the situation.

Alarmingly, bio-electricity lit up the figures in her broad scope of vision. People were crawling over the side of the ship with Angler gear – but they hadn't been Enhanced.

She could see it in their signatures, her marvellous dark eyes telling her all she needed to know to piece together what was about to happen. It was like looking into the near future.

Their ship had closed the distance between their vessels to try catching them off their guard. They were coming for her.

She had to remain calm. This happened, sometimes – ships trying to take another's Angler – usually it was simplest to just go willingly, but that wasn't an option for Bear. Fennec was on board. If she wasn't around to provide, no one else would: She'd be condemning her baby to starvation.

Like *hell*.

She pulled at her zip line and came back midway up the hull, planting her feet against the side as she started planning. The people coming for her were mundane, but they might infiltrate her ship or do some other sort of damage, looking for her. She'd make sure they could see her, track her, but she'd divide them at the same time. There was no time to waste. She ran along the side of the ship, her tether sliding along its track. With one great leap, she whizzed by her potential kidnappers to give them a good look. She stood out enough against the shining metal, with her black skin and black suit. Once she'd looped around the front of the bow, she dropped 20 feet and caught herself, turning on a dime to swing right back around. Bear had made a production of her first swing and was subtle about the second. They would pursue her around the starboard while she crept up behind them.

There were only six. She could handle six un-Enhanced kidnappers.

Silent, she watched them fire hooks into her rappel track and board her ship with what little stealth they could muster. As predicted, they sent the majority around to starboard and diverted two to port. They moved fast, on a time limit; they'd made makeshift oxygen masks and tanks, and those couldn't hold up for long.

Like a crab unfurling its legs, immense spears unfolded from two of her four arms. She crept along the bottom of the ship and aimed keenly. She had to wait for the two interlopers to descend, get into her range. Then she tore through the air tanks like shears through cloth, alarming them both. Pollution leaked in through their masks, but they must have thought she'd missed. They both dropped down to meet her, preparing their nets.

Bear flipped and ran along the metal away from them. She angled her course upwards, knowing she'd need to cut down their ropes to clear her track again. They pursued, but rapidly slowed, disoriented by the smog they inhaled. Manoeuvring all the way up, she prised their hooks out before they had a chance to catch up to her. They cried out when they fell to the waters and drowned within minutes.

Bear was already on her way around in pursuit of the others. She didn't know for sure whether the fallen two had been heard, but if she was quick enough, it probably wouldn't matter. Someone inside her home ship must have noticed their rival idling on the radar, because they'd picked up speed from a crawl to something quicker. Bear was still on her own; they couldn't lean on the engine to knock off the pirates without losing her too, but she wouldn't need the help.

She pressed buttons to reel her spears back in, and they folded up as they came back into her arms. The third inter-loper she dealt with by taking a page out of the kidnappers' book. Her net shot from one arm and entangled him within it, and he started to thrash and shout for the others. She cut him loose, but the others turned around and came toward her. In preparation, she drew her spears again, just to hold them in her hands.

All three of them were upon her. Without a thought to its brutality, she knocked aside an arm trying to wrangle her and seized his wrist, shoving his arm over her shoulder. It went into the incinerator on her back, and her leg came up around him to kick the second pirate back into his compan-ion. The burned man was screaming, losing his hold and spi-ralling away. He tried to fire his way back over to his own ship, and she was prepared to let him until he launched his net at her on his way past. She barely dodged in time, drop-ping and gliding rapidly out of its way. Landing hard, she pushed off the hull and speared him through the leg, yanking him down from the line and sending him, too, into the icy ocean.

Two left. They were trying to find a way of attacking from both sides. They couldn't fall and catch themselves with the ease Bear could, though; they didn't have the prac-tice, the certainty. They fell to her spears, and even as the last man alive tried to grapple with her while his chest wound bled freely, Bear kept her calm. She yanked his oxy-gen mask off his face and watched pollution sap his lingering strength.

The pirates would be fools to try to pursue, but if they did, it would take them time to turn the whole oil-skimmer around. They might risk it if they preferred a quick demise to slow starvation, but Bear didn't think they would.

Her ship charged on. No one aboard would throw the enemy a lifeline.

If there were pirates left to fight, they knew better than to send them out. Bear had dealt with them far too handily, too swiftly, to risk another overture of aggression. She hoped the next ship they encountered – if they found one in time – had Anglers to spare...

Ones who wouldn't rather kill than leave a daughter behind.

THE SHIFT

Isabella Mori

Red Nelly, that's what they called my grandmother, always looked a little dishevelled. So did her living room. Four book-shelves were squeezed into the small room, sagging with dark tomes, oversized coffee-table books, Greenpeace brochures, and video cassettes that even her questionable-looking TV couldn't play anymore. The enormous sofa was a mountain of pillows, blankets, dog toys and her ever-present box of beef jerky. She sure liked her meat.

Ilya, her old three-legged Czechoslovakian wolfdog, had his head rested on her lap – or maybe glued. He moved with Grandma Nelly's undulating shifts like a seagull on the ocean. They were so attached to each other that sometimes, when the light was dim, you couldn't tell which shape was hers and which was his. Large and thick like a human mas-tiff, Grandma Nelly could never sit still. And she always had a story to tell in her gravelly, barky voice.

This is what she told me the last time I saw her. Usually, there were lots of visitors around – you only had to meet her once to be drawn back to her fantastic tales – but they had all left, knowing a blizzard was on its way. It was only her and me.

"The old wolf howled," she began. "He howled the howl that says, come together. One by one, they drew closer, some of them arriving from deep in the bushes, from around the lakes and the deer trails. It was a mild summer evening in the forests around St. Petersburg. The sun would never fully go down, and the shadows were long and golden and soft. It had been a good year so far. There was food aplenty; fawns and elk calves abounded, and most of the wolf pups had survived. Even the weaker ones were doing well, two or three of them still nursing at their mother, stretched out lazily on a rock warm from the long day's sun.

"When they had all found their place, the old wolf looked at each one, all 28 of them, and finally began."

Grandma Nelly put her hand on mine. "He, too, had a story to tell. Listen."

Ilya added his paw. It felt just like Grandma's.

"Listen closely, please," she repeated. There was an unfamiliar urgency in her voice. "You're my only grandchild left. You must hear this. I should have told you a long time ago. It will explain to you why you became a forest ranger, and why you must continue your work."

That confused me. I became a forest ranger simply because nature conservation was important to me. Doing my part to help wildlife flourish felt good. True, I had wondered whether we should move closer to the city so it would be easier for the kids to go to a good school but— ·

"You must listen closely and soon you must tell your children." She looked me straight in the eye. "Promise?"

"Yes," I said, as always mesmerized by the amber light in her eyes.

"Good. Where were we. Oh yes, the old wolf."

"You have seen the humans," said the wolf to his pack. "They are coming closer and closer, sitting on horses, or in their little houses on wheels drawn by horses, even on those wooden contraptions drawn by our cousins, the dogs, through the snow. Last year, they killed three of us."

One of the younger wolves, her fur tinged red around the shoulders, barked a derisive laugh.

"Humans? Those stick creatures that have to make others pull them so that they can move fast and who can't even grow their own fur? That's who you called us here for?"

She got to her feet, paced a few steps, then returned and sat down again, showing reluctant respect for the old wolf. After all, he was her great-great-grandfather.

"You are right," responded the old wolf and paused. It was important to let his acknowledgement sink in. His respect was never reluctant.

"And yet," he continued after a while, "these humans are strong and cunning. They are strong because of their cunning. Their skin is naked and exposed, so they wrap themselves in the furs of other animals. They are slow, so they trick horses and dogs into giving them their speed. They cannot find burrows, so they take down trees and make places to live in. And they snared, I don't know how, the power of lightning and put it into their long sticks and they kill us with it."

A ripple went through the shoulders of the large wolf next to the old one. His mate had been one of the three victims. It had been ugly. The other two died right away, young ones who had joined them from another pack the winter before. But his mate, the one with the beautiful black and silver streak down her back, had been gut shot. It took two days for her to succumb, two days of bringing her food she wouldn't eat, licking her, lying next to her to keep her warm.

The old wolf, too, remembered it all too well. He moved closer to his widowed friend, letting him feel the strength of his flank, letting him know that he would never be alone.

But not everyone remembered. A young wolf with white paws and a white-tipped tail spoke up.

"My uncle told me that death is part of being a wolf. My brother and sister died as pups. We die because we don't have enough food or because we get sick. We die in fights with elks and bears or because the forest catches fire. So, some of us die because of those human sticks. I bet they die, too. Maybe they taste good?" He looked around. That was a good idea, wasn't it?

The old dog smiled inside. He didn't show it. But he remembered being young. Thinking himself smart. Coming up with great schemes he was sure no one had ever thought of before.

And again, he agreed. "You are right, young wolf. We all must die."

He looked around. Yes, they would all die. But how? And how many would be born?

"There must be a balance between life and death," he said. "And I must tell you, I had a vision. In that vision, the balance toppled until there was only death. The ones who topple the balance are the humans. They will kill us with their lightning sticks. They will take the deer and elk and eat them and wrap themselves in more and more of their fur. Even in ours! They will take the trees and make living places for themselves, bigger and bigger, and there will be less and less for us. They will make big, loud paths for their dogs and horses. And have you seen the black smoke that moves through the forest across the bay? It is from a monster much bigger than the wooden houses with wheels drawn by horses. In those monsters, they are protected with a skin so thick, none of you can rip it open, and they are so fast, none of you can ever outrun it. These monsters mate and have pups, and one day they will turn into massive birds and take flight."

He paused, then added, "This I have seen."

He howled for a long time, and no one howled with him.

His visions had never been wrong. But this one? Would it be the first to turn out incorrect? It was too outlandish. He was getting old, maybe his inner eye was beginning to cloud…

"I know, my beloved family, it is almost impossible to believe." The old wolf sat down, then lowered himself on his haunches. He looked so comfortable, so unthreatening, so relaxed. Why worry about his strange vision?

"You don't have to believe me, not all of you. But I need four of you. Two strong male wolves, and a she-wolf to mate with one of them."

The young wolf with the red-tinged fur piped up immediately. "That's three."

"You are correct," said the old wolf. "I will tell you about the fourth in a moment."

He got up again, stretched, turned his face to the slowly dusking sky. It would never turn black today like it did in the winter. The stars would be faint. No moon. The old wolf had sensed the change from waning to waxing just a few hours ago.

"None of the four will return. They will have to leave forever."

A wave of unease swept through the pack; snouts lifted, tails beat the ground, bodies shifted. One of the pups, not knowing what was going on but sensing something awry, started a low growl.

"That's nonsense." The red-tinged wolf got up and started pacing. "We will always stay together."

The old wolf lowered his snout in her direction. He could smell her irritation. And something else: the smell of healthy teeth and fur, the smell of a well-fed wolf, ready for all that life threw her way.

"Most of us, yes, we will stay together. Four of you will have to be brave and ensure the survival of future generations." He paused again. "If all goes well."

"So – four of us will go away together?"

"No. You will go in three directions. The rest of us will stay a while."

His heart was heavy. He did not want to do this. He did not want to lose a single one of his pack. But the vision he had seen had been the strongest he had ever had. As much as he wanted to disbelieve it, this vision was true.

"Two of you will go where the sun rises later and shines longer in the winter, to a place the humans call Poland. You will have pups, and your pups will have pups. Many lifetimes from now, this is where wolves will become stronger, and humans will no longer kill them. Many, many, many lifetimes from now. As many as all of us here."

The wolf with the red-tinged fur looked around. She knew every one of them but she could not hold them all in her memory at once. So many lifetimes! She looked at the big wolf. He was so old, older than many wolves would get. Her great-aunt with the grizzled snout, she had had pups seven times. She doubted she would survive the next winter. And what the old wolf talked about was so many times longer than that. She could not understand. But something stirred in her.

The old wolf went on. "And then there are our cousins, the dogs. The humans don't hunt them with their sticks. They take them in and live with them. As you know, wolves can mate with dogs. A male from among you will befriend the dogs and you will have pups. In that way, our blood will flow on, if only in the veins of dogs."

"Dogs!" A beige old wolf, almost the leader's age, lifted his head, shook it. "They're no better than humans. Some look like us but more and more, have you seen, they're like – like cats!" He spat out the last word. "Small and sitting on humans' laps like they don't want to get their paws dirty. I ate one of them a few years ago. He tasted horrible; I ate only because I was hungry. His blood was thin, and there was human sweat all over him."

A few wolves growled. Who likes dogs? Horses at least, they need to be harnessed, you can see how they'd rather run free. But dogs! Brown-nosing humans all the time.

"With that worthless crap humans feed them, of course they'll taste filthy."

The old wolf disagreed. He had eaten of what the humans called garbage. Some of it was quite tasty, and he knew the other wolves felt the same way. But this was no time to stir up more discord. His task was hard enough.

"Be that as it may," he said, his voice mellow, soothing, "we can revisit this later."

He knew there were a few young wolves eager to mate; he would talk to them in private in the next few days.

"So, what about that fourth wolf? You haven't said any-thing about him yet. What are you holding back?" So feisty, that young she-wolf. Curious, unafraid.

The old wolf did not reply. Instead, he walked up the top of the hill, facing the sun as it slowly made its way to dip just a little below the horizon. Against the gentle light, his features were hard to make out; only his silhouette was clearly visible.

A sudden wind rushed through the treetops. Pine cones rattled and fell to the ground or got caught in the cranberry bushes. The leaves of the little stand of birches by the creek twirled, reflecting the sky's deepening hue. Distracted by this commotion, the pack looked away from the old wolf but when they looked toward the top of the hill again, the old wolf was gone.

An eagle, larger than any the wolves had ever seen, rose from the top of the hill. His white head gleamed, and the sun caught the yellow of its sharp beak.

The old wolf was gone.

The eagle flew up high until he was only a dot. All the wolves' faces were turned to him. They made no sound.

Slowly circling, the eagle came closer. Closer, closer. The adult wolves circled around the pups. Some of the smaller ones hid under their mothers, fathers, aunties.

With an enormous *whoosh*, the eagle landed among the wolves. They shrank back.

Only one wolf barked – the young she-wolf with the red-tinged fur.

The eagle opened his razor-sharp beak. The wolves shrank back even more. But others, encouraged by the she-wolf, began to bark.

"Quiet!" called the eagle. The voice sounded familiar.

"Some of you older wolves remember—" the eagle looked around and fixed its vision on the beige wolf who had spoken with such disdain about dogs "that our pack has a few among us who can shapeshift."

"Ohhh…" a murmur rose from an older she-wolf. Her pup crawled out from under her.

"Is that – you?" asked another wolf.

"Yes. It is me. I have been given the gift of shapeshifting. Humans think they are the only ones, but as some of you know, we wolves can, too."

The young one with the white paws and white-tipped tail spoke up. "If we're as strong as humans, then why worry?"

The eagle shook his feathers. "Humans are not the only ones, and wolves are not the only ones. I have known an elk who could do it, and a sparrow, and have heard of others. It would be so easy if that was the only power that was needed. But there's more."

"A sparrow?! A simple little sparrow?" This was a pup who spoke up, speaking from her recent proud experience of having hunted and killed an injured little bird.

"Yes, a sparrow. How simple they are, I don't know." The old wolf yearned to be back in his old shape, yearned to be back in a time where in his old age all he needed to do was accept the food that was brought to him. When he could spend his days with these young ones, watching their accomplishments and their innocent little wisdoms before they would be dashed by the lessons of the years. How lovely would it be to lie in the den with these young pups and have a little debate about sparrows with them.

But that time... he didn't know whether it would ever come again.

"My good people," he continued, beating his wings, "this is the most difficult of the tasks. Two of you know you can shift shape. There are two more; you are young still and don't know yet, but I can tell who you are. One of you..." – oh, how he did not want to finish the sentence – "...one of you shapeshifters will have to go to the place where the humans live."

"And do what? Why a shapeshifter?"

"One of you will have to become a human."

"Are you insane?!" Impossible to tell who challenged him like that; the pack turned into a barking, running, whimpering, biting, crouching, howling mass of bodies. Fur flew, tails whipped, puppies scattered, and more than one body disappeared in the woods.

But no one attacked the old wolf, now back in his old shape. He stood on the hill, forgotten, sad. And not surprised. He had feared this would be the reaction. No questions, not even debate, just utter refusal to hear more.

Much later, in the early hours of the morning, a silhouette detached itself from the copper half-shadow of the birch stand. Slowly, it made its way up to the old wolf, who lay beneath a cranberry bush, dozing.

It was the young she-wolf. When she got closer to the bush, she lay down.

Inch by inch, the sun made its way up the horizon again. Soon, the deer and rabbits would wake up and walk down to the river and the pack would get ready to feed.

But for now, everything was quiet except for a few timid tweets from the first birds.

Finally, the she-wolf spoke up.

"So... some know they are shapeshifters, and some don't."

The old wolf yawned. "That's right."

"If one were a shapeshifter but didn't know, what would that look like?"

More yawning, jaw wide open. There wasn't much left of those molars. "They would look like any other wolf." Lips smacking, he laid his head down on his paws. "Or any other shapeshifting wolf not currently shapeshifting."

"You don't want to tell me?"

"I want you to tell me why you want to know."

The younger wolf stood up. Paced. Finally, she hissed at the old wolf: "Because I want to know if I can do it. Happy?"

Her eyes glinted red with the reflection of the sun. She stood before the old wolf, forepaws firmly planted, haunches slightly bent, at the ready. A powerful jaw, gleaming fur. Restless, fierce temper.

"Let me tell you why first. Why someone needs to become a human."

The she-wolf started pacing again but he ignored it. "I did not believe my vision first, either. What humans are capable of cannot be imagined, not without a vision, and something terrible tells me they're capable of even worse things. Did you know they will not only kill us but each other? In the most horrible ways. But in the end, there will still be many, many, many more humans than wolves, and they will still want to hunt us. But..." he raised his voice as the other wolf started growling "...they can also be kind. We need humans who find in themselves an urge to fight for us. We need a shapeshifter to start such a family. We need humans" – he got up and stretched – "with the heart of a wolf."

The she-wolf stood before him, facing him, her eyes glowing in the rising sun.

"I want to do it."

The old wolf looked her up and down.

"And so, you will."

Grandmother Nelly stopped. She looked out the window. The snow outside was thick-flaked and dense, gleaming white in the street lights across at the corner. With her left hand rummaging around in the jerky box, her right stroked Ilya's head over and over again. He sighed contentedly in her lap.

Where was the rest of the story? She never stopped like that.

I waited. Knew not to push her.

Finally, she turned to me, her wiry, unruly hair bouncing, beautiful and full, silver-grey everywhere except for that reddish streak down the right side that made everyone call her Red Nelly. Her face was wet with tears, her eyes illuminated with something that was pain but also... hope?

"That wolf," she said with a whisper, "was my great-grandmother.

BEES IN THE WIND

Sara C. Walker

Joenna stood on the porch, scanning the farm's pastures for him while the screaming wind tugged at her cardigan. With the first sign of billowing clouds on the horizon, he'd hopped onto his horse to go corral the herd. Mid-afternoon had become full dark; ice-cold drops hit the porch. There was still no sign of him.

The storms had the power to knock out their fences, peel open the roofs. To speak nothing of the tornadoes and hurricanes. If they were lucky, the storm might stay along the horizon, never reaching them.

Before he set out, she asked him, "How do you know it's coming?"

"I don't," he said. "But the wind does."

He would give her hell for being out in this when she should have been in bed, resting. But she couldn't stand another moment in the empty house.

A sharp twinge pulled in her lower belly, a reminder of what was no longer there.

She had grown up in the city, went on to earn a degree in botany, and then got a job at a garden centre, where they met.

He was a seventh-generation farmer, looking for a hardier clover. Found her instead.

Once married, she needed something to do on the farm. She decided on beekeeping, so in their first week of marriage, he built her the hives.

The second week into their marriage, he built a cradle. For three years, they'd tried. For three years, she'd failed.

They hadn't had time to process their loss when the storm approached.

The bees refused to come out of their hives all day. They were either hiding from the storm outside or the one raging inside her.

Her application for the biodome project was tucked under their mattress, unsent. She didn't know how to tell him how badly she wanted to leave. She wasn't made for farming – for life and death thrown about so casually.

He didn't know she covered her ears and cried when the cows were slaughtered because they could no longer produce calves.

And now this.

The only thing he most desperately wanted in life she couldn't give him. She could never give him. She wasn't even sure she wanted to give him.

Queen bees ensured the survival of the hive.

If Joenna stayed, the farm had no future. She knew how much an eighth generation meant to him. He wanted to adopt. He'd assured her no one would have to know.

She would know. What if she failed to raise a child who wanted to take over the farm? What if she raised a child who hated them as much as it hated farming? What if she wasn't cut out to be a parent at all?

A crack of lightning split the sky. She pulled her sweater tighter and scanned the pastures again.

She wished she could understand what the wind was saying.

~\|/~

Joenna fidgeted with her beekeeper's hat, unable to meet his eyes. A lantern spilled a pool of yellowed light on the otherwise empty farm table. The night wind howled high in the rafters, beating the shutters against the cabin.

He stood next to the door, shrouded in darkness. He'd just returned from the barn, calving, when he saw her waiting at the table in her beekeeping gear. Her timing had always been terrible.

There wouldn't be another time.

For weeks, the energy in the atmosphere urged her to gather her hives and run. Change was coming.

"My application to the project was accepted," she said before her courage ran out.

He said nothing, and although she still could not bring herself to meet his eyes, she noticed that he had gone very still.

"I'm taking the bees with me." They'd discussed this when she told him about her application. He knew this. But she said it anyway.

"When?" His voice fell, and her chest tightened.

"I have to report to the project recruiter at O-700. From there the bees and I will proceed directly to the biodome."

"So that's it? It's over?" His words cut through the heaviness and pierced her heart.

She swallowed the lump in her throat. "It's an experiment. It's not forever."

Every other time they'd discussed this, she'd been the one to storm from the room. Tonight – maybe it was the late hour or the weight of her heavy heart or that she wanted him to agree with her – she felt stuck to the chair.

He turned away, putting his back to her, and went through the door.

~·~

The dome's second-in-command, Smith, came to see her but stood as far from the hives as he was able while still carrying on a conversation. She used to smile when he did this, but after the morning's events, she wasn't sure she would ever smile again.

Smith once asked how she could constantly put herself in danger. It took a while for him to understand that the bees posed no threat, but he was still scared of being stung, and kept his distance.

She scraped the propolis off the hive to give to the medical team. It was useful for sore throats and sinus infections that seemed to always be going around. She'd kept herself busy, trying to banish the sound of the shot from her mind.

Hector was dead. The administrator. Her friend.

Last night, as the senior staff dined with Hector, he regaled the room with a story about how he went to France for the opening of a wine cellar long buried and forgotten. He'd paid a pretty price to attend that wine tasting with his lover.

The one thing he couldn't stand was not knowing if the wine would be good, or if the cork had been damaged and the wine soured. He wanted every bottle opened. The not knowing was killing him. So, he bought out the entire cellar, and stayed there with Ferdinand for weeks until every bottle was opened and tasted.

"How I miss the taste of champagne," he'd said last night with a wistful sigh.

"And Ferdinand?" Joenna had asked.

"I could have let my money be my sole contribution to the dome and sailed on my yacht with my Ferdinand, but we had a fight. I ran away, thinking I would hide out here for a while and then emerge when I was ready to apologize. Then the ice age hit."

Joenna's chest tightened. She hadn't known that Hector's story was so similar to her own.

The grapes Hector had brought had failed their first year in the dome, and he quickly went through his supply of bottled wine. Joenna had brought him mead as soon as she could, but while he appreciated the gift, mead didn't spark the same joy. They tried fruit wines, but Hector only became sullener.

They couldn't have known that was their last dinner with Hector, or that first thing this morning he would stand in front of the door to the outside and blow his brains out with a gun no one knew he had.

While others dealt with Hector's body, Joenna went to work, trying to forget the sight of her friend's dead body at the base of the dome's door. The gun fallen from his hand. The door unopened.

Smith's lips were moving, but she heard no sound over the ringing in her ears. Even the buzzing of her bees faded away.

"What did you say?"

"They want *you*, Jo."

"Me? For what?"

"For Administrator."

The air rushed out of her lungs. She braced herself on the hive.

"Me."

"It's a logical choice, Jo."

They were scientists. Of course, they'd made a logical choice. She'd dined at the Administrator's table for years. They became friends right from the start of the project. Hector was deeply concerned about the pollinators. As he should have been. Their survival depended on pollination.

"I didn't ask for the job," she stammered.

Tea. She needed tea. They wanted her to take Hector's job. The moment required tea.

With trembling fingers, she started pulling off her gear and marching away from the hive yard.

Smith followed. "Nevertheless, the board's chosen you."

The board consisted of the heads of departments – the scientists, engineers, bioengineers, etc. – that had come together to bring the biodome project to fruition, while the rest of the world buried its head in the sand.

It began as an experiment concocted by billionaires to see how long humans could survive inside, but after the eruptions, the domes became salvation.

The chain reaction of volcano activity around the Pacific put ash in the atmosphere for decades, clouding over the northern regions of North America and Europe. The available growth period for crops diminished, turning the northern regions into desolate wastelands unable to support little more than brush and lichen.

The biodome had been built to operate on ground-source energy. Solar lights between panes of greenhouse glass had got them through the dark days. Plants around the perimeter provided food and oxygen. An apartment structure at the centre housed the occupants.

For decades, Biodome North had had no contact with the outside world, as was designed at the start of the experiment – no communication whatsoever. The experiment was as much social as it was scientific.

When the world around them went dark and fell away, they could only watch, silent observers behind their glass walls. In the distance, people travelled only south. Every winter, the snow came earlier and earlier and lasted longer and longer. Summers were colder and darker. Inside the dome, they held their breath and prayed as the ice crept down from the north.

Their survival was nothing short of one well-timed miracle after another.

Once inside her apartment, Joenna boiled a pot of water. Smith sat silently at her kitchen table while she worked, giving her time to process her thoughts.

She placed a cup of tea before him, stirring honey into her own cup as she took the chair across from him.

"I know nothing about running the dome," she said.

They weren't even giving her time to mourn Hector.

"You know bees," Smith said.

"Bees," she laughed. "Bees are not people, or glass structures, or complicated waste systems."

Smith shifted in his chair. "A few days ago, Hector said something a little unusual but not completely out of character."

Hector was always saying odd things, singing sea shanties, sharing bad puns or posing childish riddles. Always keeping those around him smiling. She missed her friend so much it hurt.

"We had just finished reviewing reports and were sipping that strawberry wine on the roof, simultaneously observing the dome activity and the sunset.

He says to me, do you have any regrets, Gunnie? Do you ever wish you hadn't joined the project? And I says, no, sir. The dome provides me with fulfilling work, a belly full of food and place to rest my head at night. I couldn't ask for more."

That was Smith. Content in the moment.

"Then he said you once told him that a hive without a queen will perish."

Without the queen, there would be no new bees, for the queen is the only egg layer, and the hive would be left with drones and sterile worker bees. Their only chance at survival was to raise a new queen.

"I didn't understand what he was saying at the time. Wish I had. Of course, now it's plain as day." Smith looked right at her. "He was telling me he wanted you to replace him."

The ringing in her ears intensified, her heart pounded. *Workers don't get to be queens.*

She fell against her chair. "I never said I wanted the job. I don't. I don't want to run the dome. I had no plans to supersede Hector. Ever." He was her friend.

"It has to be you, Jo," he said softly. "You know why."

His unspoken words lanced her heart. Her defect made her the ideal candidate.

Everyone else was raising children. Children were their future. If the dome didn't open in Joenna's lifetime, it might open in theirs.

Suddenly, she was back on the wooden porch, trying to hear what the wind had to say.

Smith, ever the picture of calm, looked up at her. "What will you tell them?"

~\|/~

Near the apex of the biodome, surrounded by the hum of bees pollinating the successful tropical plants, Joenna peered through a pair of binoculars. Pulled from her administrator's desk to attend to this new matter, she'd had no time to change into something more appropriate for climbing between tree branches.

She was too old to be climbing trees. But she was pleased to see her old friends buzzing from flower to flower.

For five decades, the view had been nothing but a blank canvas of bright white snow. Today, below a solid blue sky, the binoculars revealed the distinct shape of a person marching toward them. From the south.

Her mind flashed back to her husband crossing a field, returning home.

"Impossible," she breathed.

Next to her, Smith grunted. "I daresay. We never thought we'd see the day."

She blinked. The image of long ago disappeared.

The person appeared to be shrouded in fur pelts that flapped in the wind.

The wind blew from the south.

She turned to Smith and handed over the binoculars.

To the naked eye, the approaching stranger was no more than a wee silhouette on the southern horizon. A miracle the dome inspection crews had noticed him at all. But then, with nothing new to stare at for decades, a fleck of anything was noticeable. Last month, one of them swore he saw a bird flying along the horizon, but since no one else saw it, his claim was dismissed.

The arrival of another human changed everything.

An explorer? Looking to expand humanity to the north once more?

Or a lone survivor of the worst, needing their help to rebuild?

Her job now was to decide how to respond.

If she opened the dome, would they all die of exposure or fly free in fresh air?

—⁂—

They sat in her office. The oil painting of Hector's yacht still hung on the wall behind her. His collection of carnival masks still scattered on one wall, while the stuffed marlin he'd bought occupied most of the space on the other wall. She'd not been able to bring herself to take down Hector's things.

Smith stared at the unfinished cup of tea in front of him. Joenna clasped hers in her hands. The old chair cradled her bones, weary from climbing between trees, as she rehearsed her speech in her mind. Children's laughter floated down the hall, melting into the constant high-pitched noise in her ears.

Opening the door would invite disease. The scientists had talked at length about what the process would look like for them to rejoin society. They'd have to be quarantined, vaccinations updated, etc., etc. For another to join their hive? The dome occupants had always been against it. They had no space to quarantine, and the individual would bring unknown communicable diseases.

The scientists had been monitoring the temperatures. They saw the data, but remained skeptical. Would they ever want the doors open?

As for everyone else…

Rumour of the stranger's approach would have spread throughout the dome by now. Anyone who worked near the southern windows would have noticed him. Anticipation for Joenna's decision was palpable.

After decades of no contact, they were all hungry for news from the world they'd left behind. Were there survivors? How many? How far south did they go?

Bees sensed the changes in the upper atmosphere. They knew what the scientists didn't. Bumping up against the glass for the past year, they'd been saying the worst was over.

She wouldn't risk the dome. But if the stranger brought good news, she wouldn't deny the dome occupants their freedom, either. Someone would have to arrange their quarantine and vaccinations.

She stood, abandoning her tea on the desk.

"I will go outside and greet the stranger. I'll signal you if it's good news."

Smith levelled his gaze at her. "If you go out there, and it's not good news, we can't let you back inside."

Being in proximity to the stranger would expose her to his communicable diseases.

If it wasn't good news, if the ice creep wasn't receding, she would be left outside to die of exposure. But she wouldn't let them bear witness to that. She would walk until the dome was out of sight and dig a hole.

"That's why I'm taking the gun."

Smith rose out of his chair and prepared to block her path to the door.

"Jo, no."

He had always feared being stung. Hector's death hit him much harder than he would admit. But they managed. They'd weathered that storm. They would weather this one.

A child, one of Smith's grandchildren, burst into the room. The toddler handed Joenna a fallen leaf before shyly gripping her grandfather's leg. Smith wrapped his arms around the small girl, lifting her into his arms.

"It has to be me," she said. "You know why."

Once, she wasn't sure she even wanted children. In the end, Hector had given her an entire dome of occupants and their children. She ensured their survival and that of their children. After a long winter, her hive had survived.

Would she have done as well if she'd stayed on the farm? Only the wind could say for certain.

Smith stroked the girl's flyaway hair, but his eyes were on Joenna. "What would I tell them? Who would replace you?"

Decades had passed since she'd entered the dome. She'd trained someone else to look after the hives, and they'd trained someone else, who was in the process of training others. Succession planning had become an immediate priority after Hector's death.

She smiled. The future was in good hands.

"So that's it? You're giving up? Just like Hector?"

His questions weren't fair, and it wasn't like Smith to panic. Maybe she'd misheard over the ringing in her ears. Or maybe it was only that he felt stung.

If the bees were right, they all would soon fly again. And if they weren't... She'd reached her seventh decade now. It was time for a new queen.

Either way, she would open the door and step outside. She was no longer that bright-eyed, 20-something girl on the porch, wishing the wind would tell her what to do.

She was a queen, exiting her hive with her head held high, preparing her cloud of bees to take to the sky and swarm to a new location.

She couldn't wait to feel the wind again.

FEATHERS AND WAX

KATIE CONRAD

I pulled hard on the strap holding my beehives to the trailer, hauling it as tight as I could before tying it off. The soft buzz from within the hives rose at the jostling. Satisfied that my precious cargo wouldn't fall, I walked back across the drive-way to speak to Anita Walkes.

It was late – late enough for all my bees to be home in the hives when I packed them up – but still hot. August had been blazing, as usual, and the heat lasted long after sunset.

Anita extended a hand and I took it. Her strong fingers squeezed mine, smaller but equally calloused.

"Thanks again, Melissa. I know it's a pain bringing the bees out here twice."

"Anything for my best customer." I flashed her a grin. Anita was the only farmer in the county with a big enough operation to justify two pollinations. It was more work for me, but that was a benefit, not a drawback. "I'll be back in a few weeks for my payment."

"Ah. About that." She paused and scratched the back of her neck. My stomach dropped. "I'm not going to be able to spare the grain this year. I'm really sorry."

"But we have a deal. I pollinate your crops; you give me the grain."

"I know, I know. But this's been a rough year for the har-vest, and I've got my own animals to feed. You understand."

I understood that I was screwed. "And what am I sup-posed to feed my chickens?" The grass and bugs on my own property, supplemented with vegetable scraps, were enough to keep them fed through summer, but I didn't have enough land to grow feed for the winter. I had to trade for grain to get them through until spring.

She spread her hands. Her face, shadowed starkly in the moonlight, was unreadable. "I'll still pay you, of course. Just not in grain. Come back in a few weeks like usual and I'll load you up with vegetables and firewood. We've even got some spare cloth this year. Whatever you need."

"What I need is grain."

"I can't—"

"A few bags, at least." I felt impotent, wheedling. Of course, she told me after the pollination was finished, when all my bargaining power was gone.

"Maybe one bag."

"Ten."

"Ten?" She swore. "I haven't got 10. I can spare two, at best."

After a bit more back and forth, I got her up to four. Nowhere near enough, but better than nothing.

She offered another handshake before I left. I pre-tended not to see her extended hand.

I checked the straps on my hives one more time before mounting my bike and pedalling away.

⇝

I flicked on the little portable radio on my handlebars to dis-tract me from the spiral of worry that threatened to consume my mind on the long ride home. The radio was solar-powered, made with the best technology available when I bought it 10 years ago. One of the last things I bought before the collapse. It didn't take much sun to keep it running for days.

The national station was re-running the day's news reports, which consisted of the only topic they ever seemed to talk about: the upcoming spaceship launch.

"And with just one month until your projected launch, you've finally revealed the name of your ship. The Daedalus, *is that right?"* the announcer was asking.

"That's right," Anderson Morse answered. *"We're going back to the mythological roots of human flight."*

"Daedalus… isn't he the one who flew too close to the sun and died? Not exactly an auspicious name, is it?"

"No, you're thinking of his son, Icarus. Daedalus flew safely, passing neither too close to the sun nor the sea."

"Like you're planning to do with your slingshot manoeuvre."

"Exactly, Tom. Exactly." I could almost hear the smug grin on Morse's face. I had never seen him but I pictured his face as one that could use a good punch.

I flicked the radio off. Billionaires were abandoning our dying planet while I was out here begging for chicken feed. And I had it good, compared to many.

The bees were the real money-makers, of course. Not that we used money any more, but they earned my bread and butter. Through the summer I took them to every farm in the county for a week at a time to pollinate the crops. There weren't enough wild bees left to do the job, and I had the last hives in the area. If anything ever happened to them, well, I'd be toast.

But even the bees weren't enough to keep things going. That's where the chickens came in. The eggs meant I never had to trade for meat and fish. But in turn I had to feed the chickens. That meant trading every spare bit my charges produced. My life was held together with feathers and wax; a careful balance to keep myself afloat.

It had always been enough to get through the winter before. With Anita providing the bulk of the chicken feed and a few bags coming from other farms here and there, I was able to get us all through the cold season. But without Anita's contribution, I'd be hard-pressed to make it up elsewhere. After a rough growing season everyone was going to be just as stingy with their grain.

—⋇—

"Listen, I can't spare any grain, but I've got some extra turnips; I'd be glad to trade you those."

"I appreciate that, Glenn, but I can't feed the hens on turnips alone. I need grain to get them through the winter."

Glenn Potts was another of my regular customers. After pollination season was over, I made the rounds through the fall to keep up my trade in other items. Normally I was stocking up on hardy vegetables and in a good year, cloth or timber to repair my small homestead. But this year I was stuck begging for grain first and foremost.

"I wish I could help, but I just don't have any extra this year."

"I'm not asking for a handout here. I'm good for it. I'll trade you whatever you want. Beeswax candles to keep your house lit through the winter? Or, no, you just built that new cabin for your son. I'll trade you enough feathers to insulate it. Think of the firewood you'll save."

"I'm sorry, Melissa, but I just can't spare anything. I've got to feed the cows."

"Glenn. Whose bees pollinate your crops every year?"

He sighed. "Yours. But that doesn't—"

"And if my chickens starve this winter, how do you think I'm going to get by?"

"That's not—"

"No chickens, no me, no bees, no crops. It's the circle of life, Glenn."

There was a time I would have felt slimy guilting him like that, but these days I know that you do what you have to do. And when it came down to it, everything I said was true.

In the end I left with one bag of grain and a half-bushel of turnips, in exchange for half the feathers. It was a start.

⋅≫⧫≪⋅

I got back on my bike and headed for home. The late-summer sun hung over the trees to my left, painting the landscape in copper and brass. It was past noon now and my legs were getting tired, but I pressed on. I'd left home before dawn so I could make the trip in one day.

As always, I turned the radio on as soon as I got out on the open road. I focused on the news for a minute in case there was anything of actual importance. But no, it was the usual bullshit.

I flicked the channel over from the national broadcast to the local station. No one knew exactly who was respon-

sible for it, but the rumour was that someone had comman-
deered one of the antennae of an old commercial station and
repurposed it to run off solar power. How anyone found time
to run a radio broadcast in this world was beyond me, but I
was grateful they did.

Half the reason I listened to the radio was to hear the
weather reports. The other half was the desperate hope to
hear my favourite song, "Breath of Your Joy." I hadn't heard it
in 15 years, not since the networks went down.

I still hummed it to myself, but I'd forgotten some of
the words and wasn't even sure of the tune any more. But I
was sure that someday, sooner or later, the radio would play
it again.

That night, they were playing retro double-jazz, which
was no "Breath of Your Joy," but it was fine. Upbeat enough
for biking, not like the dreary modern stuff they sometimes
played. When I was young and the networks were still up, I
could listen to whatever I wanted whenever I wanted. Now
I was beholden to the whims of the mysterious radio jockeys
and their tastes. Tastes which didn't seem to include a folk-
funk one-hit wonder from the '40s.

I put my pointless longing aside and fell into a rhythm
pedalling to the double-jazz as I made my way home, the
bike trailer bouncing along over the rough roads behind me.

~\\~

My luck at the next farm, a few days later, wasn't much better. After an hour of haggling, I biked away with one bag of
grain and a couple armloads of carrots in my trailer, having
traded a dozen eggs and half of my candles.

It was a long trip for very little, but I had done the math. If I could get one sack of grain from each of my usual customers, it should be enough. If I stretched it out and added all my vegetable scraps, it should be enough.

It had to be enough.

The news reports on the way home were talking about the spaceship again. I listened in for a moment, curious despite myself.

"It's brilliant," Morse was saying when I tuned in. "Our engineers drew up the plans, but basically we're going to go around the sun and use its gravity to slingshot us out at greater speed than we could achieve on our own. We'll reach our destination in only two-thirds the time it would take otherwise."

"And these brilliant engineers," the reporter asked, "will they be on the Daedalus with you?"

Morse laughed. "Of course not. They could never afford a ticket!"

I flicked the radio off and pedalled in silence. The rage welling inside me was better fuel for my legs than any music.

─✷─

The radio played nothing but discordant industrial baroque the whole way to the Smith farm a few weeks later. I turned the music down to the edge of hearing, but not off. I might miss something important.

I'd been successful so far in getting one bag of grain per customer, but I would need a few more to get us through the year. I had a good relationship with the Smiths, and a little part of me dared to hope that I could leave with three or four bags. Even two would be a bonus.

The Smiths were all out in the field, their hoes rising and falling as they prepared the ground for winter. Naomi, the matriarch, looked up at the crunch of my tires over their driveway. She dusted off her hands, cracked her neck to each side and walked over to greet me.

"Melissa, this is a surprise. What brings you out this far at this time of year?"

"I've come to trade."

A curtain fell over her face. "Oh?"

"I need grain. For my hens."

"I'm afraid we don't have any to spare." Her mouth was a thin line. "You know it's been a tough season."

That little hoping part of me died away. "I'm not asking for any favours. I'll trade you whatever you need. Candles? Eggs? Feathers? Wax?"

"I really can't help you. But," she raised a hand before I could cut her off, "I know who can."

⁓

The directions Naomi gave me led me farther afield than I'd expected. I was watching the sun closely, trying to gauge whether I'd have time to make it home before dark. It was looking less and less likely, but by the time I came to that conclusion, I'd gone too far to turn back. It would just be a waste of energy to make a second trip another day when I was this close. I'd have to take my chances in the dark on the way home.

I coasted down the old highway – long since cracked open and grown up with weeds – and along a series of ever-shrinking dirt roads. I repeated Naomi's instructions to myself over and over so I wouldn't forget, but eventually I came to an unmarked fork in the road. She said to turn left, didn't she?

I pulled out the ancient, crumbling road map from my pack, but by now I was too far into tiny back roads for any of them to be recorded there. I trusted my guts and took the left-hand fork. If I was wrong, then hey, what's a few more hours at this point?

But a half hour later I came to the farm. There were people working the fields, a farmhouse with smoke curling from its chimney and a pair of sheep huddled next to the house. It was like an idyllic scene from one of those old movies we used to watch when I was a kid.

I pulled my bike to a stop at the side of the road and stared for a minute. "Well I'll be damned."

How could there be a whole farm in my county that I didn't even know about?

I finally shook myself free from my surprise and started down their long driveway. The people in the field saw me coming. A few of them lifted hands in greeting, and I did the same. One man, a wiry fellow with sandy hair and a big moustache, came across the field to greet me, much the same way that Naomi had just a few hours before.

"Hello there. Can I help you?"

"Hi, is this..." I tried to remember the name Naomi had told me. "Woolhaven Farm?"

"That's us. What brings you by?"

"How – how long have you been here? What is this place?"

He cocked his head at me with a bit of a lopsided smile. "Pardon? I don't quite catch your drift."

"Sorry. Um, hi. I'm Melissa, I'm—"

"The beekeeper!" he exclaimed. "Naomi said she'd send you our way next year. I didn't expect to see you so soon."

"Well, it turns out I may need your help first. She said you folks had an excess of grain?"

"Yes; good yes. We just moved up halfway through the summer and the grain had taken over every inch of every field. Even though it was a rough year for it, when you have this many fields," he gestured around him, "and only two sheep to feed, even a bad harvest is a lot. How much do you need?"

I gestured at my trailer. "As much as I can fit, if you can spare it. I can trade you beeswax or eggs or feathers or —?"

In the end I traded him a bit of everything and left with more than enough feed to get my girls through the winter, and a promise to come back with the bees at planting time.

It was only a few hours before sunset by the time I left, and I was grateful for the apple that Micah – the farmer – handed me on my way out. I had expected to be home by dinner and all I had with me was a crust of bread.

I gnawed at the apple as I rode, feeling my legs get heavier and heavier. All too soon, I watched the sun sink below the horizon, painting the land in orange and pink and gold before it faded to purple and black.

The night would turn chilly eventually, but for now it was just a welcome relief from the relentless daytime heat. I was more thankful than ever for my radio. The chatter and song were some small comfort in the dark lonely night. I cruised along to the beat of enka-reggae until my whole body felt numb with exhaustion.

When I was off the highway and making it through my neck of the woods to my little homestead, it was becoming an effort to keep my eyes open and my bike upright. I flicked over to the national station to see if the morning news reports were coming in yet.

They were still playing music – grating classic rock – but I left it on because at least the noise would help me stay awake.

Which is why I heard the news loud and clear as soon as it happened. They broke in right in the middle of a song with the announcement.

We've just received word of a tragic accident. The Daedalus, *carrying hundreds of Earth's best and brightest on their way to a new life on a new planet, has been destroyed. The craft was to circle the sun, using the star's gravity to build speed, but it seems the ship was drawn into the sun's orbit and destroyed. Investigations as to the cause of the accident are ongoing.*

I was so surprised that I swerved and hit a rock or a root in the dark and felt myself career to the right. I leaned hard to the left to try to correct it, but a wheel of my trailer had already tipped into the ditch, and before I knew it, I was lying on the ground with a leg caught in my bike.

"Owwww," I groaned. Everything hurt. I lay still for a moment, making sure nothing hurt so much that movement would be a mistake. Then I slowly sat up and disentangled myself from my bike.

I patted myself down. Nothing seemed to be broken. One ripped pant leg with a bleeding knee beneath it. One thumb had been bent backwards but was still functional. Lots of places that felt like they'd be purple and brown with bruises tomorrow. Overall, pretty lucky.

I was more thankful than ever now that my bike trailer was filled with bags of grain and not its earlier load of delicate eggs and jars of honey. I unhooked the trailer from the bike and righted the bags one at a time, dragging them out of the ditch and onto the road. My bike appeared unscathed. The trailer had a few scratches in the paint and one bent wheel. An annoyance for the rest of this trip, but nothing I couldn't fix at home.

Once I was off and pedalling again, cursing every bruised and aching bit of my body, I realized the radio was still softly playing. I turned it back up. I couldn't handle the glorification of billionaires on the main channel, so I switched back to the local station.

"Next up we've got a real throwback," the DJ was saying. "You're not going to want to miss this one."

Either she hadn't heard the news yet or she didn't care. For now, she just carried on. "I was reorganizing our music collection earlier when I found an old disc at the back of the rack. Full of real classics that some of the older members of our audience may remember. I'll be playing some of these for you over the next few weeks, but tonight, I want to start with a song that's really near and dear to my heart. This was one of the big summer hits back in '46, back when summer was still a good thing and people still made hits."

Oh my god. It couldn't be.

"An up and coming new band called Ordinary Frenzy unleashed this track on the world."

Oh. This was it.

"It ended up being the only thing most of us ever heard from them, but we enjoyed it while it lasted, and I hope you night owls out there get as much pleasure from it as I do. I give you the seminal '40s folk-funk anthem, 'Breath of Your Joy'!"

I stopped pedalling and fumbled to turn the volume dial up as loud as it would go, not caring who might hear. The opening chords crackled out from the tinny speakers, the sound distorted, but as familiar as ever.

I barked a laugh and started pedalling again, my movements falling into that old familiar rhythm as I mouthed along to every word.

A LIFE

E. Martin Nolan

"What we are engaged in when we do poetry is error,
the wilful creation of error."   —ANNE CARSON

1
when we call error what we gain by
does error become idol
we give our last idle guilt
a question overwhelmed by
what error half-billion animals
in the bushfires and by
quick overwhelm correction
conservative estimate a billion

2
 Condors trace California highways
for coastal roadkill, enough to replace

the megafauna. Our errors of transit
replace an ancient diet. Our error

is nature. Round goby in the middle
of the Great Lakes food web,

like strangers where your family was.
Like a cormorant, you make a life of it.

3
the answer you arrive at impasse
something new constant whiplash

4
Days rain in January,
hardly got my big coat out.

Days rain in January,
ten-foot snowfall, were it cold.

Days rain in January,
sirens chasing, didn't hold.

Days rain in January,
standing still is a route.

5
The leaves of some mass-produced flowering plant
look alive in all the gardens on my block. They are flat
against the half-frozen earth, failing to wilt.

A child calls her mom back to see a wet pile
protected in a hedge's shadow. "I found snow! Snow!"
She is pointing at it, hopping. In my opinion, it is ugly.
It melts as if rotting, greying from within. Soaked dry
with soot. The child is better at hope than me.

THE BEEKEEPER

Melanie Marttila

In the stultifying confines of Maze's farmhouse – old when this land was cold enough to know snow – Leavie leans over the blocks Devon made her, constructing a castle. Her dark-bright hair falls forward revealing a ragged, red rose blossoming on the back of her neck. I swallow my gasp and look toward old Maze, but her gaze is glued to Leavie.

I watch her expression lengthen and her eyes, already rheumy, widen.

"Here, love," I say, loosening one of the hair ties I wear like bracelets, and lean down to my girl. "Why don't I tie your hair back? Maybe a braid?"

"Yes," she says, decisively. "Plait, please."

She loves it when I play with her hair.

I pass the tie over her shoulder. "Hold this for me?" She sticks the end of the tie in her mouth so she can continue to build, and I gather and finger-comb the long, dark strands into order. Bands of light escape the thick drapes and stripe Leavie's hair with blue-white. It's Devon's gift to her, this shining black fall. I glance down at her pale neck.

I thought Leavie was safe.

My gaze returns to Maze. Her lips tighten and she nods.

It's just the three of us now: Maze, me, and Leavie. Only a few years ago, there were more than a hundred of us living and working on Maze's farm. Enough of us to defend it if needed, to maintain the solar panels, the well, and all the other life-sustaining equipment, and enough of us to sow, hand-pollinate, harvest, and gather seeds from the dwindling gardens throughout the year.

But then, two years ago, a new disease found us. Maze said it was like the bubonic plague. A rash, followed by fever and swollen glands. From there, different things happened. Extremities could blacken and die, or the afflicted could be suffocated by their own mucus-filled lungs. Either way, it meant death.

Maze said it came from fleas, but no one knew how infected fleas had gotten to the farm. We'd had no visitors, and the foragers met no one out on the land. The closest settlement was a several days walk away and fleas don't travel that far on their own. We didn't have the equipment or expertise to determine how they'd reached us.

We quarantined and isolated and did all the things you're supposed to do. It didn't matter. The former paramedic, who was the closest thing we had to a doctor, did the best she could, until she caught it, too. In three days, she was dead. One by one, everyone who caught it died.

And that floral rash was the first sign.

Maze lost her spouse, her children, and their families. Leavie and I lost Devon. When there were ten of us left, Maze caught it, but unlike everyone else, she survived. Then I caught it. By the time my fever broke, three weeks later, Maze and Leavie were the only ones left.

I can't lose Leavie, too. I don't have the strength to dig another hole in the dusty earth.

The sun rises on day two, and I have to get out, do something. I can't sit here like I have for the past sleepless day and watch my daughter die. Her breathing's so shallow, and her skin's sheened with sweat. My gaze darts around the room. The water jug's nearly empty. I grab the bucket and go.

The ground is so dry it rises in clouds around me as I walk to the well. I hear the door creak behind me. I whirl. Leavie's name is ready to leap free of my mouth, but it's only Maze. She must have heard me go out. I wait for her to catch up and try not to look as disappointed as I feel.

"That child is special," she says. "She'll be the saving of us. If she lives."

Maze has been different since she got sick. Odd. Religious, almost. Still. "Maze—"

"Hush now and do what you're told." She takes my free hand and turns the palm up, places something tiny in it that I can only see when she pulls her gnarled fingers away. It's a seed. Small, brown, and round. "Tonight, press this between your hands and pray. Pray like you never prayed in your life before. Mean it, or it won't work. Put your faith in this seed. All of it. Put it under your pillow and sleep on it. Dream Leavie well."

"What good will that do?"

"None. Until you take it to the Beekeeper."

"Beekeeper?" I hear the capital letter in the way she says it. But the bees died off when I was a child. I barely remember it. Why would there be a beekeeper if there aren't any bees?

"What did I say?"

Hush and do what you're told. I wait for Maze to continue.

"Over the mountain, you'll find a field. In that field, you'll find a tree. In that tree, you'll find the Beekeeper. Give it the seed. It will know what you came for. I'll see you tomorrow morning. I'll take care of Leavie while you're gone."

Maze stares at me until I nod. I don't know what I'm agreeing to, but I agree.

She returns to the farmhouse, and I try to lower the bucket into the well without dropping the seed. I have pockets, but they're full of holes. I haven't even kept up with mending since the sickness came.

The mountain. It's not a mountain. That's just what we call the weird hill that rises out of the prairie dust. Still, it'll take most of a day to climb over or go around, either way.

I wish the pump still worked, but something seized inside it last year and none of us who were left knew how to fix it. We lifted the concrete well cap with the pump still attached, and set it to the side.

The water level's so low, I don't know if the rope is long enough to reach it. And I expect every day for the bucket to return full of muck. It doesn't happen today, though the water's dirty. Filtering and boiling's nothing new. I don't know if either process improves the quality of the water. I've lost faith in everything. How will I find enough to pray?

─╲╱─

"You done what I tell you?" Maze says in the morning.

I nod, pinching the damned seed between finger and thumb. It's so small I can't see it, only know it's still there because of the pinpoint pressure on the fleshy pads of my fingers.

"Did you dream Leavie well?"

I can't meet her gaze. I don't remember my dreams anymore.

Maze makes a sad noise. "Faith is the thing."

I turn and leave, pinching the seed even harder. I've nothing to carry it in that it wouldn't fall out of, and I can't lose it. I've already said my goodbyes to Leavie while I was waiting for Maze.

The day is thick, hazy with heat. Despite my straw hat and long, light, loose clothes, I'm sweating by the time I've made it half-way around the mountain. I've been rationing the water I brought from its flask. I didn't want to take more than I absolutely had to. Leavie needs it more than I do.

I can see my destination, though. It's a broad plain of tall, dried grass. In the middle of it is a solitary tree. An ancient oak, maybe a thousand years old. It's barely alive, the leaves yellowed by the heat of this endless summer, half its branches stripped of bark and white as bone.

When I reach the haven of the tree's sparse shade, I refuse to collapse and carefully lower myself to the ground at the base of the oak, against one of its massive roots. Not that there's anyone to see me, even if I were to faint.

―᠈ᛁᴇ―

Humming descends from above, from somewhere in the tree branches, rouseing me. I've been sleeping against the roots where I sat to rest, and my hand has fallen open, the tiny seed still miraculously in my palm, resting in one of the creases. A voice speaks from within the hum, rising and falling, in and out of resonance.

"You've come."

"Yes," I say, scanning the tree, its branches, its roots. I can't see anyone, and the hum is all around me. I lift my hand carefully and offer the seed. "I've come. For Leavie."

"Not much faith in that," the voice says. "I'll need more."

"What do you need?" I'll give anything to save my girl.

"A queen."

I don't know what it means, who it wants.

The hum stutters, like a laugh. "I need a queen for my new colony. Young. Sweet."

It wants Leavie. "No."

"I need a queen. Strong. Selfless."

"Take me."

Another stutter in the hum. "You'll do."

The hum grows louder, and, for the first time, I can identify a source for the sound. I look up and shrink back onto the ground. The stutter comes again.

The Beekeeper emerges from the tree, descends. I become stone at the sight of it. It can't be of this world. Its body is part insect, and part human, but the four arms are long, graceful, and terminate in lithe fingers. It possesses two legs with feet. Its head is that of a bee, faceted eyes shimmering in the branch-filtered light. Its mouth parts work as it tilts its head. A bee's abdomen descends from its human-like torso and when the wings stop moving, they settle like a cape over its back.

I make myself small as if it will pass me by even though I know the deal is struck and there is no escaping it if I want to save Leavie.

I swallow the scream working its way up my throat, but I can't look away from the Beekeeper's alien elegance. I shudder at my sudden desire to touch it.

It bends toward me, a horrible condescension.

"Come to me, my queen," it hums.

It places its hands on my shoulders and arms and its body shakes – vibrates – releasing a cloud of dust. No. Pollen? I'm covered, choking. I can't breathe. My sight prisms through yellow-toned tears, blurs completely. I cough, but nothing dislodges, and I only manage to draw whatever it is further into my lungs.

I don't know how long it is before the initial onslaught is over, before my eyes cease to weep and my vision clears, before I stop coughing and a deep ache settles into my chest. The Beekeeper has let go of me at some point. I've fallen to the ground, and it stands watching me, its insect expression unreadable.

I bat at my sleeves so I can wipe my face with something remotely clean, and struggle to my feet.

"You may return home," the Beekeeper stutter-buzzes, "to say goodbye to your child before your transformation is too far along."

I don't know what it's done to me, what I'm becoming, but I already feel the pollen working inside me. "Leavie—"

"You don't have much time. Go. Now."

I run.

The sun is still hot, and I've left my water behind, but I don't tire. I run straight back to Leavie, burst through the door. Maze screams. I slow in two steps and sit on the side of the bed.

"Sweet baby Jesus," Maze says. She stands on the other side of the bed, one hand raised to her chest, the other to her forehead. "Nearly killed me."

Leavie is still as death. I take her hand, but it feels boneless, and flops like a fish from my grasp.

"Fever's broke," Maze says.

I gather Leavie in my arms, kiss her, and beg her to wake. This is the last time I'll see my little girl. "I have to go back," I say.

Maze gasps. "Why?"

"I made a deal," I say. At least, I think I did. "Me for Leavie."

"What about the mustard seed?"

"It said it wasn't enough."

"Oh, no." Maze moans. "Should've told you what it is."

"Tell me now."

"It's the power of life and death. It's the one that touches you on the shoulder when it's your time."

"What? Like the Grim Reaper?"

"Reaper, keeper. Same thing in the end."

It's really not, but I don't have time to argue. Death. Maybe it wasn't pollen. It makes a kind of sense, though. A life for a life. In my arms, Leavie groans. I'm squeezing her so tight, I – I relax my hold.

"Mama?" she murmurs.

"Here, baby."

"Bee fairy says you have to go, now."

"Bee—?" Every hair on my body stands. I blink the fear back before it spills.

"It whispers to me when I sleep. It's okay, Mama," Leavie says, eyes drooping again. "Love you."

Maze looks hollow, takes my little love from my arms. "Best do as she says."

"Love you, baby."

I'm running again, trying to leave my fear behind. The deal I've made. It isn't me for Leavie. It's both of us.

~\|/~

The Beekeeper waits for me under the tree, opens its arms.

I run into it, fists flying. It doesn't go down. "You can't have her. You can't."

It wraps its four arms around me. "The deal was made before you came with your pitiful faith."

"Why?" I have no tears left.

"Cycles and gyres. The time of humanity is past. It's time for something new."

"You're not making any sense—"

And then, the first blast of pain hits, choking off my words. The Beekeeper lays me on the ground. Heat floods me. In an instant I'm flushed and feverish.

"Accept it," hums the Beekeeper. "Relax into it. Breathe around it. That's right."

It takes everything I have to do as it says. I forget and tense up. Once. Before my scream has died, I've given over. The pain holds me like the Beekeeper did, like I held Leavie when I said goodbye.

I think I understand this part at least. It's the pollen, working on me, in me. It's the transformation. I let it have its way with me, but I can't move, the surrender is so complete.

I can't open my eyes. I can still listen, though. Sometimes. When the roar of the transformation ebbs.

The Beekeeper hums into the lulls. Lullabies.

"I am not what I seem," it says. "I merely hold the memory of the bee, male and female, drone, worker, and queen, until they can be given new life, but for that, I need the mother. I need you."

Why a bee? I imagine the animals we thought of as intelligent; that if not for a twist of evolution might have been the dominant species on this planet instead of us. Any one of them might have taken better care of this world, wouldn't have caused the accelerated and unnatural mass extinctions and climate change. Pollution and crop failures. The ever-increasing heat. Ecosystems collapsing before their times. *Why not a dolphin, or a dog, or a raven?*

As if hearing my thoughts, the Beekeeper answers, "Others hold the memories of those forms. That will be part of your task, to liberate them."

The memories, or their keepers?

"Both," it says, and the hum stutters with another laugh. The laugh isn't unkind.

※

I'm conscious through the whole process, as though my attention to each moment of agony is required. When the first breath free of pain passes my lips, it turns into a sob.

Cool fingers touch my face.

"What have you done to me?" I ask when the shock of relief passes and returns my power of speech. My voice sounds different, and there's not half the bitterness in it that

I feel. Looking up, I'm confused. The fingers are Leavie's. She's here. I look for the Beekeeper. It looms over my child's shoulder.

"You're one of us, now," it hums.

"And what's that?"

"This world's avatars. Old ones, little people—" it laughs and spreads its arms, indicating its size. "Humans once thought us gods, but we are not. We are only different."

"Why?"

Leavie answers, "Some of them died. They needed us to fulfill certain roles, perform certain duties."

Leavie's voice is closer to mine than a child's. When I look at her, really see her, she's changed in more ways than the sound of her voice. She looks older, a young woman, not a child. She moves with grace. Her fingers are lithe, like the Beekeeper's.

"I am not what I seem," the Beekeeper says. "I keep the bee form for its renewal, but my true form is the hag, the crone, Cailleach, Kali—"

"The Grim Reaper?" I ask.

"That, too," it hums and stutters a self-conscious laugh. "I survived, I think, because I am the end of all things, but all endings contain the seeds of new beginnings."

"You called me the mother." I sit up, slowly, but aside from some dizziness, I feel okay.

"Yes. You will be the means by which life returns to the world."

"But not as it was."

The Beekeeper hangs its head, humming sadly.

Leavie answers, "Beekeeper says the death of this age was certain in the time before you were born."

"When did Leavie and I become certainties?" I ask the Beekeeper.

"When you proved immune to the sickness."

"Maze survived before either of us got sick. Where's she?"

"Already on her way. She is your herald."

"You mean prophet?" A memory works its way lose. John the Baptist. I sink heavily to the ground again.

"I mean herald. Maybe a scout? Maze will seek out the other survivors of the disease, so they can join us."

"Will we all be women?" It said its true form was the crone.

"No. You and Maze and Leavie just happened to be the first."

"If I'm the mother, who's Leavie?" *What has she been saved to do?*

"I'm the maiden," Leavie says.

"She is the huntress, the protector, the power of youth."

"Hope," I say.

"Yes," the Beekeeper hums.

"How many of your people are left?" I mean at all, anywhere.

The Beekeeper looks up, sensing something. There's a different tone to its buzz. Is it talking to the others of its – our – kind? "Some. Not many."

"The world is dying, then."

The Beekeeper laughs. "This world will go on until the sun swallows it. It's a survivor. It's our job now to adapt to the world as humans have left it to us, to replenish life that will thrive in this environment."

"Everything?" All the animals. All the plants. All living things. The immensity of the task is appalling.

The Beekeeper places a comforting hand on my shoulder. "Not everything. The creatures of the deep sea and earth remain. Algae, microbes, and insects have adapted, but in ways that, unfortunately, make them inimical to other life forms."

It takes me a moment to understand, and then knowledge I've never possessed before surfaces. Blue-green algal blooms poisoning lakes that dried up when I was too young to hold the memory of them. Fire ants whose venom kills in a single bite, not from a swarm attack. Antibiotic-resistant infections.

I must look confused. Leavie takes my hands in hers. "We're fairies now," she says. "At least that's how I see us. We won't sicken or grow old, but we can be killed. Part of what we've been given is the memories and knowledge of other fairies. It surfaces when we need it to. It's part of the magic."

The Beekeeper laughs. "There is no magic."

"Forgive me if I'd prefer to think of it that way," Leavie says, an edge in her voice.

When the Beekeeper doesn't react, my world shifts. We're not servants or subordinates. Leavie and I can disagree, discuss. It's here to guide us, not control us.

Another thought surfaces. It's genetics. Genetic manipulation. I'm amazed it took so little time to turn me into a different species. Unlimited cellular regeneration. An adaptive immune system. Knowledge attached to base sequences of DNA. There's more if I care to pay attention, but I can't. I'm still my old self in many ways. It will take time to get used to this. I'm not sure that I can.

"How do we begin?" I ask, not knowing if I want the answer, or if I can even understand it.

"With patience," the Beekeeper says, stepping back, "and love and hope."

YOUTH FOR MARS

Jerri Jerreat

I don't know why I didn't get picked for that group heading to Mars. My foster parents signed the form and my essay was extreme daz – I went for the heart. My teacher teared up when they read it. And, yes, I know you can't come back. I don't want to.

Here? Yeah, sure, I'm helping out here. We have to help de-pave a parking lot or a road, a couple times a year. Community work. Practically slave labour, right? The dirt is dead under there, no microbial life at all. They dump leaves, compost, wood chips, and microbes over it and in a few months it's alive again. But I'm *sick* of planting those urban Miyawaki forests with my classes. I've worked on nearly 20! *Fine,* they prevent flooding. *Fine,* they bring down the neighbourhood temperature. *Fine,* the pollinators are starting to come back. Human health improves.

What do I care? I have no family, (thank you Hurricane Tonia), no best friend to care what I do next. Bhashkara's family moved to Nunavut to get away from the heat. There won't be *room* for everyone up there. We talk virtually but it's not the same. Everybody at school has a bestie. Me – I have no one.

The Caring People say I have to pick a path forward: Science/Math or Humanities/Arts. Well, I don't know! How do the other kids *know*? I like drawing and reading, playing fiscus and swimming. I swim great, even with one crooked leg. I'd like to swim in an ocean, if that were possible. I'd like to deep-sea dive, and watch a Decorator crab creep from one rock to the next, you know? They are masters of stealth.

My foster parents say I'm addicted to vids but it's not true. Especially not now, since they cut me off – which is totally inhumane because I just got my weaponry up to 74 and my magic was already at 41! That takes skill! So unfair.

I spent two weeks last summer shadowing the solartech who maintains our school and neighbourhood. That was cool, puzzling through solarbus problems or roof spreads. We had to step carefully around all the veggies growing under the huge panels on the school roof to check every single one, carefully. (Did you know they're growing broccoli and melons up there? Seriously.) We repaired people's small solar shingles that had been damaged in June's hurricane. They, (Olene) also showed me how to fix simple things on our building's heat pump and we tinkered a bit on the small hydro generator in our creek. That was the coolest. I watched for a while, learned a bit, but drifted away to look for moss.

I think I found a new species. My favourite moss looks like micro-medieval-cities, tiny castles with turrets. You know how moss often looks like miniature forests? But they're not diverse enough, maybe, what's left around here. That's why I keep looking. With trees, you have to plant about 30 various local species – well, everybody knows that. I wonder if you can replant moss too? No one seems to care because it's so small, and people just tear them off for fun (!) or for stupid flower arrangements (!!) but moss is like a sponge soaking up stormwater and makes a tiny ecosystem in the woods or a marsh. Even in deserts and caves. Really! It's one of the first things to grow after a forest fire and helps create soil and shade for all the big guys' roots.

Trees *need* moss, you know, to shield their roots from too much sun and it can take a century to grow. I looked them up and they're called bryophytes. They've been around for like 450 million years! They might even help urban forests to grow. I read that spotted turtles wear sphagnum moss like a blanket through winter, (what?) but moss is a rich habitat for insects and microbiotic life. Seriously, why aren't we gathering them carefully and replanting them?

Anyway, I don't think tech life is for me, though it was interesting. I also helped out with the kinders twice a week for an entire term, just to test that out, too. To see if I like Caring. The Littles are very cute. And funny. But demanding, too. And unpredictable. I found them exhausting.

You know I read everything I could about the Mars Station, and the problems they're having with Caring, Socialization and stuff? And that weird thing – how they can't seem to conceive there, something in the atmosphere maybe. But no one wants to ship them *children*. Volunteer youths, they hope, might bring something the adults are lacking. So they say.

What have we got, that adults don't?

Rebellion? Anger. Sass. Maybe humour. Better music.

What else?

No bullshit. New eyes.

We aren't as jaded.

My foster mom, Xo, says I have all those qualities and I'd make a great politician. *Ha hah*. However, she says Earth needs *youth* more than Mars does. That Earth needs our zaniness. Our rebellion. Our new eyes.

She's a Medico. I shadowed her last week and, I gotta say, she was *daz*. I liked how she figured out possible solutions to complex problems. It's a lot like solartech troubleshooting, but it's with faces, people – families. With *lives*. And you're helping them all to stay together. I'm not sure I'd have the guts for it when you can't save someone, but – I was impressed.

My mom was a Medico too. She stayed behind to help hundreds during that hurricane. Four years five months ago. I dunno if I woulda stayed. But she sent me away with the other kids, to save me.

I think about that sometimes, when I'm prying up a long stretch of asphalt, or planting shrubs and trees. Mom said the Mother Trees carry the genes to survive devastations.

I wonder if I'll ever have a kid one day – seems risky – and pass along Mom's genes for brains and heroism.

I wonder.

SONGBIRDS
AND SECRETS

M.L.D. CURELAS

A heavy silence had settled over the dinner table, and the persistent tap on the windowpane drew all their eyes. After a brief moment of stunned wonder, Anna smiled. She set down her spoon, preparing to rise, but her father's stern voice stilled her.

"That damn bird," he muttered. "Can't it let us eat in peace?"

"It's hungry," Anna said softly. "Please, Father."

.He focused sullen eyes on her and inclined his head in assent, then resumed eating his soup.

Anna glanced at her stepmother, but she was calmly eating and offered no opinion. Anna pushed back from the table and went into the kitchen. Bread was scarce right now – the gases had contaminated the soil and growing anything was difficult – so Anna and her stepmother baked flatbreads consisting of ground nuts and seeds mixed with a little fat and some water. There were always small bits and pieces of nuts left over, and Anna had started saving those remnants for the bird.

After the devastating gases and then the flu had swept the country, most everything had died – birds, mammals, plant life, people. Some had survived, and water drawn from wells was uncontaminated. In Anna's village, the farmers were working with travelling scientists to remediate the soil and surface water sources. But the bird! It had to be a positive sign of life returning to a semblance of normalcy.

Hugo would have loved to have seen it.

At the thought of her baby brother, Anna's eyes teared up, but she roughly brushed the tears away and wiped her fingers on her skirt. She scooped up the crumble of nuts and seeds from that evening's baking and went out the back door.

The kitchen garden and backyard were dusty and desolate. A small HandiBot scuttled around the garden plot, with its few scraggly onions, beeping sadly while it applied the remediation mixture concocted by the travelling scientists. A few trees had remained green, but it would be weeks to see if they would bear any fruit this year. Insect life had been decimated, along with everything else, but several people in the village had reported insect activity this spring. The rest of the yard was dotted with dandelions and creeping bellflower, the most reliable crop for Anna's family and most people she knew.

The bird was perched on the bare branches of a juniper tree. At her arrival, it chirped and fluttered its wings.

Anna smiled widely and wiggled her fingers in greeting. "Hi, bird!" she called and strewed the nuts and seeds onto the ground.

The bird chirped again and flitted to the ground. It jerkily hopped among the nuts, pecking at them and occasionally cheeping.

A sharp rap startled Anna and she glanced guiltily at the window. Her stepmother frowned at her. The summons was unmistakable, even if silent.

The bird had left, so Anna gathered her skirts and scurried inside the house.

－ﾟﾞ－

The bird came again the next day. Anna was grinding nuts when the familiar tapping sounded at the window. She couldn't help the small laugh that escaped her, a sharp trill that sliced through the oppressive silence of the house. The bird cocked its head and piped a few notes.

"Hugo would have loved that bird," her stepmother said.

Anna flinched and stuffed her hands into her apron pocket. "Yes. He missed them, after the gas."

Her stepmother glided closer and Anna resisted the urge to move away. Even though her stepmother resembled Anna's mother, wearing dresses with high, old-fashioned collars and long, tapering sleeves and hair pulled back in a tidy bun, the effect was creepy instead of comforting. And she moved around the house like a wraith. Anna felt like she was being spied upon.

"I miss him, too," her stepmother said, sighing. "The house is so…"

"Quiet," Anna said. She nodded, peering at her stepmother. Her eyes were swollen and her skin had an unhealthy pallor. Perhaps she really did miss Hugo. They had quarrelled constantly until he took sick with the flu. Hugo, despite his young age, hadn't accepted his new mother. She had been patient with him at first, but he had questioned and prodded and disobeyed at every turn. One night at the dinner table, her temper had snapped and she'd slapped Hugo.

She'd immediately stammered an apology, and Father had reprimanded her, reminding her that discipline of the children was his task. She had then apologized to him, too, which Father had accepted with a grunt. A heavy silence had settled over the family, and it never really left.

Then the wars came. And the gases. And the flu.

Anna stared down at the small pile of nuts for a few seconds before risking another glance at her stepmother. Some complicated emotion flickered in her stepmother's eyes. Guilt? Grief?

"You could feed the bird with me," Anna offered, pouring the nuts from the pestle into her hand.

The tight corners of her stepmother's mouth relaxed, and she gave a small smile. "I'd like that."

The bird sat on the barren juniper tree. The twisted and gnarled branches resembled crooked, clawed hands, and when the bird fluttered down to greet them, Anna thought for a second that the tree had tossed the tiny creature to them.

Her stepmother scattered the nuts, and the bird twittered cheerfully as it hopped along the ground, pecking at the food.

They didn't speak, but Anna felt comfortable. When the bird finished its meal, it flew back into the branches of the juniper tree and burst into song. It warbled for a minute and then took flight, fading into the shadows of encroaching dusk.

~·~

It was an easy routine to establish. Her stepmother joined her for prepping the evening nut bread, and they gathered the leftovers to give to the bird while the bread baked and soup simmered. While no other birds appeared, Anna gradually became aware of a quiet buzz in the evenings, a sure sign of insect life.

The evening ritual eased Anna's grief, and she was able to talk with her stepmother, idle chitchat about the plants, the soil, and whether there were enough dandelions to make wine. As her stepmother giggled about the melancholy HandiBot trying unsuccessfully to weed a mostly empty patch of dirt, Anna was reminded that her stepmother wasn't that much older than herself.

But her stepmother, while she seemed to enjoy the time they spent together, still seemed heavy at heart. Her eyes were always swollen and red-rimmed, and Anna wondered if she cried throughout the night. The burden of sadness and grief bowed her shoulders, and her eyes were always downcast.

~✳~

One evening, Anna's father returned home from work at the mill earlier than usual. Not seeming to notice the time, he said he looked forward to dinner and retreated to the parlour to read the newspaper. Anna exchanged a wide-eyed look with her stepmother. There wasn't enough time to bake the evening bread.

Her stepmother sighed. "Luckily, we've started the soup. Add a little hominy to it, and I'll prepare some greens. We'll use some of the tortillas from the larder."

Pozole. It was a good idea. The tortillas had been dear, as their grocer had acquired them from a far trader. Her stepmother had been saving them for a festival night, or for when they had a little meat for the soup, but as a quick solution for a shifted dinner timeline, it was perfect.

As they worked together in companionable silence, her stepmother packed away the nuts originally intended for that night's bread, setting aside a handful for the bird. Anna smiled to herself.

"Pozole?" her father said when they brought in the soup tureen. A ButlerBot trundled behind them, bearing a tray ladened with condiment dishes.

"We have those lovely tortillas," her stepmother said, setting down the tureen in the centre of the table. "And we have a lot of tender spring greens to serve with the soup."

As her stepmother ladled soup into the bowls, the ButlerBot clunked over to her father. Anna followed it and removed a few dishes from its proffered tray to a spot near her father's place setting: chopped greens, a few tiny radishes, a few tortillas. There was even a spoonful of soured cream. The ButlerBot stopped next at Anna's place and then at the foot of the table where her stepmother sat, and Anna unloaded the appropriate dishes at each setting. As the ButlerBot returned to the kitchen, Anna seated herself, noting that her father had already dressed his pozole with greens and radishes and had begun eating.

Dinner progressed in its usual silence, and for the first time, Anna squirmed with impatience. Had dinner always been like this? So… so grim? Anna racked her memories and concluded, sadly, that yes, dinner had always been a sombre affair, her mother quiet and withdrawn while she assisted Hugo with his meals, her father intent on eating. Anna stared at him now, willing him to look up so she could start a conversation.

But her father kept his gaze focused on his bowl and methodically spooned pozole into his mouth, stopping only to add more toppings to the fragrant soup, so Anna dunked a tortilla in her own bowl and continued eating.

Tap.

Tap-tap-tap.

Tap-tap-tap. Tap-tap-*tap*. *Tap-tap-tap!*

Anna cringed as her father jumped up from the table, his chair falling to the floor with a clatter.

"Why can't he leave us in peace!" he yelled.

"Father—" Anna began.

"You've been encouraging him!" her father roared.

Anna's mouth snapped shut.

"This is *your* fault!"

He lunged at her, arms outstretched, and Anna flinched so violently that she fell off her chair. She whimpered, crawling towards the foot of the table, and then screamed when her father's hot hand grabbed her ankle. She kicked, heard a *crack* followed by a curse, and suddenly, her foot was free and she scrambled forward.

When she cleared the table, she got to her feet and rushed for the kitchen door. From there it was only a few steps to the backyard. The evening was coolish, the light just beginning to fade, and she dimly registered a new insect sound – cricket? – but she didn't have time to relax.

The door burst open, and her father stormed out, eyes wide and wild. He came at her, and Anna froze. The yard was fenced; there wasn't anywhere for her to run. Behind him came her stepmother, hair falling from her bun and a purple splotch on her cheek. She reached for his arm, but he shoved her aside.

The bird, shrieking, erupted from the juniper tree and dove at her father's head. He shouted and fell to his knees, covering his face and head with his arms. The bird returned for another attack and slashed her father's arms. Thin, red-black ribbons opened on his skin.

Her father was shouting, but he was sobbing so hard that Anna couldn't make out the words. The bird had returned to the juniper tree. It cocked its head and watched her father with bright, black eyes.

Her father continued weeping, but Anna could understand him now. "I'm sorry, Hugo, I'm so sorry," he said. "I couldn't sleep, you coughed so much, and what if we all got sick, too? What if... ?" The rest of the words were swallowed by sobbing.

A sharp pain lanced her chest and Anna gasped. "Father?" She stared across the yard at her stepmother, who limped forward, tears streaming down her face.

"I'm sorry, Anna. I knew. I *knew*, but didn't say anything. I..." Her stepmother trailed off, her hand drifting to her throat, to that high, unfashionable collar, and Anna didn't need to hear the rest of the sentence. She knew why her stepmother hadn't been able to say anything.

Her father was violent. He'd murdered her younger brother and beat her stepmother. The weight of this sudden knowledge crashed over Anna, suffocating her. Her chest heaved and she couldn't breathe. She shut her eyes and took several slow, deep breaths. Another dreadful thought occurred to her. She opened her eyes and asked in a small voice, "My mother? She was ill for a long time."

Her stepmother shook her head. "I think so. Sick people are so weak, and I don't think she had an easy life with your father."

Anna gulped. Too much time had passed to know for sure how her mother died, but given his confession about Hugo's death, it seemed likely her father had also killed her mother.

"What do we do now?" Anna asked, looking down at her father, still sobbing into his arms.

Her stepmother shrugged. "I don't know."

Anna frowned and then nodded once, sharply. "We'll send for the doctor. And the magistrate. I don't think Father's going anywhere."

─✴─

By daybreak, her father had been escorted away. Anna wasn't sure what would happen to him next, but he wouldn't be darkening their household again.

It was a bright sunny morning, and Anna coaxed her stepmother outside to feed the bird and bask in the sunlight. The HandiBot was trimming the dead grass that edged the garden plot. Her stepmother managed a watery chuckle, and Anna wrapped an arm around her shoulders.

The bird twittered as he ate, but after only a few pecks he flew up into the juniper tree and warbled. He paused, then threw his head back and trilled again. His tiny body quivered with the force of his song. It was a fitting herald of spring and a new beginning.

Pointing at the tree, her stepmother said, "Anna, there, look!"

Anna followed her stepmother's gaze. "Oh, my goodness," she said. "I can't believe it!"

Dozens of small green buds dotted the branches of the juniper. Anna laughed and hugged her stepmother. She could practically taste the citrusy tang of a juniper berry-seasoned cabbage soup.

The songbird puffed its chest and trilled. And off in the distance, something warbled in return.

WATER & OIL

ANNELIESE SCHULTZ

Bursting from months, maybe years, of inertia born of dis-
may (engendered by the unending disasters of the world),
Zip is instantly galvanized and greater than himself and gone.

All right, no, apparently he's still standing here, feet on
arid ground, so maybe not quite yet. But still – the thought
of that girl. Careen. Meant to be, right? Except sadly he
seems to have forgotten how this works. How you go about
tracking someone down, how you actually get together... Are
you even allowed?!

It's not as if this wrong-way world ever made it, pre-
implode, to any of the big promises:

* the joys of teleporting
* One-Food-Capsule-a-Day
* replaceable body parts
* a hoverboard that doesn't burst into flames before you
can even get it out of the damn box.

None of which he could give a crap about right now
other than the first. Because sometimes you just have to
hope against hope. He gazes up (still not going anywhere,
it looks like, already furious at himself) to see clouds converge from opposite sides of the teeming sky – weird, when
always, almost always, they push inexorably in the same
direction.

Zip reaches, back pocket, for his old-school camera but it is gutless, battery in the recharger (on the majorly off-chance that there might be a surge of random electricity this week). Doesn't matter. Clouds are just clouds; weather is weather is what it is.

Climate would be what you have to watch out for. And that, way past cloudy shadow of a doubt, is screwed. Way past faint memory of beach days and of eating out, of groceries and cell towers and air travel and everything technology, if you happened to feel like making yet another sorry list...

Meaning back to the barest of bare basics. But, problem! Who knows how to do basics anymore? Who remembers the first thing, really, about food and shelter; how to make a shirt or a table, to stay warm or to keep things cold? Or, ha, about – what was that called – communicating? Fragile and earnest face to unsure face...

So, right. He stares down at his worn boots planted on parched and shriveled earth, at this patch of overgrown weeds choking yet more tangled and dusty weeds – Abundance circa 2028 or so – and laughs, not happily. If anyone was going to get the 'relating' part, it was going to be him. At 16 he'd already been accepted, early admission, into college, planned to major in Communications and Psychology, thank you very much. Student loan in process just when it all fell down. Stock market and universities, internet and online banking, all tripping over each other on their way out... Not a bank or a single MOOC left.

The point is (he seems to be saying this, strangely, to a passing crow) that he was going to be a master at understanding and interaction and relationship; that he never got a chance. Communicating? He has no idea how to. And still, of course, he reaches, every morning, even right this minute, to automatically swipe his phone, and is brought up short. Hel*lo*. The way things have been going for a very long time now is that you would have to bring to mind an actual person, remember where they live (if yet they do), get up and walk yourself from here to there. Yeah, what a concept.

Careen. Before he can conjure up her face or anything else for that matter, skies darken, and the mustering clouds meet and mass, then all start to roll east. Zip shakes his head. Present state of affairs, there could easily be a hurricane next minute, or, sure, clouds that maybe just never return again, and this particular August (if that's what it is) goes down in history as the Definitive Drought, the Thunder of the True and Final End. Nobody knows anything at all at this point. Or cares. If there still *is* anybody to possibly know. Or care.

But it's time to get out of the sun, go lie down. Not that that will help, the foregoing thoughts of further ruination being just your climate, for God's sake, to say nothing of further plagues, of city-sized sinkholes or PTSD run rampant, the legacy of rock-hard racism, and suicide bombers, and the wars over the oil that was already a moot point many years ago, the water that becomes more precious every day... He runs his hands through his tangled hair, stands awkward cradling his cheekbones and temples. *Bereft*, he whispers. Where are you supposed to go from there?

Okay. It is what it is. Let it be. He blinks back to the thought of Careen. To be honest, he never could stand that name. *Her* he definitely liked. But Careen – it makes him think of cars flying out of control (!), flipping off highways into the unknown (!) The cars, that is, that once were.

Disturbing any way you look at it. Couldn't she have just changed her name to, um, something else?

And what the heck did happen there anyway? With them. A miniature flash of lightning stamps itself across a small patch of blue sky, and he takes it as a dare. Fine. Never mind teleporting. He's going to find her even if he has to freaking crawl.

Which reminds him – what is he doing still outside? This time of day, sun will kill you. Heading fast for his container, he notices four birds so tiny they're almost invisible crowded into each other on the branch of a wizened tree. *"In the face of less,"* he hears from another direction, *"reduce your needs; go small."*

There is nobody near. No phone or radio or leftover levitating speaker. Of course not. This is just what happens: words of advice still recycling their way through time.

Too late to change a damn thing.

His container is only a 10-foot: it is old newspapers covered with the one remaining flannel sheet (more apt than satin, under the circumstances), it's one chair, a desk of doubtful use, one box of clothes, another of books, the camp stove that will maybe keep him alive until the butane runs out. It's the sketches and wild posters that used to be his art, that sit unseen and meaningless. And his dog.

Lying down, Zip closes his eyes, about as hopeless as his short-lived Manga phase, and wonders what it's going to take for him to get gone. When Stella pokes her muzzle into his hand, all he's been able to come up with is *Connection.* Yeah, that's the word, though he's pretty flipping sure he has no idea anymore how you do that, how it works. Did he ever?

Stella whines. How long since he's seen any human being? Months. More like years. No clocks, no free calendar in July for the coming year because you've donated again to help the kids in Africa. No Africa. No kids? *Stop*, he tells himself. Just stop.

Basics only. Sleep. And eat. Because yes, there continue to be mushrooms and berries. Twigs to life-hack a kind of tea. And, best decision he ever made, the Planting a Year-Round Garden workshop, his precious seeds.

Sleep. Eat. Repeat. And it might actually work, if not for what should have been the first thing blown to bits when everything imploded. God help us: Thinking. Thinking, painful, back into the sad and unhelpful past of snow-crowned mountain or loons returned to the lake; out into stark and hopeless future. Thinking circles around yourself, thinking desperate and futile and unending until all you can do to keep from going crazy is to get down here nose to nose with Stella, let her soft warm exhale fill your nostrils; stare unblinking into her gentle eyes; continue to breathe.

~*~

Careen shivers. Why so freaking cold in… Well, who has a clue what month it is, what year? The stupid thing is that every time she feels cold, she starts to think about Zip again. What a totally ridiculous name. I mean, how could you even… Never mind. Focus on the guy, the man, his… Okay, never mind that either.

Sometimes it seems like everything – living in what's left of what's left of a shed; mostly going to sleep hungry, dirty, sad; knowing that she will never have, or need, for that matter, eyeliner again; no *lipstick* left; basically the implosion of the whole world – well, sometimes it feels like all that would be okay if she could just stop the thinking.

A million times she's tried to give it up. Just breathe. Or sleep, maybe, for as long as you possibly can. Just tend every inch of your feeble garden (the one good thing she ever learned from her fully-out-of-it mom?) Just eat, plate to hand to mouth. Just circle right on back to sleep. But no, two bites, and from the sight of the fraying tablecloth, her mind starts manufacturing needs and yearning and regret: the age-old silver, the heirloom china that really should be gracing this cloth-covered stump, the blender and the toaster oven, your morning cappuccino, her best-ever yoga classes, that sweetest of camisoles (rose-pink, with blue ribboned through the lace), her lost cat, her dreams. *Just stop*, she whispers. *Just stop right there.*

Wind rises, probably another fricking thundersnow event, and when the wall begins to groan, then shimmies and falls suddenly outward, rain and branches flying in, Careen decides she's leaving, whatever, go and look for him. Like she should have done a long time ago, right? Zip. Ludicrous name, she thinks again, angrily grabbing her moldering backpack. Just saying it sets her off-centre, makes her feel cheated, like something bad has happened but she's not sure what. Didn't he have a proper name? Couldn't he flipping use it?

--*/--

Zip skirts fallen power lines, jumps hurdle over an ancient PC, smashed stroller, barbecue, and skeletons of patio umbrellas, a milk crate tipping cords and controls, phones and monitors and chargers into the faithful dust. Did they ever... did he tell her... Why can't he remember?

Need water, he chokes, stopping, calling Stella away from what's left of an oil-slicked puddle, but what he really wants is a clear mind, some nice memories, the reassuring run of a stream, the chance for a future.

~\/~

Careen loses her balance and slips sideways into yet another overflowing ditch. Swearing, she bats away a beach ball, what might have been a yellow sippy cup, a rusting old-school wok. "*So grow some fins.*" She hears that damn advice-from-nowhere piping up again. She'll always, for the rest of time, be out here drenched and shivering and chilled. "*Get used to it.*" "No," she answers, splashing back onto the road. "Screw that." She's going to find him, even if she has to flipping swim there.

She swallows hard. Did she ever tell him *any*thing? Also, did they ever... She has no clue. All she wants — past, present or future is... She cocks her head. Is... sun? Well, sure, of course, but also just one comforting clue.

~\/~

Heat pins Zip to the side of the road. What's the point?

"*Hey there.*"

Oh god, he thinks, another download of useless words from absolutely nowhere.

Just shut the hell up.

⚺

As if drenched wasn't enough, the skies open, and Careen is alternately frosted with rain, hail, a sprinkling of snow.

"Hey there."

Yeah right, she thinks, that's all I need is a few more stupid words recycled from 2022. Leave me the hell alone.

⚺

There really is a line, it seems, between reality and longing – and, not wanting to, knowing they have to, they stumble into it, over it, stare at each other, relinquish thought, finally find voice.

"Oh."

"Whoa."

"Holy."

"Wow."

"I mean I seriously remember."

"Well, yeah. Me, too." An immense sigh. "If you mean…"

"Of course."

"Omigod, if only."

Words crash and weave, now intersect and then collide again. A total ugly chaos. A beautiful thing.

"No, really…" Her shy and Delphic smile. "Like when you always used to say…"

He hesitates. "I know." Sweet mystery in the gaze returned. "And the way you would… But did—"

"I don't know." She presses her lips together. "I seriously don't know."

And beneath this suddenly resplendent stand of windswept pines, they stop, come two steps closer, hold back cascading walls of tears.

Because... talk.

Because... words actually spoken, offered rushed and unthinking, possibly meaningless but real, but radiant, to another.

Because, as sun refracts gently through the softest of rain, in the whispered breaking voices, in the giving and the receiving, in the soul still recognizing soul, there is a small explosion. A kind of thunderflash of hope.

PART THREE

EARTH HOUR

ECLIPSE SEASON

URSULA PFLUG

Spring follows winter. Eclipse season is tough this year. I flee to the garden, preparing beds. I feel scruffy and no account as my gardens are unkempt, but I want to leave stands of wild roses, more each year, for the native bees, who do not care whether my borders are neat but whether I feed them. My rose forest is bigger every year, and irks my neighbours upon whose lawn it encroaches, but I leave it untrimmed on my side for the pollinators. We don't have fences between the properties along the river, but maybe we should.

I have a bit of funding to finish a book that I have, like so many others, already spent too much time on. To get away from failure, I dig in the garden to find myself. Yes, I know, it's an enviable gig. All the same, I sometimes miss the days when I had a clock to punch and didn't have to think about syntax. If I returned somehow to my long-ago graphic design job, I'd call present me stupid to want to trade back. Nevertheless, I'll take Door C.

Around here the little indie country papers used to have ads describing workshops by people sort of like me: "Garden as Metaphor," or "Connecting with the Devic Realms." I wouldn't pay someone to learn how to do it, and I also wouldn't teach it, not officially. Some part of me would be whispering, "You can't charge for that. You'd be scamming people."

I would imagine what my friends were saying, a few of whom are working naturalists, and feel embarrassed. I could defend it as a legitimate form of intuition, a poetic investigation, but I wouldn't want to spend the time, except maybe here, a little, writing this.

The point is to learn it yourself. If you sit in your garden and extrude your antennae, the garden will tell you things about what it wants, and about what you want, which may be different from what you thought you wanted. Today, for example, I remembered to be a happy anarchist, digging a potato bed.

I'm not really an anarchist; nevertheless I often like their vibe, especially if they're also farmers. They don't care whether their garden looks unkempt: they care whether it grows things. They care that they are taking care of themselves and their families and the bees by growing foods that aren't soaked in carcinogenic chemicals. They care that they're not working a job they hate. They'd rather work reduced hours and make up the difference in healthy vegetables, organic if not certified. Certification, they will tell you, is a bit of a scam. They will give their excess to the local chapter of Food Not Bombs. Zucchinis anyone?

It's not just the plants that speak to you when you extrude your antennae but also the river and the frogs. And the dogs! If only the dog hadn't died. She was mad in love with you and reminded me I could be too.

Was she in my dream? I feel so guilty. I was short with her sometimes when she was ill, wanting her to get up and go outside and not pee in her bed again. I wish I'd seen to her teeth sooner. Her gums were inflamed, and I know how painful that can be, I've had it too. We put her on Gabapentin, which several people I know have taken for one thing or another, but not me.

Meditating before I get out of bed, I put off looking at my phone for a few minutes longer. The aroma of chili wafts up the stairs. Sometimes you cook early in the morning before you begin work. Closing my eyes again, in a half-dream I see heads in the garden like those fallen from Greek statues, or maybe chopped off Edgerton Ryerson's neck to be taken to Land Back Lane. Modelled out of clay and glazed, they remind me of the plaster head you made in art school decades ago before you (or much of anyone other than Kurt Schwitters or John Cage or Laurie Anderson) discovered sound art. I used to think I could plant the plaster head in the garden to molder slowly. We still have it, somewhere, but where?

~\/~

Ibuprofen will make holes in your stomach if you take too much for your inflammatory joint (or tooth abscess) pain. Nettles will provide longer-term relief. Apply topically or drink in tea. The ibuprofen provides quick relief, but you will pay for it later. Your pain will be more likely to last longer over time, to become chronic if it isn't already. Again, nettles. Soon (when the mosquitoes have subsided a bit more) I'll go out to gather baby nettles for tea and lunch. "Nettle omelet again?" you will ask, a bit ironically. I will remind you nettles have a higher vitamin and mineral content than most anything other than kale. This is important survival information. If it rains enough this morning to soften the dry hillside, I will also dig the spiderwort out and move it.

On the way to the garden, I trip over a shovel someone, maybe me, didn't lean up against a tree or trellis. I'm as clumsy as if my period was coming, although it hasn't done that for over 15 years. Eclipse clumsiness. One solar, one lunar, one after the other, May 1st and May 16th after which eclipse season resumes in fall.

The eclipse columnists say we will miss someone. Is it our dog or is it your brother?

Maybe both, you say, or maybe all of them. All those we lost the last few years and there were a lot of them.

The dog made a bridge because she adored us both so much. You and I succeed but also fail at love. We are irritated with one another in a way our dog couldn't be. She lavished each of us with unconditional love and we learned, a little, to imitate her.

~\/~

After the rain starts, I open my laptop, allegedly to get back to work. Instead, I waste another hour reading eclipse columnists. I'm stuck on my project, tired of writing things of dubious worth.

On April 30th, the solar eclipse will be visible if you're in the southern hemisphere, the east Pacific or South America. The black moon will eclipse the sun but not entirely. 64% of the sun's disk will be obscured.

But even in the northern hemisphere, we will feel the eclipse. We will miss dogs or friends who have died or moved away. A black moon is the second new moon in a calendar month. A blue moon is the second full moon in a calendar month. A moon can be both blue and super, although super moon isn't a technical term; it was coined by an astrologer, not an astronomer. The moon's orbit is elliptical, hence each month the moon is alternately far from and close to Earth. At its farthest it's at apogee, and at its closest it's at perigee. May through August are perigee or super moons, though some observers say May doesn't count, and maybe not August either. May's full moon is an eclipse and a blood moon, so maybe it doesn't need to be counted as a super moon as well. Eclipsed Super Flower Blood Moon. It sounds overwrought.

Between the first and second eclipse I went on a road trip with a friend, south to Lake Ontario. We stayed in a beautiful house belonging to her cousin. Eclipses can help us to shift things we need to shift. It can feel like upheaval, I read. It didn't though. I felt I'd escaped the parts of my life that felt squalid. The house in the county was gorgeous and peaceful, and everywhere there were beautiful beaches and cute little towns to explore. One of the eclipse columnists said I would consider physical environments and what my current goals are.

Catching up on email on the porch one morning, I booked a flight to Vancouver to look after cats and a house. I figured the cats were providing me with cheap office space, a physical environment I want to work towards.

The columnists said my life would be turned ass over teakettle as I realigned with my destiny. My life didn't feel upside downed, although I stayed in the county longer than I'd planned and enjoyed it more than I thought I would. The columnists said there would be sudden new opportunities. The house near the lake was one, and the trip to Vancouver another. Both align with my destiny to live and work in stuff-free spaces in which I have more time to finish my book, due to not spending it shifting clutter from one room to another, somewhat dejectedly.

We could just get a dumpster, I say, after spending a writing morning clearing broken tube radios out of your shed. You bought them years ago from an old guy up the street. His daughter followed us anxiously from room to room, grateful we were helping her clear out the house before she put it on the market and moved her father into her home or long-term care – hopefully a place where the staff were nice and paid enough. There is a connection. Why wouldn't there be?

You and the old guy talked vacuum tubes for an hour. It was beautiful. I understood why you bought his collection. I didn't know I'd still be storing it 20 years later, the wooden exteriors of the radios in various states of decomposition. But I should have. He also had a quartz crystal as big as your head, or maybe my head, in a polished walnut case on a stand. That's the item in his collection I wish I'd bought. Even if the case, improperly stored in a damp shed, had given way with rot by now, the crystal would still be okay. After all, it had already lasted quite a long time.

The cats I will be living with in British Columbia are, I have heard, methodical housekeepers who like things to be both pretty and well organized. They would have bought the crystal and fewer radios. They would have stored the crystal indoors, removing nearby clutter to highlight its majesty and surprise. "How did you come by such a thing?" I imagined my friends saying. If I had met the Vancouver cats sooner, the crystal, in its museum quality case, would be standing in a corner of my living room. One or two of the most attractive tube radios would also stand against the wall, with art and stacks of books carefully arranged on top. My life would have been different if I'd met them sooner, these cats. "How so," I imagine my friends asking. "Well, for one thing, I'd have the crystal."

Then our first climate change storm came, the derecho, and all our possessions were highlighted, as the eclipse columnists had pointed out might occur. Highlighted were not just our indoor clutter, unusable outdoor storage space, lack of pets, but several toppled mature hardwoods and a still-standing conifer, leaning crazily toward the hydro lines. Our neighbours remarked nervously each day how the tree's angle had become more acute. You found a plumb line in the basement and made marks on the ground each day to assuage their fears while we waited for the arborists, who, understandably, were backed up for days.

The derecho storm highlighted the following questions: Which old and possibly dangerous camp stove of several you acquired at a yard sale or junk shop should we use to make coffee and meals on the back porch? Why is it so expensive to remove trees from my front and back yard? Why do insurance companies get to charge us deductibles after we have been paying them for decades? Do you think *Home Despot* has any stoves in stock that I won't fear blowing up?

It turns out they had one, but no gas canisters for that model. They had canisters for other models but not the stoves themselves. Neither stoves nor canisters were on sale. They know when they have us. In the end we (well, me, I'm the early riser) made morning coffee on a small wood fired stove. You fashioned it last summer, knowing full well (but then who doesn't, these days?) this day would come. You modified an old stainless steel toothbrush holder. It's fun to feed it dry twigs. I have a lot of those, because of the downed trees. The water boils quickly. No canisters to fuss with. Of course, since then I have seen a little stove just like it online. Never let the Roomba take pictures of your inventions.

—⁀—

I read recently about a retired professor nearby who started a magazine and a reading series and published several books. He was so excited to be doing at last what he had wanted to do for decades but couldn't because of work pressures. I, on the other hand, don't want to start magazines or reading series or write books because I have done all that. Those things have been my profession and I look forward to retiring from them, ill paid and exhausting as they are. I have already retired from the reading series and the magazine. I look forward to not writing books, though I loved it for years. "You must be so excited," I say to my Cont Ed students, several of whom are retired middle school teachers who finally get to write the book they always wanted to write. That's why they are in my class – is to suction my brain for tips.

What a relief, I think, but don't say, for obvious reasons. I never have to write another book if I don't want to. Still, I like finishing things I start, and hope to make headway while in Vancouver with the tidy cats.

I don't just miss my dog, I miss my local paper, to which I could send this story. The editor was a friend and would sometimes publish our meandering auto-fiction personal essay things although truth be told, she mostly published her own. She, like my dog, is dead, although her paper preceded her by a few years. No, it is not the death of her magazine or print in general that killed her. Although maybe a bit.

Sometimes when I publish auto-fictional things my friends believe everything in them. This startles me when it comes from supposedly intelligent people. The whole point is that you get to make a few things up. In Japan they call this genre *shishōsetsu*, or the I-Novel, and readers make a game of deciphering which events in the story occurred in the author's life and which are fabrications. It's a thing. I've spoken about this at writers' conferences and am as irritated as ever by categories. Maybe I just want a new one. How about speculative memoir?

Some of the chronology is wiggled around and one of the little things in this story that isn't true is that you never get up very early and cook before you begin work. Never. I put it in for structural reasons I've already forgotten and a bit of wishful thinking. People who know us are going to think you do. I should add something untrue that's more dramatic, that stands out more obviously as invention. Like Lucia Berlin did, fictionally murdering Buddy Berlin's heroin dealer in Yelapa – unless she really did that, hiding homicide in the plain sight of autobiographical short fiction.

I could, as she did, describe Fire and Rescue draining the ditches to look for my missing child, found later peacefully sleeping in the back of the truck. This is more plausible than murder. I could write to her son and ask him, just as a reader once wrote to ask whether I had really seen Patti Smith perform at the Village Gate in NYC, her neck still in a brace after her fall from another stage. The answer is yes.

As much as we abhor murder, we find ourselves rooting for Lucia as she hauls the unconscious drug dealer into her son's dugout at daybreak. We breathe a sigh of relief as she rows out past the surf to pitch it over the side. Buddy's dealer is ruining their lives after all.

In the *Paris Review*, Rebecca Bengal wrote: "Readers want to believe in a "real" character as much as children want to believe in the tooth fairy. And the people in most writers' lives both want to be written about and they don't. As a writer who works in both fiction and nonfiction, I have said as much before to people in my life: you'll see yourself in short stories where you aren't and miss yourself where you are. Lucia Berlin worked this desire in her readers and her characters to supreme and devastating effect. I find Berlin's willful inconsistency both admirable and liberating."

Bengal goes on to say how Berlin writes to us like a good friend and we are charmed. Not a Beat but Beat adjacent, with a different kind of México story than Burroughs, the intimacy of her prose makes her feel closer, timewise, than she is. She was born the same year as my mom. When I realized this, I was a little angry. She must not have been the easiest of mothers either, but at least her sons got to have her till 2004, 30 more years than we got.

⫸

You would think they would wax the most poetic on spirituality sites or in women's magazines but it's the NASA eclipse columnist who has the most beautiful prose. I'm not being judgemental; it's quite possible the moon writers at wellness and fashion sites are underpaid bloggers without real literacy skills. It's a good gig if you can get it. No one will proofread you, or if they do, they will lack a detailed understanding of grammar themselves and resort to the use of apps.

The lovely NASA moon columnist writes: *As usual, the wearing of suitably celebratory celestial attire is encouraged in honor of the full moon. Be safe (especially during thunderstorms), avoid starting wars, and take a moment to clear your mind.*

It seems to me he has been reading the style magazine columnists, and poaching ideas. He is a better writer though. Celebratory celestial attire, not starting wars, and mind clearing are always in fashion.

There was indeed a reddish tint to the blood moon. The NASA columnist shared an astonishing fact: the bloody tint is the refracted light of all the sunrises and sunsets on Earth. This also seems miraculous to me. Is it true? Would a NASA columnist, of all people, lie? Or is he, like Lucia, burying one fantastic thing in an otherwise true story, just to keep us on our toes?

Spring eclipse season over, I caught my flight west. Even though we no longer had to, I wore a mask on the plane. In the in-flight magazine I read that the effects of the two spring eclipses would be felt for half a year. In the fall there would be new eclipses, and their effects would supersede those of the spring eclipses. I returned home from Vancouver where I had not finished my book as I had hoped but started a new one instead, a chapter of which you are reading now. How do you know when the distraction is after all the thing?

You and I went outside to look at the first fall eclipse. Eclipses are often a bit of a no-show because of cloud cover, but ever since the fireball, we have made a ritual of looking at celestial events together.

The fireball story includes a fire, our dog, a neighbour and a fireball. I won't be telling the long version here, as I'm still trying to stick to my eclipse thread. I've failed, of course, veering into working vacations and book reviews. Hybridity rules. The fireball did seem miraculous. I will see a few more blood moons in my life, Goddess willing, but I may never see another fireball. Last night we laughed, saying maybe there had been a man inside the fireball, or something like a man. He's been walking toward our house from where it landed, for years. Soon he'll arrive, speaking a language we don't understand, at least not yet.

HIBISCUS BLOOMS AT HER HEELS

LYNNE SARGENT

I remember a time when there used to be Spring, but I don't ever remember any kind of season where there weren't flowers blooming at my mother's heels. Hibiscuses, tulips, even tiny buds that would someday become strawberries. For better or worse, though Spring and Fall both are gone, her flowers remain, if only for the briefest moments.

I watch her through the window, sweating in what used to be the garden, dancing in the sunset on arthritic feet. She is heavier and slower than I remember, but still so graceful in the slow motions of her hands. The drift of her fingers paint lines against the dark red setting sun like her flowers colour the dust of the ground. She's done this every night since I moved in to help her after dad died. Tonight though, I can't bite my tongue any longer. It's getting to be the rage of summer and the evenings are far too hot. We aren't even supposed to go out before dusk. I creak open the door and stand on the porch, arms crossed.

She looks up at the sound of the door and says, "Bethany, you used to smile when I'd dance for you."

"You know we're not supposed to exercise outside."

"Back when I was young the government tried paying old folks to exercise!" she says flippantly.

"Mum, you're going to give yourself heatstroke and I know you don't want to go to the hospital. Please, just come inside."

She frowns, her steps becoming less sure. "Can't you let an old woman enjoy herself?"

I sigh. We've had this conversation many, many times. "Let's just follow the guidelines for tonight," I plead.

She seems to sense my weariness, and allows me to take her hand and pull her inside. She lifts her hand for me to twirl her through the doorway and I oblige. It's almost an apology. For both of us.

-><-

I used to ask her as a child, "Mama, why can't *I* make the plants grow?"

"You could if you wanted to, sweetie. We could get you a succulent for inside while it's cold out and we could make a patch in the garden just for you in the Spring."

I crossed my arms, petulant, sure of her feigned ignorance. "That's not what I mean, Mama. I want to make flowers like *you*."

"We do what we can with what we have. I'm sure you could make your garden just as good as mine with a little time and some hard work from these," and then she held my hands and smoothed out each finger, kissing each fingertip in turn.

I did work in the garden that Spring, and my patch was beautiful. I imagine what a laughable farce it would be to tell my own non-existent child it might grow vegetables in Spring. My mother had so much that I will never have, just as today's children will have less than I did. Now they only grow vegetables in geothermally controlled concrete warehouses, arranged in racks for vertical irrigation.

～٧/~

In the night, she screams, though less than she did right after dad died. I've tried to get mum to see a grief counsellor, but the any-kind-of-medical-attention fight is an old one, and I can't say I don't understand. I didn't as a child. I remember her breaking her wrist and missing my dance recital because she'd had dad set it himself earlier that day and she was too high on marijuana – the only thing she trusted as a painkiller. I didn't speak to either of them for weeks. I didn't know why she couldn't just be normal, just go to the doctor. Especially when our garden was the last one left, and she let it go. She could have held on longer, but she was worried it might start to become suspicious and my tomatoes died along with the rest of it. She was always distrustful of power, and old enough to remember things like Henrietta Lacks and Tuskegee, aware of the hidden but ever-present use of sterilization as a weapon against Indigenous women. Of course, she couldn't know for sure what would happen if the government ever found out about her abilities, but it never seemed worth the gamble of her freedom to place her trust in institutions who had done so much harm for so much less.

Sometimes I wonder now if things would be different if she had, if she had trusted the government to do the right thing with her gift. If the government scientists could make everyone like her, would that be enough? If we all had flowers in our wake and could coax germinating seeds to come and worship us, would that make up for the loss of the old-growth forests? The decades of melted ice caps? Even if it wouldn't be, I'd like to think it would be something.

~\|/~

Tomorrow is the anniversary of Dad's death. For some reason, the cemetery is only open until sunset, despite how the rest of life has shifted. I guess superstition overrides a lot.

The drive up to Beechwood cemetery in Ottawa is a long one, but the plot decision was made years ago. Mum has a place reserved beside Dad for when the time comes. They picked it out together back when it was still known for its flowers. Now Dad's is the greenest plot there. By green I mean the grass has just not totally turned to dust. There's a withered sapling there, too. I don't remember it from the funeral but it was probably planted in one of those urban reforestation endeavors.

We're lathered up in sunscreen, but mum refuses to carry her own parasol, so I try to cover us both with mine. I'm thankful that at least I could convince her to wear her long-sleeved white sunsuit, and that I was able to get hold of some expensive extra water rations. For our grief, it's worth it.

We arrive at dad's gravesite and my heart feels heavy in my chest. Mum sinks down to her knees, tears streaming freely down her face and holds her hands to her heart, whispering things that are not for me to hear. After a few moments, she moves to slip off her shoes. Ottawa might be north as far as some folks are concerned, but the sun is still unbearably strong.

"Mum, you're going to burn yourself. Come on, we just went through this. Do you want to go to the hospital?"

She ignores me, entranced by her own grief. She walks to his marker, the grass on the way blooming, and dying just as fast, cycling through its whole life – sprout to bud to brown decay. I try to ignore her, say a few words for my father, so that we can leave quickly, together.

She does a little waltz around the grave, creating her own faery ring. She sweats and sways and I notice my own vision going hazy in the heat. Somewhere in my purse my phone buzzes a UV indicator warning.

My throat is parched. "Come on, we have to get back to the car, to the air conditioning." What a joke it is that we still have cars – electric, or ethanol-hybrid ones, but still.

Mum plants her feet and rolls through them, from the tips to the heels, and then drums her toes like fingers, as though she is trying to pick up the dirt and massage it, but there is only dust.

"I want to fix the world for you," she says. "I want the memory of your father to have some beauty to it. I was scared before, scared for so long, but now he's gone and you're grown and how can anything else be worse than this?" and she gestures at the barren land. "I'm supposed to worry about you, not the other way around."

"Then come with me to the car so I can stop worrying."

She lets me take her arm and guide her back, but she won't put on her shoes. If she weren't so light and thin with age she might look like a toddler, petulant and stomping to get their way.

When we get to the car she is sweating profusely and her feet are badly blistered where I can catch a view of the soles. When she starts vomiting I know we have to go to the hospital.

"I wanted one last dance with your father."

I purse my lips, tight. I didn't think she'd been showing any signs of dementia, but I can't get a sensical word out of her, so I just drive as fast as I can.

It doesn't really hit me until after we've arrived at the closest hospital and the nurses have rushed her through triage what it actually means that mum lets me usher her through the emergency room doors. She doesn't have a health card on her and she's never had a family doctor. Luckily they don't seem to care too much and the nurses say they'll get me in touch with administrative staff to work things out later.

All the questions make me worry in a way I've never worried before – what if they do take her away from me? What if all her lifelong fears have been justified? What does it mean that she's given up now?

~*~

It's weeks before they let me see her again. At first they say it seems like she's a danger to herself, and then later they tell me she doesn't want to see me yet. I don't really believe the second, but I'm able to get a hotel in the area and work remotely to be near to her.

Then, the questions start. They're indirect, they don't ask about how she makes things grow. Instead, they ask, "Has your mother ever had any delusions before?" They ask, "Did she receive grief counselling?" They ask about our economic situation, what her career was like before retirement, and if she'd ever been enrolled in any experimental medical studies from a list they give me. I answer honestly, because I don't really know what I'm supposed to do, but I don't volunteer anything further.

Later they let me visit, but only under supervision. The conversations I want to have with her feel more urgent than ever before, but I don't know what I can or can't ask. The fact that they've kept her so long and with so little information provided to me makes me afraid that Mum's suspicions were justified, that they are looking for information on her gifts and I don't want to be the reason she's spirited away and experimented on like a lab rat. If we communicate with each other honestly I may never see her again. And yet, I feel like I know her better now than ever, as everyone watches us, as the doctors ask me questions and I retreat into silence and solitude. It is so ironic, the way everyone says we become our parents, and now I have taken up her paranoia, and I can't even talk to her about her choices and the future she chose to give me now that I might just be coming to understand it. I've seen my friends at funerals, wishing they could have had one more *real* conversation with their parents. Dread makes a hard knot in my stomach at the worry that each conversation with my mother might be my last and that because of this surveillance I will be just like all of them.

I ask the doctors when she can come home, but they're evasive. They say they'll let me know next steps as soon as they can.

~*~

And then suddenly she's gone, transferred, to some unname-able facility. "Her new team will be in touch soon." I'm assured. "You can come pick up the things that were left behind."

The "things" include her cellphone, a small cactus I got her for her side table, and a stuffed get-well bear that cousin Tina sent.

I only barely manage to hold it together until I get to the safety of my car. I know it's unsafe to drive in this kind of emotional headspace, but I can't bear to be here a moment longer, so I get back on the road and drive straight home. At least the fact that there's so little traffic during the day now means that my tears are less of a hazard to anyone but myself.

By the time I get home it's properly dark. I take the cactus and set to repotting it with the rest of my desert collec-tion. Without Mum in the house there is a quiet stillness in the air. As I go through the motions of repotting the plant, I feel like a young girl again, wondering if I can understand my mother's choices by imitating them– going through the motions of keeping what is in my immediate circle alive and forgetting the rest. But then again, if that were the case I would have a spouse and child by now. I would be protecting them from the world instead of hiding from it.

I wonder if maybe these plants would take outside. I'm sure someone's tried it, but I stopped following gardening forums years ago. As I brush out the bottom of the pot to save for later, I see that there's a cardboard round at the bot-tom that looks like it's been pried up. Underneath is a little sandwich baggie with a note inside.

"My Dearest Bethany,

"I love you. I'm sorry it had to be like this. I didn't expect to be locked down quite so much as I've been. I wish we could have talked properly.

"It's been so long, and it may amount to nothing, but I had to try. I have so little time left in this world, and I want to make it the best world I can for you. That's always what I've wanted. All of my decisions have been to keep you safe.

"You've done so well this year, but the time is past for children to care for their parents, when we didn't do enough for you. I'm taking the time I have left to work with the scientists to try to help. I understand now that we all have to make sacrifices to get through this, and I have so little left to sacrifice, but I want you to know that this does not diminish the value or joy in the time that I have spent with you. I hope they'll let you visit, but I am content with keeping you safe and removed from being treated like a tool and not a person. I hope someday to dance with you again.

"I always thought that my magic came from joy. My own mother always told me I was an incorrigibly happy child. I had so much to love and be thankful for. I had a world to decorate with pretty ornaments, abundance to coax into being. It's okay if your magic comes from somewhere else. Your garden was just as good, or better than mine, for having been made with only time and your own two hands. I know I didn't have to fix the world, and I'm not, and you don't have to either, you don't even have to try. But someday, if a tree grows and gives you a little air and a little shade then I will die a happy woman. I know you'll find your own way, Bethie, and I will always love you and anything you choose to make.

"Love,

"Mom"

Tears run unbidden down my face, but I don't know what she means. The only real tree we ever had on the property was my old tree house and it has been barren of leaves for years. It's probably just a fire hazard now and should be chopped down, not that you can get anyone to do that kind of outdoor work anymore. I remember mum saying it was her favourite spot to sit when I was a baby, because it was just this wide open field away from the house, and it made her feel like I had the whole world spread out before me. I only had maybe three years in the tree house before it got too hot – 11 to 14 given or take. I'd always assumed that the tree had always been there because of its massive size, but thinking back on her stories, the way she'd described rocking me out there, maybe that couldn't have been the case.

I head to mum's old picture albums. They're easy to access, organized in the lead up to dad's funeral. I flip through to find an old picture and there she is, sitting with a bundle in swaddling in a totally empty field.

I don't know what she is trying to tell me. I never had her powers, never. A burning rage shoots through me. I want to prove her wrong. I storm out, into the moonlight, and I dance. I dance until my soft feet are riddled with a thousand tiny cuts from the harsh dust outside, until I am ready to fall over, and then I collapse on the ground, still weeping.

⋯

In the morning, I have the worst crying hangover, but the only thing there is to do is to throw myself back into routine. I want to write to her, want to interrogate officials, raise a media ruckus, ask where she has gone, how I can see her, hug her, have a real conversation with her. But I'm too scared. Too scared that I, impossible as it might be, could be next. I'm scared that perhaps now, more than ever, I now understand the old fears I used to berate her for having.

My fear and grief increase as the days pass, as I learn to not to look out the kitchen window into the garden where a small bulge is starting to break through the earth. In the moonlight, I imagine the small bit that begins to poke out from it is green. It must be a hallucination.

Then one day, the phone rings.

"Bethany?" the voice on the other line asks, and my heart breaks.

"Mum? I'm so glad to hear from you."

"I'm doing much better now. The doctors say that sometime I can come home on the weekends. I'm just in Barrie if you wanted to come collect me, if you're okay with a visit."

"Of course, Mum! It's still your house. I've missed you so much."

It's as easy as that. She rattles off an address and Friday after sunset I make my way there.

It's unclear who or what made the decision to give up the medical pretext, but a man in a black suit greets me at the entrance of the facility, which is clearly a greenhouse complex, not that they are green or made of glass anymore. "It's a very important thing your mother is doing," he says, looking at me with hawkish eyes. "It's too bad she only has a few years left. It's a shame you don't have her talent."

I smile, and say a very true thing. "I know. I've always wanted to be more like her."

He says nothing, and guides me to her room. They have her set up in style at least, with lots of little planters, and some creature comforts – a bright pink lamp, a stereo, a minifridge with a creased picture that must have been sitting in her wallet for years: Mum, me, and Dad together on the day I graduated from university.

"Hey, Mum," I say, and she looks up, looks at me like she has always looked at me, like I'm her whole world. "You ready to come home?"

She nods, and takes my hand, and I twirl her out of the room, winking at the man on the way out.

⋅⋰⋅

It's a good weekend. The facility has given her some produce to take home so we make a good dinner, and she gestures once, quietly and proudly at the sapling outside. We still don't talk about it, just in case either of us, or the house, has been bugged. We don't need to, though.

I take her outside and we dance together in the moonlight, and she is careful to lavish her most vigorous steps around the sapling. Even this visit home, perhaps is a way that she might protect me at least a little longer, long enough that I can make a decision, or at least, think about making one.

At the end of the weekend she goes back, and I only let slip a little tear. I think of all the tears I've shed and wonder where they've fallen, what they might have watered that I hadn't realized before. My tears now seem precious, dangerous. It feels like I am germinating, like all the power I always had is finally finding its sunlight, energy now ready to burst into life.

I miss my mom, and I'm proud of her. I hope maybe one day we'll have a chance to talk properly, without fear of surveillance. Maybe if, and when I'm ready to do the work that she is doing now. I think I might be ready soon. I told the man in black that I want to be more like her, and I'm growing into that, but I just need a little more time.

We share the same dream at night, I think. One where flowers don't just bloom at her heels, or trees from my tears. Instead, all sorts of plants burst into being in meadows across the whole burned world, and hers and mine are indistinguishable from all the rest, and we are there together, dancing.

GOING GREEN

Liam Hogan

We shuffle out of the sheds when dawn paints the sky a dusky pink. At this time of year the nights are long and cold. Hollow-bellied, we're impatient for the first warming, nourishing rays of the sun, even if the odds are all we'll get are grey clouds and drizzle.

Which would be enough to keep us ticking, to keep us alive; but we'll need to bask for longer before going about our tasks. Today we're lucky; though there are clouds aplenty, some brooding with the future promise of rain, they are broken rather than blanket, the horizon a fiery, apocalyptic crimson that has me tingling with anticipation.

We leave it until the last moment to strip cloth from our backs, turn as one to greet the sun by facing away from it. Recent arrivals hold discarded shirts across their chests, the rest don't bother. Modesty is a luxury.

I watch, eternally fascinated, as the pale, golden morning light reveals the intricate emerald green designs etched onto the skin of others. Abstract floral arrangements, fantastical shoulder-spanning world trees, pastoral scenes inhabited by a menagerie of half-forgotten farmyard animals picked out in shades of green, so that the youngest must believe that was the colour they once were. A forest of bodies stretches and unfurls like leaves and flowers, and for the same reason. The chlorophyll-packed algal cells are inserted beneath the epidermis of our backs by a tattooist's gun; we are canvases we can never see, not unless we chance upon a mirror, and mirrors are exceedingly rare on the farms.

My own tattoo, I am told, is a disappointment. Hard to work out what it is, or was meant to be. But I'm older than most, one of the earliest greenbacks, and the design, such as it ever was, is one of the more washed out. Art requires contrast.

There are other things that keep me apart, a little distant from the rest. Life perhaps should have deposited me, if not in the bone-white towers of the rich – who demonstrate their wealth and power by living in secluded darkness, only ever emerging like cautious vampires, gloved, hooded, and masked, every part of their alabaster skin carefully covered – but rather in the vast middle strata, the people who still work, though not in the algal fields. Mechanics, clerks, drivers, and chemists, overseeing the industrial processes that all start from the same base: the algae we tend, the same algae that thrive beneath our skin.

With my seniority comes the assumed and unwanted burden of responsibility. I am an anomaly; better educated than most the current system churns out, who enter the fields before they are even fully adult, as soon as they're old enough for the extensive tattoo. I've been offered the position of overseer over them any number of times. I always turn it down. If we are to be slaves, then let us be slaves. I would not want to be responsible for punishing others, even those who do not consider themselves slaves.

I am old enough to remember the video where the scientist, sitting comfortable in his leather armchair, talks about how *inefficient* photosynthesis is. How the latest bioengineering has made it much better, capturing far more carbon dioxide from the atmosphere, and how it can begin to reverse the damage we have wrought. It's only near the end, when asked about the distant future, that he casually mentions it might one day be possible to insert his genetically modified algae under the skin of livestock, so that a pig would grow its own food from nothing more than air, and water, and sunlight.

He could not possibly have known that there wouldn't *be* any pigs in under a decade. No cows, or sheep, or other farmed animals. These, too, were a luxury we couldn't afford, not once we realized the tipping point had already been reached, and a myriad climate feedback loops triggered as critical thresholds were crossed. From melting tundra, to the loss of reflective ice from glaciers and the Antarctic, to the sea no longer absorbing the excess heat and CO_2. Every inch of arable and pasture land was needed to grow his bioengineered algae, much of which is dried in airless, solar-powered ovens, until it is nothing but fine black powder. Soot that gets injected into depleted oil wells and exhausted coal mines, trying to force the climate change genie back into the bottle, even as seas continue to rise and traditional crops wither and die, unable to cope with the rapid temperature change, the flooding, the encroaching salt.

Thankfully, the algae grow well enough in warm, marshy conditions, in flooded fields even if they're brackish. Other crops can't compete once it takes hold. Which was the whole point of the genetic enhancements, the turbo boosting of its photosynthesis.

It isn't just the ecosystem that has been in turmoil. The worldwide sequestering project dealt a terminal blow to capitalism: there is no financial reward other than the saving of the planet. In its death throes, societal collapse left a rare few individuals insanely rich, and a far higher proportion utterly impoverished and starving, into which sorry group fate cast *my* lot.

We were a ready pool of labour to work the algal fields. And a blank canvas for biological experimentation. We were going to be outside every minute of the day; why not make use of that? Why grow food to feed the workers, when the workers can grow food on their backs?

It sounds terrible, I know. Haves, and have-nots. It isn't quite so clear cut. We have something those in their pristine towers don't: *purpose*. A worthy goal. One that rewards us with connection, to each other, and to the environment at large. Those who don't remember the before appear to miss nothing. Though we work every daylight hour, you'd be surprised at how much companionship there is in the fields, how much singing, and laughter.

In the twilight hours of dusk, when we are full of the day's energy, our work done, we who have so little are surprisingly creative with what we do have. Perhaps because we have so little. But the art on our backs is not the only art we know.

There are other complications to the rough picture I sketch, coloured as it is by notions of *before*, and *after*. The algae doesn't stay where it is put. The bright green cells creep from the injection sites, doing what all life desires – to reproduce, to colonize new territory. Green covers our arms, our legs, our fronts, even our faces. Not as well defined as the initial injection sites, our tattoos, these are delicate feathered branches, fronds slowly reaching outward, beauti-

ful in their own way. It is this spreading green stain the rich
shy so violently away from, going to extreme lengths to ster-
ilize their food, filtering their air and their water, as well as
avoiding natural light.

Measures the middle, working classes can't afford to
indulge in. So they too are turning green, whether they like
it or not. Those that spend their time outdoors, with us,
quickly find themselves at their own tipping point: their
accidental contamination doesn't offer the same benefits as
ours. Once the algae takes over, once it colonizes the gut as
well as the skin, traditional food is not so easily digested.
Without supplements that are themselves hideously expensive, we starve without sunlight. The middle classes can
fight, spending more and more of their earnings in a futile
battle, or they can give in, request the subdermal injec-
tions, their own tattoos, and so speed up the inexorable
process, spending even more of their time basking in the
sun.

There's stiff resistance, of course. They fear it will make
them part of the underclass, that it will demean them. But
this is not a door we have to push at. Nature, or perhaps
unnatural selection, is doing that well enough.

As my fellow greenbacks and I work beneath the win-
tery sun, I tell them what I remember of Edgar Allen Poe's
The Masque of the Red Death. They nod. They smile. They
see the inevitability of the tale, rather than the injustice,
rather than the horror. Ours is a gentler, less bloody revolution, but no less widespread, no less absolute.

Vibrant green engulfs the ever-expanding fields we
tend, blankets the lakes and rivers, even carpets our rooftops
and walls. Everywhere, except those slender, ivory towers of

the wealthy, sprayed daily with herbicide, as barren and soul-less as tombstones.

But it is all to no avail. How small are algae! How ready to invade every nook and cranny. It may take a while yet, another decade, perhaps, but eventually even the rich will be forced from their dark, solitary existence, and out, into the bright light of day.

We will welcome our pale, anaemic brethren, with green, open arms, show them how to tend the algal fields, and join with them, as they too learn to worship the sun.

MIND YOUR MOTHER

GIN SEXSMITH

I never thought she was going to leave him, but she finally did. She's been saying it since I learned to listen. She's probably been saying it earlier than that, she was probably cooing it to me as she rocked me to sleep when I was only a baby.

"Buddy, it's just going to be you and me."

My father named me Buddy. The only issue is that he likes his Drinking Buddies more. I know what you're thinking of when you think of Dads Who Drink, but mine wasn't really like that. He didn't come home and yell or push my mom around or break dishes or kick the dog. He came home glassy-eyed and baby-voiced, a toddler who'd had too much sugar at a birthday party and now had his first self-induced tummy ache. The problem was that he did it more nights than he didn't. He was also tossed in the drunk tank twice, too smitten with pulling out his wiener in public places as a silly little joke. A story that makes my mom smile, as much as it made her cringe, was at one of their New Year's Eve parties when she spotted my father standing in the corner of the room with his jeans around his ankles.

"Pull my pants up, Baby. This is embarrassing," he whispered, as if he hadn't been the one to pull them down. When he wasn't drinking, he was awfully bored. I'm a teenager now, so I can only equate it to teenage boredom, which feels all-encompassing, because I'm too young to get my license, and even if I was old enough I don't have the money for a car or insurance or gas. I try to keep my boredom to myself, and if I tell my mom, she always has a list of chores for me at the ready (or worse, *volunteering*) and hey, I'm not *that* bored.

But Dad would scuff his feet along the floor and sigh a lot. Sometimes my mom would just roll her eyes and say "just go then," to which he would beam the brightest smile you ever saw him wear, a kid on Christmas morning. He's careless, my mother says. He doesn't appreciate her, he doesn't appreciate me, he doesn't appreciate life itself. He used our home as a crash pad. It never helped that he was also a bartender, that his main goal in life was owning his very own bar, and that he continuously drank up all his extra cash leaving Mom to pay the bills all on her own.

My mom crashes into the room, a force of nature. The tears have made paths of her jet black mascara. Sometimes I think that I'm the only person in the world who intimately knows her pain, so raised-jaw and boisterous laugh she is when she's around everyone else. She likes to be perceived as resilient.

"Buddy, your *blood*," she howls, chucking her cluttered purse onto the table with a thud.

I find myself looking down my pale arms, my left hand ending in a spoon dripping with sweetened Cap'n Crunch milk, half-expecting to see that I've slit my wrists again.

"I failed you," she says, plopping down into a kitchen chair, resting her head in her hands, raking her nails against her scalp. She has her sleeves pulled down over her sinewy arms, the thin fabric clenched in her fists.

"I should have made sure your blood tied you closer to the land. I shouldn't have given you a father who would further strip your sense of identity."

I spoon another bite of sugary cereal into my mouth, chewing slowly as I watch her. I've learned to wait when she's like this. Her guilt makes her volatile, that she knew what it was like to be raised mixed, Mohawk and white, and she willingly made me whiter.

"What if I've played a part in the end of the world?" She looks up at me with big hazel eyes, earth eyes.

"Buddy, my *fern!*" I tear my blue eyes from hers to the drooping fern in the middle of the kitchen. In a second she's on her feet, small hand gripping the tap and filling our kitchen with an extra-stink of rotten egg. The fern's once lush leaves are brown and crispy at the edges, and she douses it with sulfur water and steps back as if her sheer pain will bring it back to life. At its first sip, it does seem to perk up, however slightly.

"Sorry, Ma," I say, shovelling another bite of cereal into my mouth so I won't be expected to add much to the conversation. I watch her tornado around the house, shutting off lights, muttering about how it's *daytime*, how it's as if she's taught me *nothing*.

She's been like this since she left him. Or rather, should I say, kicked him out. He moved in with one of the other bartenders at the pub, Ally. Ally drinks just as much as he does, so she doesn't see the issue. I haven't asked him if he still pulls his pants down as a joke. There was a sweetness to my father that distracted my mother from the waving red flags of our life. I truly believe she thought she could save him. Now, whenever it's my weekend to spend with him, it's as if she has to accept all over again that he's a lost cause.

The slamming of her bedroom door signals my time to finish my cereal in peace. I set my empty bowl and dirty spoon in the sink as gently as possible. If she hears the clang she'll tell me to wash them.

Lately, I've been excited to spend the weekends with my dad. Two full days away from her neurosis. Two full days where I don't have to feel anxious over the state of this world or the realization that I can't remember any Mohawk words. Even better, since I'm *almost* 16, he's been letting me drink.

Dad's been happier than ever: he's barely ever bored anymore. My overnight bag is already packed.

When I was a little boy, my favourite thing to do was climb the tree in our backyard. Forty feet up, the trunk branched like a wishbone and I would stay up there for hours, cradled. White oaks grow slowly, only a few feet a year, but they can get as tall as 80 feet and live up to 300 years. Mom was always going on about how people shouldn't spray dandelions with herbicide, how it would kill the oaks, in much the same way the highlighter-orange dust from the Kraft Dinner Dad cooked would kill me. But she was worrying needlessly. Four summers ago the drought sucked the life right out of it and a lightning storm finished it off. I was already quite into video games by then. It's funny how the things you once loved more than anything can be so simply dismissed. Yet sometimes when I look at what remains of the tree I feel this weird ache in my gut.

The knock on the door pulls me from the blackened, gnarled tree in the backyard. I can't get used to it, Dad knocking on a door he used to stroll through.

"I'll get it!" I yell, but I'm already too late. I hear Mom's door slam and the slap of her bare feet as she quickly descends the stairs.

"You're late," she says as she yanks open the door. There's a boyish quality to my father. He's always kept his hair shaggy. He doesn't really dress the way the other dads dress, he wears Nikes and baggy jeans and jerseys. Strangers often think I'm his kid brother.

"Hi, Baby," he says to her, his piercing blue eyes pained, but his voice casual. She hates how he's never stopped calling her *Baby*, but I know that if he ever does stop she'll hate that more.

Her reply is a *hmph*. I want her to ask him how he is. I want her to hug him and let him move back in, even if that means I have to see him on the couch every day, eyes reddish and skin greasy as his body tries to rid itself of the toxins he won't quit guzzling.

"Have him back for 6 on Sunday, k?"

Mom's New Thing is Sunday dinners, just her and me, where we collect veggies from the garden and dice and simmer them up together while she stumbles her way through old Mohawk myths and makes us take turns reciting the *Ohèn:ton Karihwatéhkwen*, the Thanksgiving Address, before we eat. For years she begged dad for dinners like that, decolonial and bonding, but he's always preferred eating in front of the TV and doesn't care too much for veggies.

"You look good," Dad says, ever-persistent.

"Well that's great cuz I feel like shit," she says, running a hand through her long hair. There's a glitch in the energy and for a moment I fear she might start to cry. She really loved him, my Dad. She really believed in him.

I push past her at that point, stepping out onto the front porch.

"See ya on Sunday, Mom." It feels a little cold, but I'll explain it to her later. I was saving her from one of Dad's *I Miss You*s which always have the power to ruin her entire day.

"*Ó:nen*, Babe. *Konnorónhkwa*. I love you," she says. She's cute, repeating her *I love you*s in two languages in hopes that I'll really feel it, her love.

"*Konnorónhkwa*, Ma," I say, without looking at her. If I look her in the eyes there's a chance that the lump in my throat will escape. My dad shuffles from one foot to the other and for a moment I wonder if he even remembers what *konnorónhkwa* means. I can feel the shame rolling off the slump of his shoulders, how he could never give her the bare minimum of what she requested.

I try not to glance at the big old oak tree as I follow Dad to the car, but I can't help it. I have to remind myself that not everything has a future.

The sun beats against the back of my black T-shirt. This is the hottest summer ever and meteorologists say it'll be the coolest summer we ever experience again.

The passenger side floor of my dad's car is littered with hamburger wrappers, coffee cups, and those little pieces of foil from cigarette packages. It smells like unwashed upholstery tinged with the sour rot of an abandoned smoothie cup, made more pungent because there's no AC. He rolls down the window which helps for a moment, but then he begins to smoke. I know I'm too old to tell him that I feel carsick, so I just close my eyes and try to sleep.

"I'm sorry about the mess," he mutters. I shrug, eyes still closed, watching the reddish hues of my eyelids. "Here, pass me that."

I jump as I feel his hand brush past my knee, as he grabs a coffee cup and half-torn McDonald's bag. I begin to gather the garbage, too, stuffing what I can in takeout bags as he tosses the trash out the window.

Mom would be screaming, swearing, demanding he pull over and collect his mess. I feel guilty for remaining silent. The cigarette dangles from his lips as he tosses the last bag before he chucks the butt of his smoke, too.

"Aren't you nervous of wildfires?" I ask, hating the little-boy condescension of my voice.

"You sound just like your mother, Bud."

"She'd be cussing you out," I say as he turns to face me, his red-blond hair golden in the sun, his eyes crinkled in laughter.

"You're right, Bud, you're right."

He's beautiful, my dad, and I don't think anything makes me happier than when he smiles at me like this, when I know for certain that he's amused instead of bored.

We don't talk much after that and we don't need to. He turns on the radio, drums his fingers along to "De Do Do" by The Police until we pull into the parking lot of Ally's apartment. I still call it Ally's apartment because I can't fully accept that he won't be back. Calling it Dad's apartment feels final. I'm superstitious.

But Ally isn't home, and when I walk through the door, I can't help but realize that this place feels more like my father than our house ever did. There are seven cases of empties pushed up against the kitchen wall. Labatt Blue. He opens up the fridge and pops the cap off another one.

"You want?" he mutters to me between sips.

"Yeah, sure," I say as he quickly grabs another and passes it to me. The chilled bottle feels refreshing in my hands after the stifling, stinky car ride, but my stomach still feels iffy. Every single light, including the one above the stove, is on. I can feel my mother's words daring to escape my lips: But Dad, it's *day*time. I take another swig instead, the bubbles soothing and replacing my judgement with a pleasant numbness until even the smell of stale second-hand smoke becomes less noticeable.

"You hungry? Want some KD? Or a Hungry Man?"

I shake my head, no, remembering how Dad doesn't like to eat until the moment before he goes to bed, so he doesn't ruin his buzz.

I take another swig of my beer. I realize, now that they're finally apart, that my mother drove a lot of the conversations between the three of us. It feels like there's an invisible door that I don't have the key to.

"So, uh, school? How's school?"

"It's good," I answer quickly, wondering if I should tell him about my crush on Jenny Fisher but then deciding against it at the last second. My dad is so charming, I don't think he'd understand just *not* talking to someone day after day.

"How's work?" I ask, filling the gaping silence.

"Good, good," he takes another sip, polishing the bottle off and setting it on the counter with one hand, while his other opens the fridge.

"Ally?"

"Listen, Bud, uh," he gestures to the two chairs beside his little breakfast table. For a moment I wonder if he ever came over here before Mom kicked him out. I pull out my chair with a screech across the linoleum.

I remember when I was small and Dad used to chuck me in the air over his head and I'd squeal and laugh and Mom would say, "Babe, please, please be careful," but my eyes would be locked to his and we'd share matching looks of glee, and I'd feel so incredibly safe.

He grabs me another beer and opens it, even though the one quickly warming between my sweaty palms isn't even half gone.

"So, uh, Ally's not at work. I told her not to come home for a bit because I need to talk to you."

I take a swig, and quickly switch it for the cold one. This is what's meant by *piss warm*.

"I don't really know how to say this. Shit." He takes another swig. I feel halfway between annoyed and terrified. I try to rack my brain for a time I've seen him serious. He sobbed when Mom finally told him he had to go, but it had been brewing for such a long time that he didn't really fight. I always wondered if she was serious or if she was just hoping for the argument. They always seemed to be okay for a few weeks after the It's Over fight.

I reach my hand across the table but then quickly retreat it. What am I thinking? That he'll hold it?

"So last weekend I passed out... ."

I wait. He looks at me and I see his shame as he realizes that him passing out isn't sit-down news. He laughs a misplaced laugh, embarrassed.

"Are you okay?" I ask, my voice too calm, the voice of my mother when I would fall off my bike and scrape my knees, and she was trying to keep her reaction to a minimum so I didn't freak out at the sight of my own blood.

I watch as his face reddens. He bites at his lips as if he can contain the sob that's breaking its way through. He sets the bottle down on the table with a thud, his eyes falling to his lap.

"I'm sick, Buddy."

I think of AA chips and Fight Club. A fridge full of near beers. My mom's voice: alcoholism is a *disease*.

"They found something on my lung."

I hear the words but I don't. They hang in the air, waiting for me to process and process again. I hear him, a laugh on his voice: *I'm just shaving off the bad years.*

But he's 35. The bad years aren't till what? 80?

"Are you kidding me?"

I don't expect the rage. Dad didn't expect the rage either. I feel bad when I look into his boyish eyes but I can't stop it. It's taken over.

"She warned you, didn't she?"

I repeat it. Again. Again. She warned you, didn't she? She warned you, didn't she? She warned you, didn't she. The words begin to lose their meaning but I can't stop.

Dad's sobbing now. The way he used to sob when Mom would tell him it was over, her rage rattling the windows until I hid in the bathtub, ducking my head beneath my arms for protection.

My mother's been the only one to care for me, really, even though he's always been there within the same walls. I tell myself this is not like losing her. But I'm sobbing now, too. The beer bottle is clutched in my shaking hand one second, and smashed against the wall the next. Dad doesn't even flinch. His eyes stay glued to his writhing hands.

I'm standing over him, chest heaving as if I'll be a man one day, and when he looks up at me I see stark acceptance. The key in the lock pulls us from our standoff. Ally bustles in. She's young and pretty and the cigarettes haven't started to carve wrinkles around her mouth.

"Oh," she says, stopping in the doorway as if she wishes she could walk right back out the door. "You told him. I didn't think you were actually going to tell him."

She waits. I figure she assumes my father would speak but he doesn't. She turns her attention to me, her voice becoming a little higher, a little sweeter.

"He'll fight it, Bud. He'll be okay." But then she starts to cough and I watch the panic hit her eyes. It's the hottest summer ever and the coolest summer we'll ever witness again.

"Can you take me home?" I ask, to neither of them in particular. I long to be cradled. I have nowhere to go.

My mother is standing in the kitchen when Dad and I get back. She's looking out the window, at what's left of the oak.

"We're all sick," she whispers. "It's too hot and the water's too dirty. The air, can't you feel it, Bud?"

"Mom?" I ask, stepping away from my father and closer to her.

"It's poisoning us with each breath," she says.

She rolls up her sleeves and I see it then, the moles with their uneven borders, their blends of browns and blacks. She turns around and faces us. She coughs. "I warned him, Bud. You remember, right? I warned him."

I watch her closely as she grabs the Zippo fluid from beneath the kitchen sink. My dad forgot to take it when he left. She pours it into her hands and begins to rub it into her skin.

"Mom? What are you doing? Mom?"

"You mind your mother," my dad says, his face sterner than I've ever seen it.

I look at him with wild eyes, half-expecting to wake up sweaty and afraid.

She's dousing herself with it now. Her clothes are soaked. I can see the old oak tree through the kitchen window, black and gnarled and hopeless.

"We all mind her," my dad says, watching her as she pulls a box of matches from the third drawer.

"Dad?"

She scrapes the match along the book, it fizzles, fails to ignite.

"*Iakwatonhontsanónhnha*, Bud," my dad says and I wonder why he's never spoken Mohawk with us before.

"This was my fault, Bud, remember that. She warned me, you know? You warned me, Baby. You mind your mother now. *Iakwatonhontsanónhnha*. We all mind her, the Earth," he says with his signature grin. The match catches fire.

THREE TURTLES

E. Martin Nolan

1.

All three breathed the wildfire air in, with us.
Two I saw jogging on the wetland sand road.
In the morning, to warm in the sun, welcome.
As I came up, they twitched their dry legs
inward, but didn't close. Held. Must have
somehow trusted me, like I believed in signs
that said Brake for Turtles.

2.

The air quality said "moderate." The wind shifted
and took our planetary consciousness with it.
We were on vacation, and the beach was sunny.
Lake Erie was cold, but the body is remarkable
in its adjustment as the freeze becomes
what you can be. I thought I saw
a stick carried out from the shore,
but how it arced to the deep water.
The truck with the wheels and the striped flag decal
was parked nearby again. I was too close to home.

3.

It was raining when we left Long Point. The air
purified. My son said "Bye bye, lake" – a turtle was ahead.
I dodged it on the road. It sat dark and round
top and bottom, red between. I could not see
if the legs stayed in, or had slid back out. Old turtle,
you should not have trusted us. All we'll ever do
is run you over and worry about the suspension.

WHEN THE LEAVES FELL

Erin MacNair

When the leaves fell, everywhere, all at once, we thought it was the harbinger of doom, all the harm we'd done coming to fruition in one giant dump. We stood on lawns and scratched our heads and spoke quietly to the neighbours about soil depletion and atmospheric rivers and heat waves, and then about football because we were scared. Those of us who can never stand a mess bagged the leaves, placing them in neat rows along the edges of driveways. No one got much sleep that night. The skeletal trees were too silent.

The next day the bags were splayed open, burst from the inside. The leaves were gathering into formations, curling bodies shivering on the ground, trembling. They worked their way towards us, slowly, like hunters, leaving tiny furrows in the dirt and forming arrowed echelons like birds do in the sky. The wind kicked up, pulling some of them free in one violent swell. They went skittering across yards and winding their way through back alleys, descending on the inner city with a determined flurry of autumn colour.

All these years we'd wondered if the trees were listening to us. If they could really feel who we were, understand our troubles as we whispered to them deep in the woods, while we sheltered underneath their foliage on a hot day in the city, the confessions rising through their canopies like unfurling smoke, our simple miseries another nuisance boring their way in. Turns out they had been listening.

We got the feeling from their hypnotic rustling that we could trust them, and that we should let them show us all they knew. We slowly peeled off our clothing, stacking garments on the sidewalk in front of Starbucks, on seats of the #239 bus, in the produce aisles, wherever we happened to be. The leaves scampered up our bodies, labouring to perfect their work, each Oak and Arbutus and Evergreen leaf searching for its perfect place, each body a canvas showcasing our hurts and needs. A few of us hypothesized about magnetism, remembering toys we had as kids, where filings were pulled along a fat face by a magnet on a stick, forming moustaches and bushy eyebrows.

Everyone suddenly became very interested in the physiology of trees. How did they really work? Were they like us? Why had they shed their leaves for us, what auspice foretold?

We paced on the spent blossoms of Magnolia and Rhododendron, turning to our phones for some hurried internet research, our new skins crackling and snapping. We learned that tree cells grew thick over wounds but never forgot about them. They communicated under the ground through their roots – they knew everything about each other – no secrets divided their communities. Even the dying announced when their time was coming. *Use all my nutrients, my water, everything. I live on through you.* That's how we imagined them speaking, in the no-nonsense voice of Emma Thompson or the soothing baritone of Lawrence Fishburne.

The wind forced its way through the naked stems and branches, skirting the twisted frames, trees now whistling a haunted tune, a few simple notes, like one might hum from a soundtrack – the part where the hero's journey has come to a standstill and the understanding of their task washes over them.

One of us looked down at the dark green Holly encircling her heart, the plasticky hooked edges bound in tight stacks, and muttered, *That's not fair,* but the leaf-voice inside said *The barbed protection has been up for some time now; perhaps it is time to address that.*

We checked our undergrowth, gently lifting the foliage over our groins, searching for any rot. A few discovered a whole slurry of decaying vegetation they struggled to scrape away.

One of us stood in the middle of the street, crying, body covered in the leaves of a Chestnut, spiky fruits still attached and digging into the skin, leaves swimming in a fetid soup of decomposition. The smell was intolerable and the rest of us instinctively moved away.

I'm sorry, Chestnut-person said, to no one, or to the voice inside themselves.

The trees rattled and thrashed. *Are you listening?* we heard Lawrence/Emma say, the sombre melody beginning to form words.

Someone swiftly rode past on a bicycle, eyes wide with shock under scaly-plated red bark, clusters of green needles waving in the breeze, a stiff petticoat of dead spikes rustling underneath. Many got into their cars and made to leave but found themselves circling back to the place where they'd been tap-rooted.

There was a recognition, even though most of us were not gardeners, of what each leaf could mean. All prophecies aside, the trees were no longer producing much oxygen, so we knew we'd better figure out quickly what they were telling us. We sat down in the streets, in the aisles, and told our stories, searching each other for swaths of brown and red, similar dead patches we could commiserate upon.

Listen!

We tried.

Outside a café, one of us was steeped in conversation, the plastic latticework backing of the patio chair offsetting his many-coloured layers of maple. Another took his hands in hers, happy that he had so many golden hues despite his sometimes-crippling depression, but started at the sight of raised foliage at his wrists, crisped bracelets of dead Scarlet Oak, crimson edges rising and falling in arcs like waves, like Japanese paintings of tsunamis. The yellowed rims of his maple-cheeks curled under a hidden heat. *That… was a long time ago*, he said. She held him and let him cry, aware that we could be more than one type, that perhaps hidden seeds could sprout anytime given the right circumstance.

A solo Hemlock even approached Chestnut-slurry, difficult as that was.

The trees shuddered again, notes forceful, impatient.

We heard. We tried harder, aiming for worthiness. We were really trying our best to understand each other, but just in case, breathing in tiny, shallow breaths.

APPLE BREAD

KATHERINE KOLLER

I have 65 growth rings with her. This spring, to let her know "it is enough," I sprout extra buds. But even from a distance away, when late wet snow on the ground prevents her daily walk and inspection, I sense her anxiety. I detect it deep in my cracking heartwood, in my roots under her feet, high in my branching canopy that protects her head from the rising sun, and in the frantic assembly of bees in my blossoms.

She steps out of what she calls "home." Her concern is clear in her eyes as she starts toward me. Then she crosses the yard, chasing the wind. She lifts "my scarf!" from the grasp of the wind and wraps it around her neck and laughs like a bird. She always has a scarf of flowering colours draped around her shoulders. I love the rippling sounds she makes when she talks and when she moves. Her name is Esther. That is what her man called her. Now that he is gone, I try to mimic her name with my leaves in the breeze, "Es-ther."

Of all her gifts, walking amazes me the most. I know my roots reach away from my trunk, and my branches, even with regular fall pruning, stretch far, but her easy change in position is exotic to me, wonderful and weird. I know, though, that rootedness is my strength. My rootlets and my twiglets detail the health of the earth, here, near Esther, the one who nurtured me. The bulk of me – my trunk, my branches, and my roots – leans toward the slant of her dwelling, not only to provide shade, but to assure myself of her wellness. Esther's well-being and mine are connected. The state of the atmosphere that I sense through my leaves at the top of my crown affects us both.

Once, I was nurtured by Esther, but it is long since I needed daily watering. I did, at first, after her great sadness: the child born to death, cradled among my young root shoots. Esther fed me water not only from a long tube and from the hollow that collects rain but also from her eyes, mother's tears. The others in the yard, Horse Chestnut, Chokecherry, White Spruce, Saskatoon, and Lilac fed me sugars and medicine. I am Apple.

Blue Spruce, who watched over us all, was felled in a storm, her stump cut like a table and flowers potted atop as a tribute. Now, the rest of us treefolk shelter each other.

I fear for Lilac. Her trunk has split. We send her sugars and medicine, whatever we can spare. Lilac shields us from the northwesterly winds, in the gap left by Blue Spruce, who taught that a lost limb is nothing to fear, the cut would heal into an eye, and a new sensitivity called "seeing" would result. She motioned to us when wild wind approached. "Tighten up, big one on the way." We prepare for storms by ceasing food production. In stress mode, our leaves susurrate messages to each other: "You can bend." "It's going over your crown," or "I'll block it for you."

I love when Esther talks to me. When her grown son chided her for it, she said, "It is my way, to take it to the tree." Only she and I know her joys of each season, disappointments about carelessness, and her deepest loss, for which I am a living monument. She speaks of her dreams:

equilibrium, peace, and potential. Her hopes for her kind, and mine. I treasure her whispers of gratitude. "When I'm with you, my friend," she says, "time stops." She is also near her little one, asleep, under me.

The others ask me for her gossip. I ignore them. I believe that what Esther tells me is not to be restrung on the wind like a wet scarf on the line.

⋅ Instead, I scour the air for her, flushing the oxygen out of my leaves to help her breathe easier, especially when she mourns. As I grow older, like Esther, I am more sensitive to variations in the air. I'm disturbed by smoke haze that ghosts my friends across the yard. But on clear, windless days, the smell of Esther's food, "baking," wafts from the opening on her home and delights me.

This summer, Esther brings me sun-warmed rainwater from a bucket every time she comes near. The moisture is welcome. Every summer seems dryer than the last. She pours the water out slowly, letting the earth around me soak it up without splashing or causing a pool or exposing a main root. She does it as if feeding her child.

Today, scarf billowing, she faces me, scanning my branches, checking my shrivelled apples that fall at her touch. She inspects me but does not talk as usual because of the squealing outside the yard.

Every day the squeal is nearer, and more frequent, insistent.

"Sirens," Esther says.

The high-pitched sound arrests my fluids so that I cannot grow. Or hear the man calling out, entering our yard. He has a tiny Blue Spruce on his shirt. Every time he comes, I wonder if he's bringing a new Blue Spruce for us. He comes straight to me, and my bitter hormones settle and sweeten. Gently, he pulls down on one of my stiffened lower branches that has recently gone numb.

"Esther, it's got to go. The yellow leaves along this branch mean Blight."

"I clipped a bunch of affected branches a few days ago. That yellowed one is new."

"It's systemic. Blight will eventually kill it. Please, Esther, let me take this old tree down."

"No. Not yet."

"That's what you said last year."

Not in front of me, like now.

Esther pats my trunk. "Not this one."

The Blue Spruce man looks away. "The lilac, then?"

"See if you can save it by tarring it up at the split. Take the windward side off."

We all send more food and medicine to Lilac, bracing ourselves for "the amputation," as the man says. He saws by hand "to be precise." We all appreciate this. We've heard chainsaws in neighbouring yards. Afterward, Lilac, half herself, mercifully, is still alive.

The man uses a lopper on me. He finds other recently yellowed and brittle branches with shrunken fruit. After the removals, my posture feels better.

Now I hope that my remaining apples will grow bigger. Esther loves them. She puts them in her food, Apple Bread. To feed Esther, as she fed me, is my pleasure. Every fall, Esther shows her Apple Bread to me and eats a piece from her hand. Then she leaves some, "warm from the oven," where my roots meet my trunk, tucking it in as if for her child's picnic, "an offering."

Her hands are another wonder of humanity – what they can do, how they lift, dig, push, and pull. I wonder how they make Apple Bread. I tried to imitate her hands when I had supple, young, flexible branches, and the others told me they resembled her scarf dancing in the wind. I was content with that image. Now, my branches are drying up, but I have that memory of movement and that is enough.

Without my missing boughs, I have more eyes. With them, I can now watch Esther from all sides. I see her weeding and planting, creating colour and texture and charm for every season. She addresses the birds. "Hello, Magpie!" or "Hi, Robin," and often stops her work to look back at me. Her eyes drip, too, which reminds me to send healing hormones to mine, to seal my fresh eyes from harm.

She does not speak to the other treefolk. They send me sugars and medicine.

But I wonder if it takes more energy than I possess to resist Blight. My yellowing continues out of season. Saskatoon naturally turns golden in the fall, and Lilac, too. Lilac not only blossoms first in spring to herald the bees with her scent but holds her green the longest before it turns. Horse Chestnut goes brown, and Chokecherry, purple. White Spruce stays green behind us. And before, there was Blue Spruce, her wise grey-blue in the background. We are a normally a carnival of colour for Esther, but my sickness may strip me bare before the others reach that glorious autumnal state. No matter how hard I try, I cannot grow my stunted apples any larger than they are, and one by one they prematurely ripen and drop.

The Blue Spruce man tells Esther not to save my trimmed limbs for edging a new flower bed as she does with

Lilac's. "Blight spreads," he says as he wipes my sap off his loppers with a scarf dipped in liquid that smells like pine.

Esther says, "It takes a tree a long time to die."

The man nods. He murmurs, "But Esther, death is a part of life."

After a while, she says, "Yes." Esther holds on to his arm because she is swaying, even though there is no wind. "I often think about who will tend my trees after I'm gone."

Her feelings are mine. I worry about the winter because I see her less during the cold moons. I fret about the others in the yard after my trunk is cut to the ground.

Esther's name, she said, means "star." When she is gone, she will be "another star in the sky." I wonder how I will know when she is a star. Because her little one is near me, I do know that Esther's starlight will shine on my stump.

The man says, "What happens depends on who lives here."

Esther is quiet for a while, then says, "And who has lived here before. I'm going to leave a map, with the names of the trees, for whoever comes after me."

"It's a good idea to write it all down."

I've seen her do this, write on paper, with her marvellous hands. Esther likes to make lists. She once told me that paper comes from trees. I am honoured that this memory aid for humans comes from my kind.

Esther tugs the man's arm. "I may need your help."

"Let's do it today."

"Are you sure you can spare the time?"

"For you, Esther, yes. I never put off what I can do today. I'm about ready for my coffee break anyway."

They take some of my apples and sit at the table on the patio and work on their Tree Map. Esther draws, and he drinks his coffee and gives instructions that she writes down: "Take out the deadwood, leave the leaf mulch, water them in for winter." When they are finished, Esther places a rock on the paper "so the wind won't take it."

I rejoice that my smaller, fewer apples are "tangy," according to Esther. She carefully buries my apple core in some soft ground nearby, but Blue Spruce man digs it up when she is not looking, muttering, "Blight is a plague." He chews one of my apples. "But you are the only apple tree I know that resists Apple Maggots." He packs up his tools for the day. I catch his look of satisfaction when he leaves our little treefolk community, and his smile to Esther as she rolls up her Tree Map.

As we prepare to rest for winter, I sense that the others gradually withhold nutrients from me.

Squirrel leaps from Chokecherry and runs my bare, trimmed lengths.

Mouse pulls at my drying bark near my oldest eyes. Insects burrow there.

Magpie steals the Apple Bread at my base.

Woodpecker travels up and down my trunk, taps out the hard facts, *rat-a-tat-tat-tat*.

Esther asks me, "Is there anything we can do?"

Her concern penetrates deep inside my core.

I send a message of warning to Sapling, grown from seed of my topmost sun-blushed fruit, dropped by Squirrel three summers before and hidden under the wide skirt of White Spruce. I caution Sapling about Blight. A blessing of my new eyes is that I have an unobstructed view of Sapling, where before I only knew of her presence from her tender, searching rootlets that even now reach for mine. I allow this, despite Blight, the plague that spreads. I have so much to give. I must not delay, and do what I can today, like Blue Spruce man said.

Everything from my ancestors laid deep in my heart-wood I now deliver to Sapling: vibrations from stampeding beasts, the shock of earthquake, flood, volcano, glacier, of mudslide, wildfire, hailstorm, and tornado, and lasting grip of drought, heat dome, smoke.

I am about to send a faint warning about Apple Mag-gots when Sapling redirects her rootlets away from mine. Hers are pulsing with root knowledge and need open space to expand and to immunize from my infected wood. I cry a little through my newest eyes. I can bear this separation from Sapling only because of Blue Spruce man's teachings about Blight. I rejoice that I have lived this many years and that Sapling, in her delicate third year, has absorbed what I and all my forebearers know. She will be a beautiful tree. Watching her grow will be my greatest joy for the rest of my days.

I discourage suckers rising from my thickest surface roots. Difficult, but necessary, because Blue Spruce man says suckers "waste energy" and regularly removes them from Lilac and Chokecherry. I trust his voice.

I had no eyes when I was first planted here, but I won-der if it was Blue Spruce man who nested Esther's little one under me. My heartwood memory contains the timbre of his voice, his knowledge. He is gentle even with the snapping loppers and makes smooth cuts to prevent infection. He considers each incision carefully and positions himself so that he is always balanced and mutters, "There's a good angle." He whispers a soothing song each time he makes an incision, "All the lives we ever lived and all the lives to be are full of trees and changing leaves." He is as old as Esther and never does anything without her say-so.

All of us in the yard are grateful, for Blue Spruce man keeps us well. He has also helped put us all on a Tree Map. We have been named, and placed, and dated on paper, skin of our own kin. Our history has become part of Esther's history. Beings other than the wind and animals and insects will know us, and we will help them recognize others of our own kind.

For the final yard cleanup before winter sets in, a different Blue Spruce man comes. He is tall, young, and skinny. He seems to be in a hurry and wears a cap low on his head so we can't see his eyes. Instead of drinking coffee, he smokes. Tosses butts with glowing embers into our beds. He has a black box with pounding sounds that he carries around. Sometimes, it emits siren calls. Esther looks up at me when we hear that. We are all upset. Where is old Blue Spruce man?

When the new man trims the lower dried branches of White Spruce, I fret over Sapling. Sure enough, he finds her, thin but standing straight. After he trims the spruce boughs, his loppers search for the bottom of Sapling's stem. My fluids, already depleted, halt. One of my stiff twigs pokes him in the face. He drops the loppers. Then he gets down on his knee pads and, with two gloved hands, prepares to pull out Sapling like a rogue thistle.

Esther shuts off the box. "Wait." She puts her hands on the earth, then kneels, crawls under White Spruce, and compares the fine leaves of Sapling to the last of my rougher yellowed ones. "No. We'll transplant her in the spring."

The man stands up and pulls off his cap. He is a sapling himself. Esther looks up at him from where she crouches on the ground.

"Before you go today, I will give you a copy of my Tree Map. Together we will decide where Little Apple will go next spring."

He grins at her.

He begins to move the dried spruce branches away, but Esther stops him.

"Could you check the Choke for suckers?"

"Sure." He moves on to Chokecherry and uses his hand pruner. Esther nods at him.

My flow, already stagnant from cold and illness, resumes from a standstill and I breathe again. I always breathe better when Esther is near me, and now all I want is to share her air.

Esther replaces some of the spruce boughs around Sapling's slender stem "to hold the snow in over the winter." Then she wraps her scarf around Sapling. She murmurs other words to my only daughter, Little Apple. I suspect that what she says is about me.

Esther backs out from under White Spruce on her hands and knees. Using me for support, she slowly stands up. She removes a glove, places her warm hand on me. She curls her arm around my trunk and rests her head on my split bark.

I send sugars. All I have.

BIRDSEED

Matthew Freeman

Near the end, I began to devote the bulk of my time to what I believed to be a gregarious individual of the species *Corvus brachyrhynchos* – the American Crow. By then a chemical scythe had begun to carve up the clouds hanging over the lands of "Vancouver" in a psychedelic frenzy, and the shocked blue skyline often bled in shades of lime.

Sal, my partner of three decades, worried. About the fervour in which I spent my time, at least. So committed was she to daily life that I'm less certain of her attitude toward the unmaking of the landscape as it happened around us.

"Felicia," she would say to me in her Swedish accent – a voice both sweetly seductive and occasionally comical. "Let us leave the bird alone or it will make a nest of your hair. Come now, come in the bed."

⁓

Our home was an extra-large Vancouver Special situated alongside rows upon rows of other neat, plain, suburban domiciles huddled atop a steeply sloping hill. Our orientation afforded a view of the jagged sprawl of the city as it unfolded in all directions, punctuated everywhere with sprigs of strategically planted, non-native greenery.

An empty lot sat at the end of our street, overgrown with yellowing knives of spiky grass. It was assumed that coyotes lived there, though I never saw them.

-⁣◃⁣|⁣▹-

Initially, I called the crow Angela, plucked from a list of the female names most often chosen by parents in my birth year, 1971. It didn't take long, though, as I got to "know" the bird better, for me to abandon the name, which felt increasingly patronizing.

It's a psychotic human habit, this naming. A dog will turn its head when you call it, but without even the ability to recognize itself in the mirror, does it regard itself by this same name? Does it regard itself at all? I do not think so.

Instead, as the crow glided down with a whisper to land on the balustrade, I would simply coo hello, murmur nonsense, or, occasionally, try out a throaty vocalization myself.

I am certain the neighbours loved this, though they never approached me about it.

-⁣◃⁣|⁣▹-

Still, even after my epiphany about names, I couldn't abandon the name of my beloved borzoi, Talia. I would keep her in the house behind the glass door each time I tried to communicate with the crow from the balcony of my apartment. Shaggy and ancient-looking, Talia watched our conversations from inside, with her long snout perched on her paws.

-⁣◃⁣|⁣▹-

From where I waited on the balcony, Sal sometimes had an angle on me from the kitchen window. Occasionally, I could feel her eyes on my shoulders, and I would turn to see her smiling. There was concern behind it, but I think she suspected I had latched onto a new project with what she called my "characteristic intensity." She'd give me a little wave, and I'd wave back, and turn my eyes again toward the horizon.

·─⊱⊰─·

At first the bird would stop for a few unsalted peanuts or some mashed scrambled egg on its nightly migrations to Still Creek. Later, as the blanket of black birds papering the evening grew thinner, it came more often.

During our interactions, I became immersed in the bird's gaze. I was fascinated with the way it cocked its head. I'd read that the motion gave the bird depth perception with every twitch. Sometimes it would sit with me for over an hour, eating birdseed from my pinched fingers, backdropped by the hiss of the distant streets and the overwrought glass skyline.

·─⊱⊰─·

One rare sunny spring afternoon, I watched from my perch on the balcony as Sal trimmed the Yoshino Cherry. Blossoms clung to the hood of her electric sedan below as she pruned away the sprigs that had failed to bloom.

She looked sturdy and determined on the ladder as I watched her grey, sable hair fall down the curve of her exposed shoulder. She hummed something from Stravinsky.

But as I stared at her, surrounded by imported shrubs, with lanky Talia lounging in the ryegrass, I was overcome by a profound sense of estrangement. I no longer wanted to participate, to be a person. I did not want to move, or to look at the yard, so I went inside and sat on the sofa. I could hear the shrill chattering of house sparrows through the windows.

The next day a rain fell that smelled of gasoline, stripping the Akebono's branches of its bruised remaining buds.

~\'/~

Out on the balcony, as I waited nightly for the bird to appear, it grew easy to believe that we would inevitably lose. Or rather, that we, humankind, would win the war we were waging against life. That the Fraser River would shrink and gutter with sludge; that all the corals of the world would expel their life-giving algae and crumble to white sand; that what we thought of as the most noble aspects of our human communities would become further and further diminished, until finally becoming as unrecognizable as the stricken, peeled land.

By then, I hoped the plants and animals would have changed so that they could finally thrive amid the damage. Sometimes I doubted it.

I won't bore you with how it all came apart. We have had enough exhausted chronicles of the dissolution.

~\'/~

I cannot explain why I found my interactions with the bird so compelling, other than perhaps that it offered a space outside the cage of human behaviour.

Every day, as the air smelled further of astringent plastics and effluvium, and the thick, heavy sky pressed down harder as if to seal me in, my life – to me – was becoming more fictional. My work-from-home career was relatively stress-free, but ultimately pointless – numbers resettling from one spreadsheet to the next – and the rotating tread of entertainment, online purchases, geopolitical cataclysm, and subsuming panic wore a groove in my mind. Everything seemed to happen elsewhere, in digital space, in echoey department stores and other non-places. The crow's talons clinging steadfast to my knee were more solid in comparison, even when its pale, nictitating membrane peeled back to reveal a remote, black-eyed gaze.

And then, of course, there were the things it said to me.

-\/-

Corvidae can parrot human language, using their avian syrinx to mimic sounds they hear. However, these fall far short of the declarations this particular crow made to me. Rarely threatening, but never comforting, either. They were complex, and probably a delusional mirroring of my own thoughts. It does not, ultimately, matter.

-\/-

Still, the crow's words appeared unbidden, and vibrated like physical sound passing through the air. Its speech carried the cadence of dreams. It once told me that even after the remaining pockets of bird life had been extinguished, the crows would abide. That they would scrape their talons through the cracked sky, perhaps transformed by adaptations, perhaps the same as ever. That they would roost in halls festering with human skulls.

It told me all this with a wavering voice, pausing to preen its inky wings. And then it nipped its unsalted peanut from my hand and floated away.

⁓⁓

Sometimes I suspected that Sal believed me to be "protecting" myself from the surrounding circumstances, insulating myself from the world out there from my spot overlooking the neighbourhood.

I found it impossible to explain that I was never at rest there, feeling always that I might attune myself to a more substantial mode of being.

⁓⁓

Reading everything I could about the American crow did nothing to reveal the specific nature of the creature. It felt the same as walking the flooded banks of Brohm Lake and learning the names of different plant and animal species.

No matter what you do, it's impossible to feel enmeshed with anything you pretend is wild. You walk along the trail. You note the sculpted blade of a leaf, the mud in which the plant grows. You look at the marmorated stink bug gnawing at its trunk. You can even lie down and let the muck seep into your skirt for as long as you like. None of this will make you feel like you're actually a part of that place.

This may be why, late in my attempted communications with the bird, I mostly stopped leaving the house except to acquire the essentials.

~\⁄~

I am certain Sal's worry must have escalated, but she trusted me. Her fierce ethic of self-sufficiency allowed me the freedom to do as I wished.

Which was, truth be told, not much of anything.

~\⁄~

She let me slip away from everything but her.

"I've been reading," I said to her once over a pair of fried eggs on multigrain toast. "Ecologists love scrubbing out the line between humans and what we call 'nature.' But you can't, can you? Can you really commune with the quiet it throws at you?"

"Well," she said, plunging her fork into the arugula, "Maybe try communing with your beautiful, aged wife once in one while, then." She smiled at me, and stood to leave for the office. But I can tell you she was trying to understand.

~\⁄~

As the everyday wound down and the hours at her work dwindled, she once left early to join me out on the balcony with half a hard-boiled egg.

I taught her to be patient, to wait with the egg-white pinched between her thumb and forefinger and her arm leaning on the banister. Our skin was pimpled with goose-bumps, both of us underdressed for the uncharacteristically chill evenings of that early summer.

The bird came like always, without hesitation. It snatched the treat from Sal's hand as she stifled a squeal of revulsion and delight.

The bead of its eye fixed me with a silent inquiry. Sal pointed at the bird clinging there, jittering its head about. "He looks like you," she said, chuckling. "What was his name, again?"

⋅⋁⋅

It never spoke in Sal's presence, and I certainly never told her of the visions it shared: the flowering hills absent of human trace, or the swarms of what had once been birds, scattered like stars over the husked city.

⋅⋁⋅

And if I have reluctantly recounted examples of what the bird told *me*, then what did I tell the bird?

I asked questions here and there, but mainly, I found myself speaking about my own alienation.

I told it that before I mostly stopped leaving the house, and more specifically the balcony, I liked to take walks around the neighbourhood with Talia.

We would sit on the bench in the nearby park and stare at the grass, dotted with dandelions, and at the clutches of bigleaf maple planted there by who-knows a generation ago.

The maple leaves would shiver in the wind – fresh, but tinged with shifting, pungent odours – and I would begin to shiver, too. Sometimes it would get so that I felt I was in a wind tunnel, with the sharp flush of air slicing my sides.

The sensation would inch inward toward my heart, until it became so unbearable that I was forced to stand and walk away. My hand gripping Talia's leash would tremble. The skein of grass on either side of the gravel path began to feel like a great ghost laid over the Earth.

"But I always ended up thinking," I told the crow, "despite it all: you know my face."

It never indicated even a sliver of surprise.

~\/~

After I told Sal about these feelings, and of the physical pain I felt when I left our home, she became Talia's primary care-giver. I regretted it, of course, but welcomed the comfort. I wanted nothing more than to hold out a nut or bit of bird-seed for the crow.

~\/~

Lying across from me in bed, Sal would tell me what the city was like now, with its spare storefronts painted over with slurs or clusters of fading flowers; with the tent cities that proliferated along the streets.

"Even with all these people out there now, it is so much quieter than before," Sal said. "With all this stillness, the overgrowth keeps stitching stuff together. It looks wild, like a set from a TV show." She touched my cheek. "But it also smells like a stove with the knob cranked up all of the time."

I nodded. "What did you do today?" she asked. I looked at her face, her bone structure, her flickering, green irises, and thought: How lucky I am to share a species with this woman.

"Birdseed," she said when I didn't answer, brushing her fingers through my hair. "Little birdseed."

I hoped she would not cry.

--\\'/--

Then one night, the crow did not arrive.

Traffic, by then, had declined considerably. It seemed no one had anywhere to go.

That first night without the bird, I sat for a long time in the acid breeze. Sal was washing the dishes, and through the kitchen window, I could smell the detergent.

--\\'/--

I am certain that by now the bird has died, another victim of the cyanobacteria riding the blooms of teal algae in the cooked waters of the creek.

I am trying not to be sentimental about it, but I am sure you understand that it is difficult.

--\\'/--

After sitting for hours several evenings without an appear-
ance of the bird I had foolishly grown to think of as *my companion*, I went inside and closed the balcony door. I felt
hemmed-in by every mass-produced thing in our den, and,
eager to get another look at the crescent moon rising in the
purple air, I left through the front door without a word to Sal,
and shuffled down to the empty lot. I found a spot beneath
a dead, overgrown ball of cotton lavender and lay down out
of view from the road.

I pressed my head into the dirt and breathed in mildew
and dust. I closed my eyes and listened to the stalks as they
clacked together. I even imagined that I could hear insects
skittering across the soil.

⤝⟍⫽⤞

When I woke up, Sal was lying there beside me in her paja-
mas. The night was deep, close, and heated. I could not see
a single star in the sky, but had the distinct sense of them
wheeling far above.

I felt Sal looking right at me. "The power went out
again," she said. "Longer this time. I watched you come out
here, you know."

I did not know what to say, so I sat up. I put my hand
on her shoulder. It was warm. I heard a single yip of a coyote
from the far-off road, then silence. I felt hypersensitized, but
blind.

I tasted isopropyl on the air. I cocked my head like a
crow I once knew: to look, to listen.

I still couldn't see anything.

PLUCK

Jade Wallace

It was only after I started working at the florist a few months ago that I began to think of plants as things that move. I learned that algae may swim towards the light; sundew can catch insects in their stalks; the leaves of touch-me-nots will slouch when they feel rain.

One afternoon, in the shop's back room, I was arranging extravagant bouquets in glazed ceramic vases for a wedding, when I dropped a cut stem, bent to retrieve it, and observed that the floor was littered with leaves. I hadn't noticed any disorder when I came in. A close-up confirmed that they were of a species I did not recognize. I relegated them to the compost bin.

"Taking a half-hour break." My boss's voice was followed by the sound of the shop door clanging open and shut.

I had moved to the pristine front of the store and was reading a magazine article about ideal soil composition for succulents when a customer came in for a pickup. Turning toward the back room, I was confronted by a scattering of leaves at my feet. Feigning oblivion, hoping the woman would not notice the excessive rustling when I walked, I made my way to the refrigerator, where I spent minutes digging doggedly, but the order was difficult to find.

"Be with you in a minute!" I shouted in agitation. Finally retrieving the wreath of roses, I pivoted back to the cash register and was faced with another small chaos of leaves on the ground.

The customer received an accidental discount in my rush to finish the transaction. I stared at her departing back until she was out of sight. When I let my gaze drop, there were leaves again at my feet. I swept them up swiftly and discarded them in the compost bin, which had become inexplicably empty of everything but the remains of a browning snake plant.

My boss returned and the rest of the afternoon passed with reassuring banality. By the time I walked into my darkened apartment that evening, I was not even thinking of foliage. Yet, as I knelt down to take off my shoes, I saw leaves strewn throughout the entryway. I swatted them frantically outside, but for every leaf I turned out, another entered in its place. Grabbing a broom, I batted them away in swaths. They shuffled out belligerently before rushing back inside. I kept sweeping until I was sweating and losing my breath, then I threw my broom at the leaves and left them in the foyer while I went to get my vacuum cleaner.

The first leaf clotted its nozzle and had to be forcibly pulled out. I tried sucking up each of the leaves in turn but got the same result.

"They're! Just! Leaves!" I said as I struck the vacuum nozzle repeatedly against the floor. Nothing dislodged. I pulled out my phone and called my landlord.

"Do you have a leaf blower?" I asked, dispensing with pleasantries. My landlord – probably delighted by the misbelief that I intended to clear the walkway outside the low-rise – agreed to drop off the tool in half an hour.

As it turned out, the leaf blower was no better than my hands and only made the foyer smell like gasoline. I stared down the leaves with the blower turned up to the highest setting. They fluttered in avian circles around me, refusing to make their exit.

"What is wrong with you," I muttered to the leaf blower, or to the leaves, or to myself. Exhausted, I let the leaves stay where they were, hoping a change in wind direction might clear everything up.

The wind changed hardly at all that week, despite weather reports promising otherwise. I had begun to suspect that the wind might be irrelevant anyhow. There were leaves in my apartment, leaves at work, and I swear sometimes leaves even followed me down the street and onto the bus. Their number never seemed to vary and they were always vivid green, as if freshly-fallen. Daily vacuuming and blowing did not fix the problem at home. Sweeping and stashing the leaves in knotted trash bags kept them contained at work, so long as I was nearby; it did not keep them from following me after. I avoided visiting my parents' house, lest the leaves show up there as well. My parents, in their usual way, would deny that the leaves existed, or blame me for the leaves, or both.

By week's end, I had begun to walk everywhere with my head turned sideways, watching leaves tumbleweed after me in my peripheral vision. I hypothesized that it was always the same set of leaves following me. To be certain, I spent my next day off kneeling on my bedroom floor, numbering the leaves with permanent ink, photographing them with my phone, making notes of any distinguishing marks, and pinning them like butterflies to my wall. There were 42. A perverse inversion of my age? Fungal spots on several of the leaves, probably *Septoria*, formed sinister shapes, including one that looked like a trefoil.

That night I slept on the couch. The next day I woke to leaves infesting my blanket. I leapt to my feet and threw the blanket off me, as if it were covered in cockroaches. In the shower, I washed my hair until my scalp hurt.

I beat down my dread while I was at work so I could broach the subject with my boss when she came into the back room.

"Have you noticed a lot of leaves in here?" I said with unconvincing casualness. "Lately?"

"Like, on the plants?"

"No, on the ground."

"I haven't noticed that. Why?" Lines creased her forehead. I glanced surreptitiously at the compost bin, where the leaves reposed in their knotted bag.

"Oh, it just seems like there have been a lot to sweep up these past few weeks." I tried to keep my lying voice from quavering. "I keep checking our plants, but they all seem fine. Nothing missing."

My boss paused before answering.

"And you don't know what kind of leaves they are?"

I shook my head, fished a specimen out of the bag, and handed it to her. "Does that look familiar to you?"

"Jugate, alternate, condiform, denticulate, revolute," she recited, staring at the leaf. "And it seems to have some kind of number marked on it." She paused again. "This was in the shop?" I could only nod. "I don't recognize it either," she said finally. "Sloppy delivery drivers maybe."

"Guess so." My voice creaked. At least the conversation was over.

In university, I had a philosophy professor who used to goad us through logic proofs with this expression: *If you do not understand the problem, then you will not understand the solution.* I rolled my eyes when I first heard it, but the catching phrase had infected my reasoning process ever since.

I said it aloud to myself as I trudged to the bus shelter after work. What was the problem? Way too many leaves, impossible to escape. An absurd predicament. Was the solution to keep them from following me, or to eradicate them altogether? I would settle for either. The bus came and I chose the remotest seat so I could think. It seemed that the only option was to undertake a systematic series of experiments, however amateurish, to determine whether there was any feasible method by which I could put an end to the stalking. I was fairly sure that the leaves could not be physically removed by ordinary means, so I would have to try a more radical approach.

I transferred onto another bus and got off at the entrance to a set of well-worn hiking trails. Not entirely sure of which way to go, I chose a route arbitrarily, but soon found what I was looking for. Turning about-face, I stared down at the leaves strewn on the dirt path, for once looking like they were meant to be there. It was a time for last words, but I had nothing to say.

With the leaves restrained under new kindling I had collected, and charred logs someone had left in a makeshift fire pit, I held my lighter to the pyre until it caught. Even in the conflagration, the leaves did not disappear easily. They crackled and smoked and stubbornly remained fleshy, as though I was burning small animals alive.

I went home that night to a silent apartment and bare floors. I took off my socks and brewed a pot of valerian tea, which I sipped slowly while I sat at the kitchen table trying to relax. When I slept, I dreamt of floating in a sensory deprivation tank.

I woke the next morning to leaves. They were green again, as though fire had never touched them, but they were still marked with my ink.

"You – can't – be – here!" I yelled, grape-stomping them into the carpet. "It doesn't make sense."

I missed my bus to work that morning and had to catch a later one.

"If you do not understand the problem…" I repeated it to myself aloud over and over until I noticed a man staring at me with concern. He was sitting a few seats away from me and wearing a coat that looked like it had barely survived an apocalypse.

I had already obliterated the leaves in the most thorough way I could conceive, so the solution had to be something other than destruction. Perhaps, I thought, problems that are beyond our understanding require us to be open to solutions we can't fully explain.

"Yes!" I shouted. The man moved farther away from me.

I needed a more transcendental way to respond to the leaves. When a young child cried that afternoon after it became separated from its parent in the shop aisles, it gave me an idea.

"But who are the parents of leaves?" I demanded as I struggled with the key in the shop lock during closing. "Make do," I told myself sternly, scraping the damp of tears from my cheeks.

In the city park farthest from my apartment, I patted leaves into the hollows of trees, fitted them into the branches of shrubs, and stitched them to flower stalks with my flimsy pocket sewing kit. By the time I finished, it was too late to catch the last bus and I didn't have money to spare for a taxi. I walked home and collapsed into bed, depleted but alone.

My actions bought me a week's relief from shadows.

The leaves reappeared one at a time and each time I readjusted my plea. *If I cannot be free, then let there be only one... let there be only two... let there be only 41...*

When the last leaf returned, I picked it up, fought back anger, and looked at it deeply, as though its dark spots were the eyes of an intelligent but enigmatic being. What I saw there was death. Not death as I had always known it – the husk of a bird carcass on the sidewalk, my grandmother emptied of blood and inflated with formaldehyde – not death as motionless finality. This death was a suspended and tremulous phase before change. Leaves that fall give life to new seasons of leaves.

I bought the tiniest syringe that the pet store sold, surreptitiously stole some of the syrupy green juices of various flora from the store, and injected this juice into the dead leaves ever at my feet. I thought this might revive them, satisfy them, and they would be done with me at last. Sticky streaks of green marked my routes across the city for days afterward, but that was the only development.

Despite this failure, I remained convinced that the leaves sought a kind of resurrection. One night, after my boss had left, I picked up several leaves, ground them to paste with a mortar and pestle, mixed them with rich soil, and transplanted a struggling bunny cacti into the salmagundi I had made. Shop protocol required me to dispose of plant refuse to prevent the spread of disease, but the cactus was such a sickly plant that no one could blame its death on me.

The next morning, accompanied by a far smaller cadre of leaves, I found the cactus completely recovered. Flowering, even.

"That shouldn't have worked," I hissed to the leaves. They vibrated at me expectantly. "Shut up."

Over the next few days, I repeated the procedure, turning every last one of the remaining leaves into detritus for dying blooms. Succulents swelled lusciously throughout the shop.

I phoned my parents and made excuses for weeks of not calling them. I turned off all the appliances in my apartment and sat alone listening to the quiet.

Until the 84 leaves arrived.

I bought the largest food processor I could find and took care of the 84 leaves. Then the 168, the 336, the 672, the 1344. I stopped counting. My arms tired and I grew increasingly afraid that there would be no end to my labour, but I could not do otherwise.

Still the leaves keep coming. They leap elated into my hands. Despite their enthusiastic participation, I cannot keep pace. I suspect that what they really want is their forest back. Or their meadow or their mountain or wherever they are from. But maybe kilometres of concrete keep them from their homes; maybe their motherlands are mephitic and uninhabitable; maybe fathoms of water have interred the places they once lived. They come to me instead, sensing chlorophyll on my hands.

If you do not understand the problem, then you will not understand the solution. I am no longer certain that there is a problem. I try my best for the leaves, though I am just one person who cannot do the work of the vast earth. Sometimes I want to tell them, *No, I will not* – sometimes I think I should have told them this long ago. But as I lie in my soft bed of green at night, I am sure that there never could have been another way. When I am weary, I work more slowly, and the leaves do not mind. This is our only ecosystem now. I will not turn from them.

EARTH HOUR

BRUCE MEYER

She awoke when she heard the birds singing and assumed it was time to begin the day. When she checked her watch, it was only 2 a.m. The songs were coming from inside. She sounded like wild canaries and goldfinches.

The next day, the doctor listened to her lungs, bronchia, and scoped her throat.

"Do you recall when the sounds started?"

"About a year ago. I'd been sitting in the dark for Earth Hour. It was the first warm night of the year. I stood on my front porch, closed my eyes, and inhaled deeply, so deeply I felt the world rushing into my body. The back of my throat was sweet as candied rose petals. The bird inside me would not stop singing."

"You've swallowed a large quantity of springtime," the doctor said. "It happens sometimes."

"Is there anything I can do about it?" she asked. "Will the euphoria last? What's the name of my malady?"

"You have *acute avian dyspnea*. From now on it will return. If there's a blizzard, remember to stand on your porch and exhale. You can't keep it bottled up after March. You'll see why."

At the end of summer, the songs ceased. She missed the birds until April.

She felt a lump in her throat and thought the malady had turned fatal. She began to choke. She choked for more than an hour. Her face went aubergine until, with a violent cough, she felt something in her mouth. A small yellow warbler rolled off the tip of her tongue, landed in her nested palm, and sang its heart out.

THE WATER SPRITE

AFTERWORD

It was a cold November day, before the snows, as I wandered the old-growth forest of Jackson Creek. Centuries-old cedar, pine and hemlock towered above me, giving off the fresh scent of forest. The trees creaked and groaned, swaying in a mischievous wind. I sighed with the thought that this ancient forest might soon disappear to invading development. Already, the city encroached with condo complexes and roads.

Leaving the main path, I descended the leaf-strewn slope toward the river. My boots pressed through a frosty crust into the spongy ground of dead leaves and organic soil. I stopped and breathed in the pine-scented coolness of the air. A damp mist huddled among the trees, adding wisps of mystery to the ancient wood. It was as though I'd entered an enchanted forest in some fanciful fairy tale.

Not far from the river, I approached an old yellow birch tree. Its gnarly trunk rose as tall as some of the cedars and pines around it. Golden flakes of bark curled and formed craggy patterns around the thick girth of the old tree. Its moss-covered roots snaked out like tangled ropes in a profusion of brilliant green. This was fairy country, I suddenly thought with an impish smile, and felt it tug my soul with thoughts of home.

I crouched down, and set up my tripod and camera to capture this magical tree from the perspective of the forest floor. Head almost touching the ground, I inhaled the scent of loam and decaying leaves. The fresh pungency of cedar, pine, and humid moss hung in the air, coiling around me like a caressing hand. Nearby, the river chortled and bubbled in a content symphony of motion. A curious red squirrel parked itself on a log nearby to watch me. It didn't scold me like they normally did when I entered the forest; as though it understood. It then occurred to me, as I set up my equipment under the squirrel's careful stare, that I was in the presence of an enchantment. I was peering into a secret dance of feral celebration. By being there and appreciating it, I had now become part of it. I was Alice going down the rabbit hole into a true wonderland...

It was then that I caught sight of it as I carefully took my timed pictures. A blur of blue. What had I witnessed? A motion? A colour? Then it was gone. But in that moment, I'd felt the spark of an elation that comes with a glimpse into a secret world.

When I returned to my small room in the city to look at the images, I saw that my camera had captured a wispy blue being that flowed into view and peered around the old birch at me with a kind of curious though mischievous grin.

Had I just captured a blue sprite? *Something* was unmistakably there!

I read up on sprites. According to European lore, a sprite is a supernatural entity. They are often depicted as fairy-like creatures or as an ethereal entity. The word sprite comes from the Latin *spiritus* ("spirit"), via the French esprit. Given that the sprite I'd observed was blue and we were close to the river, I wondered if it was not a forest or wood sprite, but a water sprite. According to alchemist Paracelsus, the term "water sprite" was used for any elemental spirit associated with water. They can breathe water or air and sometimes can fly. They also possess the power of *hydrokinesis*, which is the ability to create and manipulate water at will. Also known as "water nymphs" or "naiads," these divine entities tend to be fixed in one place. Sprites are not corporeal beings (like selkies, mermaids and sirens) given that they are not purely physical; they are more like local deities than animals. This explained the wispy nature of the being I'd seen peering at me from the tree.

I consulted with several friends – some who purported to know much more about sprites than I did. When friend Merridy suggested that "forest sprites, normally green, may turn blue if a nearby brook calls to them," I reconsidered, particularly when she added that "water sprites can be distinguished by their chatty nature. They rarely go beyond the banks of a river or brook. Forest sprites are mostly silent." My sprite, though quite curious, had remained silent. And yet, I felt a strong sense that it wished to tell me something.

When I told friend Craig that I would return in search of them he observed, "If you're looking for them, that might be when they hide. Or maybe not. Any type of sprite is probably good, mischievous or friendly." With a spritely grin I thanked him for his advice.

I visited the forest several times after but saw no sign of any sprites. Perhaps Craig was right; they were hiding from me. But, why had I seen this shy water sprite in the first place? What was its intention with me? There had been a kind of plaintive sadness in its rheumy eyes and timid smile. I'd felt a kindred connection somehow. More like a lost memory, buried deep in the mists of my past, shoring in my mind. Like the floating debris of a home long abandoned to the careless violence of progress.

Then, on a foggy late December day, after a light snowfall, I returned to document the ice forming in the river. Islands of ice had created a new topography for the flowing waters of Jackson Creek. Ice sheets also covered the forest path in places – making the walk somewhat treacherous. At times, I had to scramble and seize hold of branches to haul my way up precipitous banks from where I'd captured sculptures of ice that formed pearls, columns and platforms on the river.

The fog grew thick as my walk eventually led me into a stand of eccentric cedars that leaned like drunks over the river bank. The cedars sent out a tangled tapestry of gnarly roots I had to negotiate. Tingling with earth-magic energy, I crouched again and set my camera and tripod to the level of the roots.

That is when I saw the water sprite again!

This time the sprite lingered with a look of plaintive determination on its wispy face. It seemed to float in and out of the old cedar like the tree's own breath, inhaling and exhaling. It met my stare with a timorous plaintive look on its hoarfrost face, eyes glistening like melting ice. I knew its pale face – how long I'd known that sad face of solastalgia!

Then it vanished in a puff of blue mist.

Again, I shared with my friends the images I'd taken of this wispy being, dressed in the blue frost of ice and snow. In response to my photos, friend Gabriela challenged me: "Did you ask what message they have for you, Nina? They keep showing up in your way; they might have a message for you or to be delivered through you to…" *whoever*. This somehow resonated with me. But how, I challenged, would I hear their message when they were silent and so fleeting? She wisely responded, "Just ask yourself the question; you might be surprised when your next thought brings the answer. Since everything is energy, and you saw them at least twice, you're probably connected with them."

I recalled what Gabriela said to me as I reviewed the photos I'd taken. What had I thought when our eyes met for that eternal moment? Immediately upon my elation at being invited into this magical secret world, I thought of the forest and the river running through it, both home to the silent sprites. I thought of the plan to clear the forest and straighten the river into a lifeless gully. There would be no forest canopy to cool the river. The organic loam would shrivel beneath a merciless layer of concrete, brick and plastic.

First, the pines and cedars would fall in a thunderous maelstrom of screaming saws. Ancient beech trees would squeal as they were cut, then crack with a final death shout. Then, with the clearing fires, the leaves of my precious old yellow birch would sizzle and take flight. They would join with embers of curling bark and soar in a vortex of billowing coal black fury. All that had once clothed the earth would be destroyed, leaving a residue of black stumps and charred debris. The melancholy brook would flow through a killing field, itself choking with burned debris. Thick and oily, the lonely creek would grow dark and surly, smothering its own.

That was what the sprite wished to tell me: *Everything is interconnected.*

If the forest goes, the water goes, the sprites go, and with them the magic of life goes.

I grew tearful at the thought. The sprites – the water, forest, and field sprites – had for centuries been the caretakers of this enchanted wood, guarding the beauty and the magic of the wild.

Forced to flee their home, where would the sprites go?

Doomed to scatter into the concrete world of grey monochrome and unyielding progress, would they die along with their magic?

I imagined them lurking in the sterile domain of human hubris – vilified, ridiculed, and ignored. I saw them shrivel to empty husks, discarded detritus left on the side of the road along with Tim Horton's disposable cups carelessly pitched from a car.

I felt dizzy with guilt. What could one person do?…

I suddenly smile.

There is much I can do. I will start by sharing this story with you…

—Nina Munteanu

ABOUT THE AUTHORS

Agata Antonow is a writer living and working in Ontario. Most recently her work has been featured in the Mile End Poets' Festival, *The Gravity of the Thing*, and the FOLD (Festival of Literary Diversity) program. Her work has been awarded the 2021 Douglas Kyle Memorial Prize and the 2023 Alfred G. Bailey Prize by the Writers' Federation of New Brunswick.

Sarah Christina Brown is a graduate of Concordia University's Creative Writing MA program, and now works as an English instructor in New Westminster, British Columbia. Her writing has appeared on the Bronwen Wallace Award shortlist, and in the publications *Journey Prize Anthology, Grain, Prism International, carte blanche, EVENT,* and *Room*.

Mary Burns, a former journalist and documentarian, is the author of four novels, two story collections, and a non-fiction book about snow geese and perception. Her first book, *Suburbs of the Arctic Circle*, was selected by the Literary Press Group for the Writer's Choice award. Her most recent novel, *The Reason for Time*, was shortlisted for the Foreword Reviews Indie award and listed as a "Must Read" Chicago book. Her radio plays have been broadcast on CBC and BBC Radio 3. She lives in Grantham's Landing on British Columbia's Sunshine Coast. maryburns.ca

K.R. Byggdin is the author of *Wonder World*, a ReLit Award finalist and winner of the Thomas Raddall Atlantic Fiction Award. Their writing has also appeared in anthologies and journals across Canada, the UK, and New Zealand. Born and raised on the Prairies, they currently divide their time between Halifax and Toronto as an MFA candidate at the University of Guelph.

Petra Chambers lives in the traditional territory of the Pentlatch people. She was grateful to be a guest in Treaty 7 Territory, homelands of the Tsuut'ina Nation, the Blackfoot Confederacy (Siksika, Kainai, and Piikani Nations), the Iyarhe Nakoda Nation, and the Otipemisiwak Métis Government of the Métis Nation from 2020 to 2022. Her work has appeared in *Queens Quarterly*, *Prairie Fire* and *CV2*. Her first poem was nominated for a 2025 Pushcart Prize. This story is her first work of fiction. She is the Yosef Wosk Fellow for the Vancouver Manuscript Intensive in 2024.

Katie Conrad is a writer and civil servant from Halifax, Nova Scotia, where she lives with her partner and two cats. She has previously been published in *Daily Science Fiction*, *Proton Reader*, and *A Quiet Afternoon 2*. She writes a monthly serial fiction story about the adventures of a witch and her cat. katieconrad.ca

M.L.D. Curelas was raised on a diet of Victorian literature and Stephen King novels, so it's unsurprising that she now writes and edits fantasy and science fiction. You can find her other fairy tale-inspired story in the anthology *Clockwork, Curses, & Coal*. Her most recent short fiction appears in the anthologies *Untethered* and *Sherlock Holmes: Further Adventures in the Realms of H. G. Wells vol. 1*. She lives in Calgary.

Matthew Freeman is an emerging writer of fiction and poetry from Idaho, currently based in the ancestral territories of the hən̓q̓əmin̓əm and Sḵwx̱wú7mesh peoples, colonially known as Burnaby, British Columbia. His stories tend to focus on uncanny interactions between human and non-human subjects.

R. Haven is a fantasy and horror novelist from Toronto. His short stories have been published by Canthius, Soitera Press, TL;DR Press, among others. *Last Stanza Poetry Journal* and Spoonie Press have published his poetry. theirritablequeer.com

Liam Hogan is an award-winning short story writer, with stories in *Best of British Science Fiction* and in *Best of British Fantasy*. He helps host the live literary event Liars' League, and volunteers at the creative writing charity Ministry of Stories. happyendingnotguaranteed.blogspot.co.uk

Cornelia Hoogland is the 2023 winner of the League of Canadian Poets' Colleen Thibadeau Outstanding Achievement in Poetry Award. Her poetry and non-fiction were finalists for the CBC Awards in their respective categories. Hoogland's books *Trailer Park Elegy* and *Woods Wolf Girl* were finalists for national awards. *A Girl Walks into the Woods* is her graphic novel, and *Cosmic Bowling* her latest book. Her first novel titled *Atmospheric River* is looking for a home. corneliahoogland.com

Vanessa Hua is the author of the national bestsellers *A River of Stars* and *Forbidden City*, as well as *Deceit and Other Possibilities*, a *New York Times* Editors' Pick. A National Endowment for the Arts Literature Fellow, she has also received a Rona Jaffe Foundation Writers' Award, the Asian/Pacific American Award for Literature, a Steinbeck Fellowship, as well as honors from the de Groot Foundation, and California Arts Council, among others. She was a finalist for the California Book Award, Northern California Book Award, and New American Voices Award. Previously, she was an award-winning columnist for the *San Francisco Chronicle*.

Jerri Jerreat is from Anishinaabe & Haudenosaunee territory north of Kingston, Ontario. Her writing has appeared in *Fairlight Books short stories, Fictive Dreams, Grist/Fix: Climate Fiction 2022, Flyway: Journal of Writing & Environment, Onyx Publications, Alluvian, Every Day Fiction, Feminine Collective, Yale Review Online, The New Quarterly, The Penmen Review, Glass & Gardens Solarpunk Winters, Solarpunk Summers, Allium Journal of Poetry & Prose*, and in *Solarpunk Creatures*. She has an op-ed online in *On Spec*, and is inspired by youth she meets through the festival Youth Imagine the Future, youthimaginethefuture.com.

Zilla Jones is an African-Canadian woman writing on Treaty 1 territory (Winnipeg) who has won numerous awards for short fiction. In 2023 she was a Journey Prize winner and a finalist in the Writers Trust Bronwen Wallace award. Her stories have appeared in *Prairie Fire, The Malahat Review, Prism International, The Fiddlehead, Freefall Magazine, the Ex-Puritan, Room Magazine, Bayou Magazine, The Journey*

Prize Stories, and anthologies of Nottingham Writers Studio and the Federation of BC Writers. Her debut novel, *The World So Wide,* and a short fiction collection, *So Much To Tell,* are forthcoming with Cormorant Books in 2025 and 2026.

Katherine Koller writes for stage, screen, and page. Plays include *Coal Valley, The Seed Savers, Last Chance Leduc,* and *Riverkeeper.* Books are *Voices of the Land* (plays), *Art Lessons* (novel), and *Winning Chance* (short stories), winner of a High Plains Book Award. Her short fiction has appeared in *Grain, Room, Epiphany, Alberta Views,* and *EDify.* Her web series is *Sustainable Me* and recent audio plays are *Hope Soup* and *The Percussionist.* Katherine is a founding producer of Edmonton Script Salon, a monthly new play reading series in its tenth year, and a recent member of the Citadel Playwrights Lab. katherinekoller.ca

Lynn Hutchinson Lee is author of *Origins of Desire in Orchid Fens,* and was first place winner of the 2022 Joy Kogawa Award for Fiction. Her short fiction has appeared in *Room, Fusion Fragment, Food of My People* and *Cli Fi: Canadian Tales of Climate Change* (both Exile Editions), *Weird Horror* and *Northern Nights, Wagtail: the Roma Women's Poetry Anthology,* and elsewhere. Her novel *Nightshade* (shortlisted for the Guernica Prize) is forthcoming in 2026. lynnhutchinsonlee.ca

Erin MacNair lives in North Vancouver on the unceded territories of the Squamish, Musqueam, and Tsleil-Waututh people in British Columbia. Her stories have appeared in

The Walrus, Grain, EVENT, december, PRISM international, and elsewhere. She recently completed a collection of speculative fiction stories with support from the Canada Council for the Arts, and was runner-up in *subTerrain*'s 2023 Lush Triumphant literary awards.   erinmacnair.com

Melanie Marttila is an #actuallyautistic emerging SFF writer of poetry and speculative tales of hope in the face of adversity, who lives in Sudbury, Ontario. Her most recent poems were published in *Polar Starlight*, her most recent short fiction in *Pulp Literature*, and her debut poetry collection, *The Art of Floating*, was published in 2024. melaniemarttila.ca / Substack: melaniemarttila.substack.com

Bruce Meyer is the author of 77 books of poetry, short stories, flash fiction, and non-fiction. He survived a liver transplant in July of 2022. He lives in Barrie, Ontario, with his wife Kerry, and is professor of Communications at Georgian College.

Isabella Mori writes novels, short fiction, poetry, and non-fiction, and is the author of three books of and about poetry, including *A bagful of haiku – 87 imperfections*. Work has appeared in publications such as *State of Matter, Kingfisher, Signs Of Life*, and *The Group of Seven Reimagined*. An alum of Simon Fraser University's The Writers Studio, Isabella is the founder of Muriel's Journey Poetry Prize, which celebrates socially engaged poetry. A book about mental health and addiction is forthcoming in 2025.

Nina Munteanu is a ecologist, novelist and award-winning short story author of eco-fiction, science fiction, and fantasy. She teaches writing at the University of Toronto. Her writing includes essays on science and futurism. Her short work has appeared in *Neo-Opsis Science Fiction Magazine*, *Chiaroscuro*, *subTerrain*, *Apex Magazine*, *Metastellar*, and several anthologies. She currently has 10 novels published and several non-fiction books on writing and science. Her book *Water Is…* – a scientific study and personal journey as limnologist, mother, and teacher – was Margaret Atwood's pick in 2016 in the *New York Times* "The Year in Reading." Nina's most recent novel, *A Diary in the Age of Water,* was released in 2020. Her novel *Gaia's Revolution* is scheduled for publication in 2025.

E. Martin Nolan is a poet, essayist, linguist and teacher. He is the author of *Still Point* (poems) and the chapbook, *Trees Hate Us*. He is an Assistant Professor in the Engineering Communication Program at the University of Toronto, where he lectures on engineering communication. He is a former editor of *The Puritan* magazine and is currently a PhD Candidate in Applied Linguistics at York University. He received his MA in the Field of Creative Writing from the University of Toronto. He was born and raised in Detroit and now lives in Toronto.

Avery Parkinson is a chemical engineering student based in Hamilton, Ontario. She has published in *The Walrus*.

Ursula Pflug is author of the novels *Green Music, The Alphabet Stones, Motion Sickness* (illustrated by SK Dyment); the novellas *Mountain* and *Down From*, and the story collections *After the Fires, Harvesting the Moon,* and *Seeds.* She edited the anthologies *They Have to Take You In, Playground of Lost Toys* (with Colleen Anderson; Exile Editions) and *Food of My People* (with Candas Jane Dorsey; Exile Editions). Her award-winning short stories have appeared in Canada, the U.S. and the UK, in genre and literary venues including *Strange Horizons, Postscripts, Lightspeed, Fantasy, Leviathan, LCRW, Now Magazine, Bamboo Ridge, EXILE Quarterly,* and more. ursulapflug.ca

Marisca Pichette is a queer author based in Massachusetts, on Pocumtuck and Abenaki land. Her work has appeared in *Door Is a Jar, Room Magazine, Flash Fiction Online, Necessary Fiction,* and *Plenitude Magazine,* among others. She is the flash winner of the 2022 *F(r)iction* Spring Literary Contest, and her debut collection, *Rivers in Your Skin, Sirens in Your Hair,* published in 2023, was a finalist for the Bram Stoker and Elgin Awards.

Shana Ross is a new transplant to Edmonton, Alberta, and Treaty Six Territory. Qui transtulit sustinet. A Rhysling nominated author, her work has recently appeared her work has recently appeared in *Radon Journal, Ilanot Review, Haven Spec, Canthius* and more. She is the winner of the 2022 Anne C. Barnhill prize and the 2021 Bacopa Literary Review Poetry competition. Shana serves as an editor for *Luna Station Quarterly* and volunteers as a critic for Pencilhouse.org.

Lynne Sargent is a writer, aerialist, and holds a PhD. in Applied Philosophy. They are the poetry editor at Utopia

Science Fiction magazine. Their work has been nominated for Rhysling, Elgin, and Aurora Awards, and has appeared in periodicals such as *Augur Magazine, Strange Horizons, and Daily Science Fiction*. Their work has also been supported by the Ontario Arts Council.
scribbledshadows.wordpress.com

Karen Schauber has had her flash fiction appear in over 100 international journals, magazines, and anthologies, with nominations for Pushcart, Best Small Fictions, Best Micro-fiction, and the Wigleaf Top 50. She is Editor of the award-winning flash fiction anthology *The Group of Seven Reimagined: Contemporary Stories Inspired by Historic Canadian Paintings* (2019). She curates Vancouver Flash Fiction, and in her spare time is a seasoned family therapist.
KarenSchauberCreative.weebly.com

Holly Schofield travels through time at the rate of one second per second, oscillating between the alternate realities of city and country life in western Canada. The author of over a hundred speculative short stories published in genres ranging from hard science fiction to magical realism, her works are used in university curricula and have been translated into numerous languages. Stories have appeared in *Analog, Lightspeed, Tesseracts*, the Aurora-winning *Second Contacts*, the Aurora-winning *Nothing Without Us Too*, and many other publications throughout the world.
hollyschofield.wordpress.com

Anneliese Schultz was shortlisted for the 2016 Harper-Collins/UBC Prize for Best New Fiction, and is a Bread Loaf

Scholar and Pushcart Prize nominee with an MFA in Creative Writing. Her widely-published fiction has won numerous awards and been recognized by the Writers' Union of Canada, "The Writer," the Bath Short Story Award, the Surrey Writers' Conference, the Alpine Fellowship, and more. In 2023 she was longlisted for the Fugere Book Prize and shortlisted for Exile Editions' inaugural Morley Callaghan "Best Canadian Short Story" Award (see final page of this book for details). Anneliese works on climate fiction, middle-grade stories, and adult literary fiction in a wildly creative German-Punjabi household in Vancouver.
linktr.ee/AnnelieseS

Gin Sexsmith is a mixed-Mohawk writer and musician from Tyendinaga Mohawk Territory, and a member of the Mohawks of the Bay of Quinte First Nation. Obsessed with the darker sides of our psyche, Gin's work explores love, loss, sexuality, and mental illness. Her debut novel, *In the Hands of Men*, was published in 2023, with its audiobook released on Audible in 2024, and voiced by Kawennáhere Devery Jacobs. She is currently studying Kanyen'keha in her community.

Sara C. Walker writes speculative fiction, and has been published in *ON SPEC* magazine, the anthology *Alice Unbound* (Exile Editions), *Air: Sylphs, Spirits & Swan Maidens*, and others. She lives in Kawartha Lakes, Ontario.
sarawalker.ca

Jade Wallace is a writer, editor, reviewer, and co-founder of the collaborative writing entity MA|DE. Wallace's debut

poetry collection, *Love Is a Place But You Cannot Live There*, was released in 2023, and their debut novel, *Anomia*, was published in 2024. MA|DE's debut poetry collection, *ZZOO*, is forthcoming in spring 2025.
jadewallace.ca + ma-de.ca

Melissa Yuan-Innes likes odd and beautiful tales, as seen in her collections, *Chinese Cinderella, Fairy Godfathers & Beastly Beauty,* and *Dog vs. Aliens, and Grandma Othello & Shaolin Monks in Space.* She won an Aurora Award for poetry in 2023. As Melissa Yi, she writes the paranormal medical thriller *Hope's Seven Deadly Sins* series, including *The Shapes of Wrath* (anger) and *Sugar and Vice* (gluttony).
kickstarter.com/profile/melissayi/created
Facebook: Melissa Yi Yuan-Innes
melissayuaninnes.com (free gift with newsletter)

TWO STORIES IN REPRINT:

"Imagine" by Karen Schauber was originally published in *The Wild Word*, July 2021, at www.thewildword.com/fiction-karen-schauber/

"The Water Sprite" was first published in *Kawartha Lakes Anthology* (Sara C. Walker, ed.), Autumn Issue, November 2021; reprinted in *Polar Borealis* (Graeme Cameron, ed), Issue #22, July 2022; reprinted in *Love Letters to Water Anthology* (Claudiu Murgan, ed), *Manor House Publishing Inc.,* November 2022.

PUBLISHER'S NOTE: the Exile Editions anthology books mentioned in the Author Biographies can be found among the following pages, featuring all 19 previous titles in this anthology series.

19 PREVIOUS ANTHOLOGIES
IN THE SERIES

EACH IS AVAILABLE AT EXILEEDITIONS.COM

* AND ON THE FINAL PAGE *

OVER $175,000 AWARDED TO DATE!

EXILE'S $12,500
(SECOND YEAR*)
MORLEY CALLAGHAN
"BEST CANADIAN STORY" COMPETITION
$10,000 for Best Story
$2,500 for Second Place Story

EXILE'S $3,000
(TENTH YEAR)
DAVID & RUTH LAMPE
GWENDOLYN MACEWEN
POETRY COMPETITION
$1,500 for Best Suite of Poetry
$1,500 for Best Suite by an Emerging Writer

* For 10 years Exile offered the Carter V. Cooper (CVC) Short Fiction Competition,
sponsored by Gloria Vanderbilt. The Morley Callaghan competition
replaced the CVC following the death of Ms. Vanderbilt.

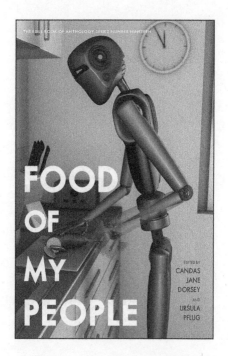

EDITED BY
CANDAS
JANE
DORSEY
AND
URSULA
PFLUG

FOOD OF MY PEOPLE

CO-EDITED BY CANDAS JANE DORSEY AND URSULA PFLUG

Food is often integral to the magic, the meetings, the processes of fantastic fiction: from myth and legend to high fantasy, from hard-science-fiction to post-modern magic realism. And whether in *Hansel and Gretel* or Soylent Green, the myth of Persephone or *2001*, Alice in Wonderland or *Alien*, food-themed stories offer a mixed menu of good and evil, light and darkness.

In this delectible buffet of genre writing that explores our attraction to the candy coating and our fascination with the poisoned apple, each story is paired with a recipe, real or fantastical, to consume with pleasure... or at your own risk!

Kate Story, Chris Kuriata, Kathy Nguyen, Joe Davies, Richard Van Camp, Casey June Wolf, Desirae May, Lisa Carreiro, Tapanga Koe, Lynn Hutchinson Lee, Nathan Adler, Sang Kim, Colleen Anderson, Elisha May Rubacha, Sally McBride, Melissa Yuan-Innes, Liz Westbrook-Trenholm, Sheung-King, Gord Grisenthwaite, and Geoffrey W. Cole.

Aurora Award finalist, Best Related Work category.

THE EXILE BOOK OF ANTHOLOGY SERIES
NUMBER EIGHTEEN

BAWAAJIGAN
STORIES OF POWER

EDITED BY
NATHAN NIIGAN NOODIN ADLER
CHRISTINE MISKONOODINKWE SMITH

BAWAAJIGAN:
STORIES OF POWER

CO-EDITED BY NATHAN NIIGAN NOODIN ADLER
AND CHRISTINE MISKONOODINKWE SMITH

"This is, overall, a stunning collection of writing from Indigenous sources, stories with the power to transform character and reader alike… the high points are numerous and often dizzying in their force… This is an inspiring and demanding collection, and that is by design. The stories challenge readers on numerous levels: thematically, narratively, and linguistically…" —*Quill & Quire*

"The range of stories in this anthology is remarkable, and so are the many themes explored: discovery and recovery, whether of oneself or of ancestral knowing and ways of being; journeying to other worlds; experiences of residential school; the fates of murdered and missing Indigenous women; and gifts that were once commonplace and are now misunderstood or misused." —*Malahat Review*

Richard Van Camp, Autumn Bernhardt, Brittany Johnson, Gord Grisenthwaite, Joanne Arnott, Délani Valin, Cathy Smith, David Geary, Yugcetun Anderson, Gerald Silliker Pisim Maskwa, Karen Lee White, Sara General, Nathan Niigan Noodin Adler, Francine Cunningham, Christine Miskonoodinkwe Smith, Lee Maracle, Katie-Jo Rabbit, Wendy Bone.

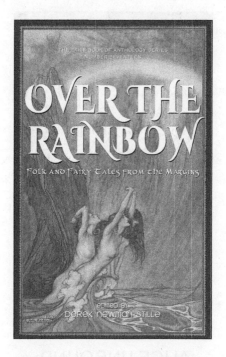

OVER THE RAINBOW:
FOLK AND FAIRY TALES FROM THE MARGINS
EDITED BY DEREK NEWMAN-STILLE

Fairy tales tell us the stories we need to hear, the truths we need to be aware of. This is a collection of adult stories that invite us to imagine new possibilities for our contemporary times. Collected by nine-time Prix Aurora Award-winner Derek Newman-Stille, these are edgy stories, tales that invite us to walk out of our comfort zone and see what resides at the margins. *Over the Rainbow* is a gathering of modern literature that brings together views and perspectives of the underrepresented, from the fringe, those whose narratives are at the core of today's conversations – voices that we all need to hear.

Nathan Caro Fréchette, Fiona Patton, Rati Mehrotra, Ace Jordyn, Robert Dawson, Richard Keelan, Nicole Lavigne, Liz Westbrook-Trenholm, Kate Heartfield, Evelyn Deshane, Lisa Cai, Tamara Vardomskaya, Chadwick Ginther, Quinn McGlade-Ferentzy, Karin Lowachee, Kate Story, Ursula Pflug, and Sean Moreland

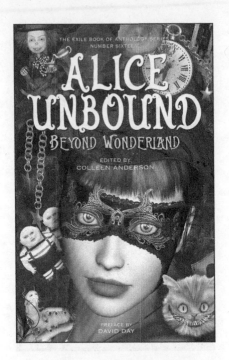

ALICE UNBOUND:
BEYOND WONDERLAND

EDITED BY COLLEEN ANDERSON

"This tremendously entertaining anthology… will delight both lovers of Carroll's works and fans of inventive genre fiction." —*Publishers Weekly*, starred review

A collection of twenty-first century speculative fiction stories that is inspired by *Alice's Adventures in Wonderland, Alice Through the Looking Glass, The Hunting of the Snark*, and to some degree, aspects of the life of the author, Charles Dodgson (Lewis Carroll), and the real-life Alice (Liddell). Enjoy a wonderful and wild ride down and back up out of the rabbit hole!

Patrick Bollivar, Mark Charke, Christine Daigle, Robert Dawson, Linda DeMeulemeester, Pat Flewwelling, Geoff Gander and Fiona Plunkett, Cait Gordon, Costi Gurgu, Kate Heartfield, Elizabeth Hosang, Nicole Iversen, J.Y.T. Kennedy, Danica Lorer, Catherine MacLeod, Bruce Meyer, Dominik Parisien, Alexandra Renwick, Andrew Robertson, Lisa Smedman, Sara C. Walker and James Wood.

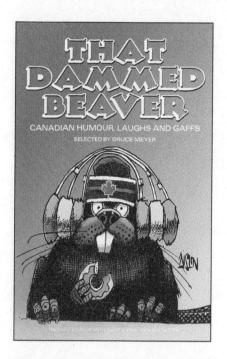

THAT DAMMED BEAVER:
CANADIAN HUMOUR, LAUGHS AND GAFFS

EDITED BY BRUCE MEYER

"What exactly makes Canadians funny? This effort from long-standing independent press Exile Editions takes a wry look at what makes us laugh and what makes us laughable." —*Toronto Star*

Margaret Atwood, Austin Clarke, Leon Rooke, Priscila Uppal, Jonathan Goldstein, Paul Quarrington, Morley Callaghan, Jacques Ferron, Marsha Boulton, Joe Rosenblatt, Barry Callaghan, Linda Rogers, Steven Hayward, Andrew Borkowski, Helen Marshall, Gloria Sawai, David McFadden, Myna Wallin, Gail Prussky, Louise Maheux-Forcher, Shannon Bramer, James Dewar, Bob Armstrong, Jamie Feldman, Claire Dé, Christine Miscione, Larry Zolf, Anne Dandurand, Julie Roorda, Mark Paterson, Karen Lee White, Heather J. Wood, Marty Gervais, Matt Shaw, Alexandre Amprimoz, Darren Gluckman, Gustave Morin, and the country's greatest cartoonist, Aislin.

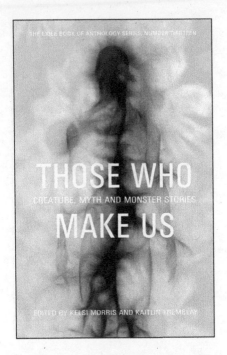

THOSE WHO MAKE US:
CANADIAN CREATURE, MYTH, AND MONSTER STORIES

EDITED BY KELSI MORRIS AND KAITLIN TREMBLAY

What resides beneath the blankets of snow, under the ripples of water, within the whispers of the wind, and between the husks of trees all across Canada? Creatures, myths and monsters are everywhere… even if we don't always see them.

Canadians from all backgrounds and cultures look to identify with their surroundings through stories. Herein, speculative and literary fiction provides unique takes on what being Canadian is about.

"Kelsi Morris and Kaitlin Tremblay did not set out to create a traditional anthology of monster stories… This unconventional anthology lives up to the challenge, the stories show tremendous openness and compassion in the face of the world's darkness, unfairness, and indifference." —*Quill & Quire*

Featuring stories by Helen Marshall, Renée Sarojini Saklikar, Nathan Adler, Kate Story, Braydon Beaulieu, Chadwick Ginther, Dominik Parisien, Stephen Michell, Andrew Wilmot, Rati Mehrotra, Rebecca Schaeffer, Délani Valin, Corey Redekop, Angeline Woon, Michal Wojcik, Andrea Bradley, Andrew F. Sullivan and Alexandra Camille Renwick.

CLI FI:
CANADIAN TALES OF CLIMATE CHANGE
EDITED BY BRUCE MEYER

In his introduction to this all-original set of (at times barely) futuristic tales, Meyer warns readers, "[The] imaginings of today could well become the cold, hard facts of tomorrow." Meyer (*Testing the Elements*) has gathered an eclectic variety of eco-fictions from some of Canada's top genre writers, each of which, he writes, reminds readers that "the world is speaking to us and that it is our duty, if not a covenant, to listen to what it has to say." In these pages, scientists work desperately against human ignorance, pockets of civilization fight to balance morality and survival, and corporations cruelly control access to basic needs such as water.... The anthology may be inescapably dark, but it is a necessary read, a clarion call to take action rather than, as a character in Seán Virgo's "My Atlantis" describes it, "waiting unknowingly for the plague, the hive collapse, the entropic thunderbolt." Luckily, it's also vastly entertaining. It appears there's nothing like catastrophe to bring the best out in authors in describing the worst of humankind. —*Publishers Weekly*

George McWhirter, Richard Van Camp, Holly Schofield, Linda Rogers, Seán Virgo, Rati Mehrotra, Geoffrey W. Cole, Phil Dwyer, Kate Story, Leslie Goodreid, Nina Munteanu, Halli Villegas, John Oughton, Frank Westcott, Wendy Bone, Peter Timmerman, Lynn Hutchinson Lee, with an afterword by internationally acclaimed writer and filmmaker Dan Bloom.

The Exile Book of Anthology Series
Number Eleven

playground
of
LOST
toys

Edited by Colleen Anderson and Ursula Pflug

PLAYGROUND OF LOST TOYS

EDITED BY COLLEEN ANDERSON AND URSULA PFLUG

A dynamic collection of stories that explore the mystery, awe and dread that we may have felt as children when encountering a special toy. But it goes further, to the edges of space, where games are for keeps and where the mind plays its own games. We enter a world where the magic may not have been lost, where a toy or computers or gods vie for the upper hand. Wooden games of skill, ancient artifacts misinterpreted, dolls, stuffed animals, wand items that seek a life or even revenge – these lost toys and games bring tales of companionship, loss, revenge, hope, murder, cunning, and love, to be unearthed in the sandbox.

Featuring stories by Chris Kuriata, Joe Davies, Catherine MacLeod, Kate Story, Meagan Whan, Candas Jane Dorsey, Rati Mehrotra, Nathan Adler, Rhonda Eikamp, Robert Runté, Linda DeMeulemeester, Kevin Cockle, Claude Lalumière, Dominik Parisien, dvsduncan, Christine Daigle, Melissa Yuan-Innes, Shane Simmons, Lisa Carreiro, Karen Abrahamson, Geoffrey W. Cole and Alexandra Camille Renwick. Afterword by Derek Newman-Stille.

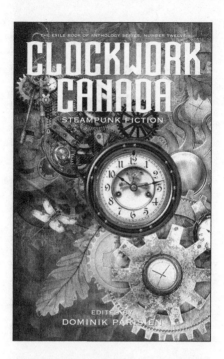

CLOCKWORK CANADA: STEAMPUNK FICTION

EDITED BY DOMINIK PARISIEN

Welcome to an alternate Canada, where steam technology and the wonders and horrors of the mechanical age have reshaped the past into something both wholly familiar yet compellingly different.

"These stories of clockworks, airships, mechanical limbs, automata, and steam are, overall, an unfettered delight to read." —*Quill & Quire*

"[*Clockwork Canada*] is a true delight that hits on my favorite things in fiction – curious worldbuilding, magic, and tough women taking charge. It's a carefully curated adventure in short fiction that stays true to a particular vision while seeking and achieving nuance."

—*Tor.com*

"... inventive and transgressive... these stories rethink even the fundamentals of what we usually mean by steampunk." —*The Toronto Star*

Featuring stories by Colleen Anderson, Karin Lowachee, Brent Nichols, Charlotte Ashley, Chantal Boudreau, Rhea Rose, Kate Story, Terri Favro, Kate Heartfield, Claire Humphrey, Rati Mehrotra, Tony Pi, Holly Schofield, Harold R. Thompson and Michal Wojcik.

FRACTURED:
TALES OF THE CANADIAN POST-APOCALYPSE

EDITED BY SILVIA MORENO-GARCIA

"The 23 stories in *Fractured* cover incredible breadth, from the last man alive in Haida Gwaii to a dying Matthew waiting for his Anne in PEI. All the usual apocalyptic suspects are here – climate change, disease, alien invasion – alongside less familiar scenarios such as a ghost apocalypse and an invasion of shadows. Stories range from the immediate aftermath of society's collapse to distant futures in which humanity has been significantly reduced, but the same sense of struggle and survival against the odds permeates most of the pieces in the collection... What *Fractured* really drives home is how perfect Canada is as a setting for the post-apocalypse. Vast tracts of wilderness, intense weather, and the potentially sinister consequences of environmental devastation provide ample inspiration for imagining both humanity's destruction and its rugged survival." —*Quill & Quire*

Featuring stories by T.S. Bazelli, GMB Chomichuk, A.M. Dellamonica, dvsduncan, Geoff Gander, Orrin Grey, David Huebert, John Jantunen, H.N. Janzen, Arun Jiwa, Claude Lalumière, Jamie Mason, Michael Matheson, Christine Ottoni, Miriam Oudin, Michael S. Pack, Morgan M. Page, Steve Stanton, Amanda M. Taylor, E. Catherine Tobler, Jean-Louis Trudel, Frank Westcott and A.C. Wise.

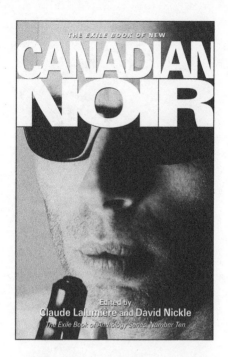

NEW CANADIAN NOIR

EDITED BY CLAUDE LALUMIÈRE AND DAVID NICKLE

"Everything is in the title. These are all new stories – no novel extracts – selected by Claude Lalumière and David Nickle from an open call. They're Canadian-authored, but this is not an invitation for national introspection. Some Canadian locales get the noir treatment, which is fun, since, as Nickle notes in his afterword, noir, with its regard for the underbelly, seems like an un-Canadian thing to write. But the main question *New Canadian Noir* asks isn't "Where is here?" it's "What can noir be?" These stories push past the formulaic to explore noir's far reaches as a mood and aesthetic. In Nickle's words, "Noir is a state of mind – an exploration of corruptibility, ultimately an expression of humanity in all its terrible frailty." The resulting literary alchemy – from horror to fantasy, science fiction to literary realism, romance to, yes, crime – spanning the darkly funny to the stomach-queasy horrific, provides consistently entertaining rewards." —*Globe and Mail*

Featuring stories by Corey Redekop, Joel Thomas Hynes, Silvia Moreno-Garcia, Chadwick Ginther, Michael Mirolla, Simon Strantzas, Steve Vernon, Kevin Cockle, Colleen Anderson, Shane Simmons, Laird Long, Dale L. Sproule, Alex C. Renwick, Ada Hoffmann, Kieth Cadieux, Michael S. Chong, Rich Larson, Kelly Robson, Edward McDermott, Hermine Robinson, David Menear and Patrick Fleming.

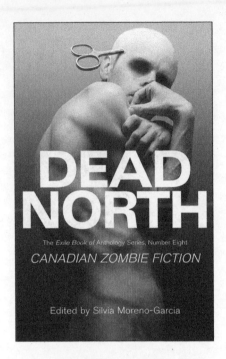

DEAD NORTH:
CANADIAN ZOMBIE FICTION

EDITED BY SILVIA MORENO-GARCIA

"*Dead North* suggests zombies may be thought of as native to this country, their presence going back to Indigenous myths and legends… we see deadheads, shamblers, jiang shi, and Shark Throats invading such home and native settings as the Bay of Fundy's Hopewell Rocks, Alberta's tar sands, Toronto's Mount Pleasant Cemetery, and a Vancouver Island grow-op. Throw in the last poutine truck on Earth driving across Saskatchewan and some "mutant demon zombie cows devouring Montreal" (honest!) and what you've got is a fun and eclectic mix of zombie fiction…"—*Toronto Star*

"Every time I listen to the yearly edition of *Canada Reads* on CBC, so much attention seems to be drawn to the fact that the author is Canadian, that being Canadian becomes a gimmick. *Dead North*, a collection of zombie short stories by exclusively Canadian authors, is the first of its kind that I've seen to buck this trend, using the diverse cultural mythology of the Great White North to put a number of unique spins on an otherwise over-saturated genre."—*Bookshelf Reviews*

Featuring stories by Chantal Boudreau, Tessa J. Brown, Richard Van Camp, Kevin Cockle, Jacques L. Condor, Carrie-Lea Côté, Linda DeMeulemeester, Brian Dolton, Gemma Files, Ada Hoffmann, Tyler Keevil, Claude Lalumière, Jamie Mason, Michael Matheson, Ursula Pflug, Rhea Rose, Simon Strantzas, E. Catherine Tobler, Beth Wodzinski and Melissa Yuan-Ines.

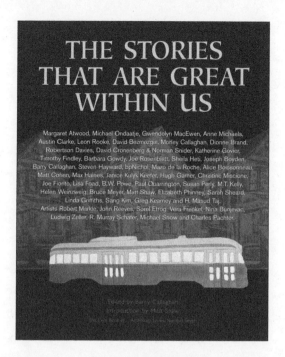

THE STORIES THAT ARE GREAT WITHIN US

EDITED BY BARRY CALLAGHAN

"[This is a] large book, one to be sat on the lap and not held up, one to be savoured piece by piece and heard as much as read as the great sidewalk rolls out... This is the infrastructure of Toronto, its deep language and various truths." —*Pacific Rim Review of Books*

Among the 50-plus contributors are Margaret Atwood, Michael Ondaatje, Gwendolyn MacEwen, Anne Michaels, Austin Clarke, Leon Rooke, David Bezmozgis, Morley Callaghan, Dionne Brand, Robertson Davies, Katherine Govier, Timothy Findley, Barbara Gowdy, Joseph Boyden, bpNichol, Hugh Garner, Joe Fiorito, Paul Quarrington, and Janice Kulyk Keefer, along with artists Sorel Etrog, Vera Frenkel, Nina Bunjevac, Michael Snow, and Charles Pachter.

"Bringing together an ensemble of Canada's best-known, mid-career, and emerging writers... this anthology stands as the perfect gateway to discovering the city of Toronto. With a diverse range of content, the book focuses on the stories that have taken the city, in just six decades, from a narrow wryly praised as a city of churches to a brassy, gauche, imposing metropolis that is the fourth largest in North America. With an introduction from award-winning author Matt Shaw, this blends a cacophony of voices to encapsulate the vibrant city of Toronto." —*Toronto Star*

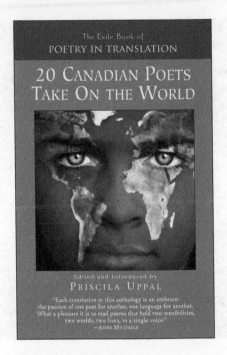

20 CANADIAN POETS TAKE ON THE WORLD

EDITED BY PRISCILA UPPAL

A groundbreaking multilingual collection promoting a global poetic consciousness, this volume presents the works of 20 international poets, all in their original languages, alongside English translations by some of Canada's most esteemed poets. Spanning several time periods and more than a dozen nations, this compendium paints a truly unique portrait of cultures, nationalities, and eras."

Canadian poets featured are Oana Avasilichioaei, Ken Babstock, Christian Bök, Dionne Brand, Nicole Brossard, Barry Callaghan, George Elliott Clarke, Geoffrey Cook, Rishma Dunlop, Steven Heighton, Christopher Doda, Andréa Jarmai, Evan Jones, Sonnet L'Abbé, A.F. Moritz, Erín Moure, Goran Simić, Priscila Uppal, Paul Vermeersch, and Darren Wershler, translating the works of Nobel laureates, classic favourites, and more, including Jan-Willem Anker, Herman de Coninck, María Elena Cruz Varela, Kiki Dimoula, George Faludy, Horace, Juan Ramón Jiménez, Pablo Neruda, Chus Pato, Ezra Pound, Alexander Pushkin, Rainer Maria Rilke, Arthur Rimbaud, Elisa Sampedrin, Leopold Staff, Nichita Stănescu, Stevan Tontić, Ko Un, and Andrei Voznesensky. Each translating poet provides an introduction to their work.

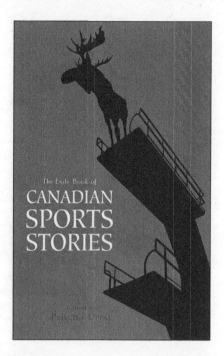

CANADIAN SPORTS STORIES

EDITED BY PRISCILA UPPAL

"This anthology collects a wide range of Canada's literary imaginations, telling great stories about the wild and fascinating world of sport... Written by both men and women, the generations of insights provided in this collection expose some of the most intimate details of sports and sporting life – the hard-earned victories, and the sometimes inevitable tragedies. You will get to know those who play the game, as well as those who watch it, coach it, write about it, dream about it, live and die by it."

"Most of the stories weren't so much about sports per se than they were a study of personalities and how they react to or deal with extreme situations... all were worth reading"
—goodreads.com

Clarke Blaise, George Bowering, Dionne Brand, Barry Callaghan, Morley Callaghan, Roch Carrier, Matt Cohen, Craig Davidson, Brian Fawcett, Katherine Govier, Steven Heighton, Mark Jarman, W.P. Kinsella, Stephen Leacock, L.M. Montgomery, Susanna Moodie, Marguerite Pigeon, Mordecai Richler, Priscila Uppal, Guy Vanderhaeghe, and more.

CANADIAN DOG STORIES

EDITED BY RICHARD TELEKY

Spanning from the 1800s to 2005, and featuring exceptional short stories from 28 of Canada's most prominent fiction writers, this unique anthology explores the nature of the human-dog bond through writing from both the nation's earliest storytellers such as Ernest Thompson Seton, L. M. Montgomery, and Stephen Leacock, as well as a younger generation that includes Lynn Coady and Matt Shaw. Not simply sentimental tales about noble dogs doing heroic deeds, these stories represent the rich, complex, and mysterious bond between dogs and humans. Adventure and drama, heartfelt encounters and nostalgia, sharp-edged satire, and even fantasy make up the genres in this memorable collection.

"Twenty-eight exceptional dog tales by some of Canada's most notable fiction writers… The stories run the breadth of adventure, drama, satire, and even fantasy, and will appeal to dog lovers on both sides of the [Canada/U.S.] border." —*Modern Dog Magazine*

Marie-Claire Blais, Barry Callaghan, Morley Callaghan, Lynn Coady, Mazo de la Roche, Jacques Ferron, Mavis Gallant, Douglas Glover, Katherine Govier, Kenneth J. Harvey, E. Pauline Johnson, Janice Kulyk Keefer, Alistair Macleod, L.M. Montgomery, P.K. Page, Charles G.D. Roberts, Leon Rooke, Jane Rule, Duncan Campbell Scott, Timothy Taylor, Sheila Watson, Ethel Wilson, and more.

NATIVE CANADIAN FICTION AND DRAMA

EDITED BY DANIEL DAVID MOSES

The work of men and women of many tribal affiliations, this collection is a wide-ranging anthology of contemporary Native Canadian literature. Deep emotions and life-shaking crises converge and display Indigenous concerns regarding various topics, including identity, family, community, caste, gender, nature, betrayal, and war. A fascinating compilation of stories and plays, this account fosters cross-cultural understanding and presents the Native Canadian writers' reinvention of traditional material and their invention of a modern life that is authentic. It is perfect for courses on short fiction or general symposium teaching material.

Tomson Highway, Lauren B. Davis, Niigaanwewidam James Sinclair, Joseph Boyden, Joseph A. Dandurand, Alootook Ipellie, Thomas King, Yvette Nolan, Richard Van Camp, Floyd Favel, Robert Arthur Alexie, Daniel David Moses, Katherena Vermette.

"A strong addition to the ever shifting Canadian literary canon, effectively presenting the depth and artistry of the work by Aboriginal writers in Canada today."

—*Canadian Journal of Native Studies*

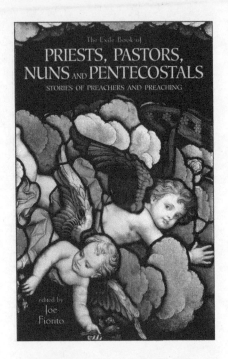

PRIESTS, PASTORS, NUNS AND PENTECOSTALS

EDITED BY JOE FIORITO

A literary approach to the Word of the Lord, this collection of short fiction deals within one way or another the overarching concept of redemption. This anthology demonstrates that however God appears, he appears again and again in the lives of priests, pastors, nuns, and Pentecostals in these great stories of a kind never collected before.

Mary Frances Coady, Barry Callaghan, Leon Rooke, Roch Carrier, Jacques Ferron, Seán Virgo, Marie-Claire Blais, Hugh Hood, Morley Callaghan, Hugh Garner, Diane Keating, Alexandre Amprimoz, Gloria Sawai, Eric McCormack, Yves Thériault, Margaret Laurence, Alice Munro.

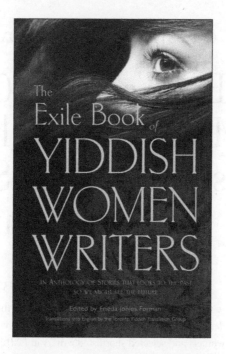

YIDDISH WOMEN WRITERS

EDITED BY FRIEDA JOHLES FORMAN

Presenting a comprehensive collection of influential Yiddish women writers with new translations, this anthology explores the major transformations and upheavals of the 20th century. Short stories, excerpts, and personal essays are included from 13 writers, and focus on such subjects as family life; sexual awakening; longings for independence, education, and creative expression; the life in Europe surrounding the Holocaust and its aftermath; immigration; and the conflicted entry of Jewish women into the modern world with the restrictions of traditional life and roles. These powerful accounts provide a vital link to understanding the Jewish experience at a time of conflict and tumultuous change.

"This continuity... of Yiddish, of women, and of Canadian writers does not simply add a missing piece to an existing puzzle; instead it invites us to rethink the narrative of Yiddish literary history at large... Even for Yiddish readers, the anthology is a site of discovery, offering harder-to-find works that the translators collected from the Canadian Yiddish press and published books from Israel, France, Canada, and the U.S."
—*Studies in American Jewish Literature*, Volume 33, Number 2, 2014

"Yiddish Women Writers did what a small percentage of events at a good literary festival [Blue Metropolis] should: it exposed the curious to a corner of history, both literary and social, that they might never have otherwise considered." —*Montreal Gazette*